CAROL ANNE D
is a Scot and a ful
She's written abou
adult and horror magazines and produced
how-to modules for a well-known writing
correspondence course. Her short stories
have appeared in many magazines and
multi-author anthologies and her first
suspense novel, *Shrouded*, was highly
acclaimed on publication in 1997.

Safe as Houses

Carol Anne Davis

BLOODLINES

First Published in Great Britain in 1999 by
The Do-Not Press
PO Box 4215
London SE23 2QD

A paperback original.

ISBN 1 899344 47 0

British Library Cataloguing in Publication Data. A catalogue
record for this book is available from the British Library.

Printed and bound in Great Britain by
The Guernsey Press Co Ltd.

FOR IAN

PROLOGUE

The body went over the cliff like a weighted rag doll. He watched it fall, half-listening for a drawn out cry. There was none, because if she'd still been alive, they'd still be at the Secret House. Right now be looking for ways to liven her up.

From first glimpse to last she'd needed livening. She'd been lolling against the bus stop when he'd driven past. Head to one side, brown hair against grey metal, legs crossed beneath a too-short skirt at the thigh.

Was she waiting for a bus or for business? He'd driven slowly round the block, concentrated hard on looking aimless. Vision trained sideways, checking for police cars, pimps.

Misspelt graffiti over damp brick walls: land of the wooden curtains. Finally he'd pulled over, breathed deeply, wound the window down.

'Can I give you a lift anywhere?'

She'd flinched, looked away, thumbed the strap of her worn plastic holdall.

'The bus service is lousy,' he persevered. 'I'm going into town.'

Silence. Insolence.

Just as his anger started to sweep over him, she'd moved towards the car. He'd opened the door, lips curving upwards, assessing but not staring as she swung into the front.

Fifteen – or trying to be. Not a hooker yet, but getting there. A Lycra scoop-neck which made the most of her budding cleavage. Food and grass stains near the midriff which suggested she'd put on the top the day before. He stared through the windscreen as the rain started up again. 'You'd have drowned if you'd stayed out in this.'

She nodded her dampened head. Her hair still looked reasonable, for a runaway. He'd heard a customer at work mention dry shampoos. The Saturday girls used talcum powder to get the adolescent grease out. Silly bitches, giggling and fussing over the powdery grey. His Sunday night girl was playing with her hair now, muttering about the May rain, looking at him sideways as she finger-combed the fringe.

He wondered what else she played with, and his groin swelled slightly with anticipation. Unlikely she'd have found a boyfriend yet. He bet she'd hitched into Edinburgh yesterday or come in on the train or a coach. Turned up in the early evening expecting soft-voiced hospitality only to encounter other runaways with street cred PhDs.

Graveyards, basements, doorways: everyone had their outdoor sleeping space and was keeping it. He bet she'd spent the night in a skip. He'd kept warm in one the first week he'd left home, nestled down beneath the upholstery and flattened cushions of a three-seater settee.

Casually he took his right hand from the wheel and reached into his top pocket. The girl tensed. Good reflexes. Good everything. He watched her sag back against the seat cover when she saw the packet of sweets.

David took his time unwrapping one, popped it in his mouth, chewed, smiling. They drove past satellite dishes, a child, a too-thin dog. As they left the housing scheme he offered her the packet.

'Thanks.' Offhand again. If he had his way, she'd learn. She freed one from the tube, then dropped it. Scooped it up from her lap, unwrapped, ate.

'Hey, you're hungry.' He reached into his other pocket and handed her a chocolate bar.

'Cheers, I owe you one.'

Up close her skin was slightly patchy. She had that slowing down look people got when they'd missed a few meals. The sweets had perked her up no end though, and now she started on the chocolate. He saw defeat, despair replaced by hope – or was it greed? – in her eyes. His palms were damp on the wheel: he had to force himself to keep speaking.

'There's this place where we could get a cheeseburger...'

'That'd be great.' She turned sideways on the seat towards him, and her short black skirt crept further up her taut young thighs. Slender, silky. God knows, he thought distractedly, how long her stockings would last. So many snags around, unexpected obstacles. Not his problem, though: he was in control.

He looked in the car mirror at himself and saw what she saw. Black, wavy hair – slightly too long to be fashionable. Brown eyes, finely-sculpted but even features, a newly-pressed grandad shirt. Looks that spoke of money, of confidence. A man like this would buy a girl a meal. Out of kindness, and natural generosity, not because he expected sexual payment. She was young enough to be his daughter. She was also – the thought jarred slightly – not much younger than his wife.

Heartbeat accelerating, he turned off the road that led into town, towards The Secret House. He smiled, forcing casualness. 'My treat.'

They drove on, the rain increasing. Perfect. Fewer people went out when it was this wet. Those who did go kept their heads down and their eyes half shut, paid little attention to passing cars. 'What's your name?' he asked into the silence. He'd wanted her to ask him first, had wanted interest, appreciation, a measure of respect. He'd given her his time, his presence, escape from the housing scheme. He'd offered his food, the watertight sanctuary of his car.

'I'm Kim.' It sounded like a dog's name: she'd probably made it up to keep him at bay. 'Yours?'

It was obviously an afterthought, a token gesture. Irritation gave him fresh energy, fuelled fresh plans. Pressing down on the accelerator, he turned the car towards the Secret House. 'David, call me David.' He'd decided not to lie about his name. He might want to see her for many months, make her his tenant. He'd be her mentor, her lover. She'd be so grateful, she'd be his to command…

'Area like this looks too good for a burger place,' she said, straightening slightly. She'd think otherwise in a moment, he thought. That was the beauty of this area, residential houses all around the slum part. He'd used it when he was younger to impress the other kids. Getting off the school bus, pointing: 'I live over there.' Prestige could be bought, for a while, with symbols and lies. Few of them knew that cutting through a sidestreet and expanse of waste ground brought them to his real house. Even fewer knew the pretty shortcut to some of the meanest and most hopeless tenements in town.

His tenement. Correction: his *father's* tenement.

He lived in a decent flat now, surrounded by decent folk. People who thought about life, and who discussed it. People who had quiet debates rather than endless days of screams and shouts.

The girl wasn't shouting yet, but she soon would be. He wanted her to cry out as she came. To moan, 'David, you're the best ever.' To beg him to make love to her again.

Fragments of classic song lyrics were raging through his head like hailstones: 'All Night Long', 'Touch Too Much'. They'd be so good together, he and his little Kim girl. His wife, Jeanette, with her long work hours and early bedtimes would never know.

Kim would lick him, suck him, brushing his juice-filled balls with her knowing fingers. She'd squeeze her tits together and he'd shoot off in between...

He turned to her, turned down the sidestreet that led to No Man's Land. That's what the newspapers had called it when he and his parents lived there. Now that it was uninhabited – was truly no man's land – they didn't call it anything at all.

'Hey, this isn't the way to the city centre,' Kim said, craning forward.

Know that, do you baby? Done the tourist bit?

He'd driven faster, faster, keeping an eye out for police cars.

'I didn't say it was.' He had to keep calm now, stress-free. Once she saw what he had to offer, recognised his gifts...

'But the burger house...?'

'We'll be there in a moment. First, I've something to show you, something you'll really like.'

As he spoke, he pulled into the kerb outside his childhood home. His was the only vehicle. Even through the darkness and rain, the derelict nature of the tenements was clear.

'I don't like it here. I want to go home. I want to...'

It was a cry from the heart: she obviously recognised his power. He liked that. Liked respect. Liked the increasing up and down lifting of her breasts beneath the clinging top.

'I could offer you a different home,' he said carefully, 'I've got this special place.' She made a lunge for the door, and he pulled her back, hooking his forearm round her neck till she started to choke. 'Don't scream or I'll tighten this,' he muttered, pushing his arm against her soft flesh for emphasis. She gagged audibly and he loosened the pressure slightly, still kept an unbreakable grip.

'Aaagh,' she said. 'Uuuh, uuuh…'

Was she pretending she couldn't breath to confuse him? He relaxed his arm another millimetre.

'Don't make a noise and you won't get hurt.'

Jesus, he sounded like someone from one of those black and white gangster movies. He hadn't meant his evening to end like this. Esmond had been screaming, Jeanette trying to comfort him. He'd felt the tension rising, had known he had to escape from the house. He'd wanted someone to listen to him, to make love to him. Someone who saw not who he was, but who he would become.

Moving carefully in the small car, he manoeuvred his body till it was over the joystick. Now he was facing the passenger window, with her body armlocked in front. 'We're going straight ahead,' he said, staring at the deserted tenement. 'Just keep quiet and we'll get along fine.'

Other than little half-sobs – quite attractive, really – she did what she was told. She obviously needed a mentor, someone to instruct and guide her, to keep her right. She could give him the female viewpoint of most situations, help him to vary his work…

Gasping slightly, he pushed forward, and got the two of them through the passenger door. Once they were out on the pavement, it was simple, easy as a lie. Just ten hurried steps, moving like a beast with two backs, to the entrance of the tenement close.

They'd just made it when he realised that he hadn't locked the driver's door. Damn and blast it. He could hardly drag her all the way back. He hoped no one took his old but very well polished Escort. Cars gave you status, freedom, power.

The close smelt as abandoned it had on his last few visits. No vagrant's faeces or signs that kids had been lighting fires. Once this place had been alive with time-killing and idly chatting neighbours. He'd bounced his ball down here, against the dusty concrete, whenever the weather was bad.

Bad to linger. Blinking slightly, he pushed her through fifty feet or so of tile-chipped passageway and out the other side. On, on, on, over the uncut grass and up the sloping grounds to his very own secret place.

His Secret House. His girl. His... Afterwards he found himself staring down at her body, wondering how much time had passed since they'd arrived here. Hours? Minutes? The shutters over the windows were fastened down. Impossible to tell if it was dark outside, or if it had gotten light whilst he lay curled here. He put on a third and fourth flashlight, and the shadows flickered. He didn't feel strong enough to unlock the door just yet. Or look at her face.

Carefully he pulled up her top and let it cover her features. He knew they'd be distorted. They had been when he'd taken his aching hands from her neck. Why had she struggled and screamed when...? He'd only wanted to... He stared into the middle distance, feeling weak and slightly sick.

The sickness passed. As it did so, he felt compelled to look at her body again, the lace-edged bra cups. Bolder now, he let his eyes feast on the swell of flesh within. That texture. It was worth a song in itself, was pale perfection. But writing was emotion recollected in tranquillity, and he wasn't tranquil – not yet.

Carefully he traced a thumb from her cleavage to her waistband. So rib-hard slender. He himself was slim, *too* slim. Better than being seriously obese, though: that took much of the dignity out of life.

Women gave a little tilt of their hips when they got out of skirts and trousers. He'd seen Jeanette do it when he'd surprised her getting ready for work. Kim couldn't assist, so undressing her was awkward. Her cool arms flopped back as he lifted her at the waist.

Finally he found two concealed side buttons and undid them. Gotcha. The stockings turned out to be tights. Going, going... He rolled them off, after removing her stilettos. Her panties came down at the same time.

He left the bra till last, though its presence irked him. He could remember once seeing his mother in her bra. He'd gotten up early that morning, feeling hungry. She'd been standing with her back to the fire, pulling on her skirt. Her face had been turned towards the window, looking dreamy, her top half immobilised in cross-your-heart cups. He'd thought that someone with breasts that substantial should be able to sort out his father. Surely any man would want to please breasts like that?

This girl had small breasts. It wasn't going to be the same, punishing breasts that small. He shook his head slightly and stared round the large, square room. What was he talking about? He didn't want to punish Kim. He just wanted to explore a little, to look...

And feel. Crouching astride her, he ran his palms over her deep pink nipples. Jeanette's nipples were larger, but they were brown. Not that nowadays he... Well, it didn't seem right, somehow. After all, she was his wife, his helper and the mother of his child.

Not like this little bint. She didn't have ties with anyone – not anyone that mattered. She wasn't deferential or respectful, or even especially nice. All promise, and no delivery – overselling her tits in a too-tight top. Now, though, she'd do anything he wanted her to. Like offering her vulva. Like spreading these pale and slender thighs.

As he parted her legs he was surprised at the temperature of her body. Ah, the inadequacies of language. She was still warm, he the stiff. He pushed forward, slid in easily. A lubricated freeway. Maybe, despite her struggles, she'd fancied him? Young girls didn't know what they wanted half the time. Take his teenage customers: they ran hot and cold, like taps.

Wetness. Warmth.

Afterwards he dressed her and carried her like a baby in his outstretched arms. She'd look like a sleeping drunk if they were seen. Or someone who'd gotten a bit too much brick dust in their veins along with the heroin. People often carried their relatives about around here.

Carry-outs and carry-ins. He daren't wrap her in a blanket and carry her fireman style. Those forensic guys weren't blockheads when it came to fibre checks. If they found the body they could trace what she'd been wrapped in. Cue Jeanette seeing their spare blanket on *Crimewatch UK*. Anyway, her body in a rug would look suspicious, didn't fit in at all with the lemming-style leap for her he'd just planned.

Breathing heavily, he covered the early-morning ground to the vehicle. Sweating anew, he squashed her into the boot. He'd made the journey to the cliffs before, with Jeanette and Esmond. They'd gone round a castle, had quite a pleasant day. Then, with its little boy stops, the journey had taken ages. Now it took little over an hour. As far as he knew, no one saw or heard him, a world using multi-coloured TV images to counteract the persistent grey backdrop of the rain.

Coarse grass, broken fences, waves far below. He opened the boot and her arm sprang out and he screamed in terror. Watched tremulously for further movement, his usually even heartbeat still thudding out of control. She could have killed him, even if it was just a reflex action. Was she truly and permanently motionless now?

Acid rising in his throat, he crept closer to the boot and studied her pale limbs as they misted in the unchanging drizzle. Her watch, in the moonlight, showed 4am.

Her underarms were still eerily warm to the touch. It took him long moments to lift and lower her from the boot, her penultimate travelling coffin. Took further moments to drag her to the cliff's uneven edge. But when he pushed she dropped towards the watery depths much faster than he'd have believed possible. Mission accomplished, yet the lack of drama left a dissatisfied cheated hollow in his chest.

Hurrying back to the car, David studied the greying sky. What was it some people called it? The darkest hour of the soul. But he didn't feel dark, not really. Just amazed at how easily and unexpectedly the girl had died. Already it felt as if she'd planned to die, a virtual suicide. Had teased him and struck out then expired the moment he fought back.

Now he had to get back to Jeanette. Hurriedly he slid behind the wheel. She'd be surprised if she got up and found his bed empty. She often brought him his breakfast cup of tea. He'd have some water when he got in: tonight's exertions had made him unusually thirsty. Keeping within the speed limit David set off for home.

CHAPTER ONE

J eanette took the eggs from the refrigerator. *Damn it!* – they were three days past their sell-by date. Unfortunately these were one and the same as far as David was concerned. Not that he was difficult, not really. It was probably just a reaction against life in his childhood home. The little he'd said had made it clear that he'd had to eat what he was given. Eat it, or…? God knows what, he wouldn't say.

Now he liked the eggs new and free range, the wholemeal bread lightly toasted. The butter had to be at room temperature – which was awkward in summer – and spread out evenly to encompass every millimetre of the crust.

Not that she begrudged David his way of doing things. He was definitely a special type of man. No one else she'd known had ever gone to University. Not neighbours or workmates or friends. OK, so David hadn't stayed the course, but he'd had his reasons. What was it he'd said? 'The truly intelligent know when to quit.' What he was doing now proved he wasn't a quitter: the singers of the future would pay thousands for words from his pen.

Returning the eggs to the fridge (she'd make an omelette for herself tomorrow) Jeanette switched off the grill and removed the toast. If eggs were out, it would have to be soya beans in sugar-free tomato sauce. David said that protein was important first thing.

Jeanette herself rarely bothered with more than a cracker or two. After feeding Esmond and David she often didn't feel like eating. Luckily the launderette had a chocolate machine for mid-morning snacks. On cold winter days she waited till Susan provided lunchtime cover, then nipped out to the cafe for soup and bacon rolls.

Roll on next weekend. Roll on family life – well, a semblance of it. David was still in bed: last night he'd gone out in a bit of a rush. She wished he coped better when Esmond was crying. She wished she'd had an education and could speak to him as an equal about such things. He was fine when the child was playing and sleeping, but if he was ill…

She wondered if David had gone to the pub yesterday to console himself. That would be unusual – he rarely drank. Still, a three-year-old with a sore throat was not the most pleasant companion. He'd snuffled and wailed so much she'd been ready for a drink herself.

No, David hadn't planned on fatherhood, and it hadn't come naturally to him. He was a man who needed space and lots of time. She looked round the kitchenette almost guiltily: he should have a full-sized kitchen with an Aga cooker, a freezer, units that matched. He would have had them, too – or would at least have been getting there – if he hadn't had to marry *her*.

She popped her head into the lounge, already smiling. Esmond was sitting up in his divan in the recess. 'Toast?' she asked hopefully.

'Toast,' he replied. He had a habit of repeating what others said, regardless of meaning. As she hurried back to the kitchen, Jeanette wondered what purpose the repetition served. He often did it even when they asked him a question, as though the sound of the words was more important than what they meant.

Maybe all kids did this? She didn't know any other three-year-olds. As ever, when he stared at her with those unfaltering eyes she felt strangely at a loss. Did other mums know what to say or do to get a proper reaction?

'Breakfast.' Pushing open their own bedroom door, she tried to say the word calmly. Her true inclination was to half-sing it: it was a word which contained a lilt. One morning – had he just received a rejection slip? – David had referred to her 'exhaustingly high spirits.' Since then, she'd tried to keep the inflection under control.

Two steps took her to the bunkbeds, to the lower bunk. David's head was tilted, face upwards, on the pillow, long lashes darkly fringed across the faint shadows beneath his eyes. His breathing was shallow, but he was clearly asleep. She loved this moment best of the entire day.

'Breakfast,' she said again. If only he would smile more often when he saw her. Drawing over the occasional table, she put the tray on top, then touched his arm: her proud and talented prince.

He whimpered in his sleep, pushed an arm from the duvet. Said something unintelligible, then his lids snapped open to reveal confused dark eyes.

'Someone was after you there,' she said, surreptitiously sniffing the air for alcohol. He shuddered, rubbed his face, began to focus. She smiled: 'You were having a bad dream.'

'Not me – I never dream.'

She let it go: he seemed to regard a nighttime nothingness as a sign of intellectual superiority. Yet she regularly heard him cry out in his sleep.

'Brought you toast,' she said, taking a reluctant step back. 'Esmond has had his. The mail hasn't arrived yet. I'm about to leave for work.'

'Oh, right.' He really must have had a skinful yesterday. Or maybe driven around, searching for new ideas for his songs. He did that sometimes, just searching, thinking. Without connections, it was hard to get a break. As he said himself, the ones who'd been to music school got their names known. Or else mummy and daddy were in the record business, and pulled strings. Daddy certainly wasn't a labourer, like his daddy. Mummy hadn't... whatever mummy once did.

David didn't talk much about those days. He'd said that his parents had been bastards, that his mother was dead. Once they'd driven past a cemetery and he'd said she was buried there, another time he'd driven within blocks of his childhood home.

She'd only found out what his father had done for a living after her own mother had asked him point blank. That had been a few days before the wedding, as part of her 'Are you good enough for my daughter?' questionnaire.

Jeanette snorted, remembering; that had been a laugh. By then she was already morning-sick with Esmond, teenage dreams of a white satin church wedding replaced by a cream cotton suit worn for half an hour in a stuffy registrar's.

'I've got to go. Thought we'd have fish suppers for tea,' Jeanette said.

David had pulled himself up and was rearranging the pillows. His bare arms reached out for the tray.

'You'll bring them in with you?' Already he looked distracted, gaze flitting away.

'Yep.' Hurriedly she reminded him what to give Esmond for his lunch and for his afternoon snack. 'You'll keep popping into the lounge to check on him?' Esmond was so self contained and quiet that David tended to forget that he was there. 'See you later,' she added, hurrying into the hall for her anorak. As she walked towards the door, the mail shot through it in single file.

A bill, then another bill. She read the return addresses on the envelopes. And more to follow: the monthly hire purchase payment was due on David's CD-player any day. Still, as he'd said, he needed it for his creative compiling. Those who missed out on research missed out on rewards.

Another music catalogue – this time a list of golden oldies – lay in the doorway. She picked it up, fighting a sudden urge to throw it in the bin. Not that she begrudged him his pleasures, far from it. Only the frequency of his purchases made her bite her nails. A little restraint wouldn't hurt their hunger-lunch finances. But when she'd mentioned it he'd made the research remark, then immediately gone for a solitary drive.

Shrugging into her anorak – why was it that, no matter how early you got up, mornings were always a rush? – she backtracked into the lounge. In her haste, she'd forgotten Esmond had been ill last night. Fine thing to leave without checking how he was.

She studied the three-year-old closely as he reached for the toys in his box. His nose looked unblocked today, skin free of blotches, eyes fixed on his small metallic cars.

'Hug for me?' She noticed that he'd finished his weak tea and toast. 'Daddy's taking care of you till teatime, Esmond.' She wondered if the changing schedules were confusing for the child. One day his dad took care of him, the next his gran. She'd voiced her fears out loud and David had looked it up in a book. The experts had said that a child simply needed lots of love and attention, could cope with more than one important person in their life at a time.

Mrs Landrew was important all right, especially in her own eyes.

'Don't know what you'd do with that child if it wasn't for me,' she often said. Which wasn't quite fair given that David took his son on his songwriting days and she, Jeanette, was available every weekend. In less than two years he'd be going to primary school. Thereafter he'd hardly need his gran.

After giving her child a hug, Jeanette set off on the twenty-five minute walk to the launderette. What had her mother said? 'I've already brought one child up and don't see why I should have to bring up another.' Wanda, who did the sewing alterations for the shop, had overheard her. She'd said she'd babysit for Esmond if it would help.

Walking on, Jeanette felt pleased with herself. She'd handled the situation well, managed to find things to say to the student-turned-seamstress for a good few minutes. She might never find another babysitter as clever or as nice. She'd introduce the girl to David: he was a good judge of character. He'd know if she was the right type.

CHAPTER TWO

David put down his fountain pen and switched on the CD-player. He leaned back in his swivel chair as his son walked in. 'Lo.' Esmond walked up to the desk holding his small stomach. That was his usual sign for hunger pangs.

Tomato soup, a brown bread roll and a Milky Bar. He found them grouped together on the floor of the fridge. There were also eggs which had passed both their sell by date and Jeanette's attention. Grimacing slightly, David threw them in the kitchen bin.

Waste not, want not, his mother had said throughout his childhood. Christ, such ignorant fucking cliches. It was a waste of energy if you vomited your breakfast, a waste of human spirit to be made to clean it up.

Mechanically, he heated the soup, spread the roll and cut it into quarters. Jeanette had gone on to margarine again, worse luck. Maybe he'd bring home butter from the Health Food Store. They gave him a discount, though not as much as he deserved.

Thinking of what he deserved, David felt the familiar rage start up behind his breastbone. He did everything in that place, was assistant manager in all but name. It was ridiculous that the Saturday girls got the same percentage off as he did. Some of them didn't even know where everything was kept.

He winced as he loaded his son's meal onto a fluorescent tray. Its yellow pattern blurred before his eyes. He'd only had three hours sleep after... after driving back from the cliff-top. He shivered, assaulted by a sudden mental image of a choking, flailing Kim. He stared more intently at the tray and the image faded. Wished Jeanette's mother would stop giving them such gaudy gifts.

One day they'd be able to afford all the luxuries they wanted. Don McLean had said the money from writing 'American Pie' gave him the option of not working ever again.

'Here we are.' Back in the lounge, Esmond was already sitting on his little black plastic chair behind his equally sized-down matching table. Jeanette's mum had actually bought the child the set in red. Red, the colour of notice-me Post Boxes, the colour bored house-wives wore on their rare nights out. David had driven back to the shop and changed it for black pieces that matched the rest of his furniture. A man needed a masculine, restful room.

Not that his own settee was black plastic – rather black leather. The portable TV and CD were on similar black and chrome stands. Esmond's bed, in the recess, spoiled the effect somewhat – but Jeanette had refused to let him curtain the area off. 'He'd be frightened' she said, 'He might even feel claustrophobic in the dark.' Honestly, she didn't know the meaning of the word – like he did. Though her mother was stupid, he doubted if she'd ever been deliberately bad. He could tell Jeanette things that would make her tremble. But would they also make her see him in a different light?

That was the trouble with relationships – there was always someone ready to screw you. If she saw him as a victim she might start to defy… Not that he wasn't a match for her – for any woman – but she was the full time worker, brought in most of the cash.

She was also the one who got the child benefit. Without her he'd have to relinquish his health shop three-day-week. David shivered, imagining the restrictions of a full time nine to five existence. He'd have to meet schedules, follow others – he'd never find the time to write and perfect his songs.

Not that he was finding much time now – there was so much to think about. If only Kim hadn't been so foolish last night. He'd been so peaceful these last three months, doing up The Secret House; happy, almost, imagining a respectful naked mistress at his feet.

Not that Jeanette wasn't respectful – she showed due deference. But when it came to appearances she didn't try very hard. He never felt like holding her, far less fucking her. He wanted someone with big breasts and long, dark hair.

Kim hadn't been quite right – but she'd been available. He'd thought they could have sex together, take it from there. He'd put so much thought into the place: cleaning, furnishing and painting it. Changed its interior from a large disused makeshift canteen shed to a veritable wendy house.

For Adults Only. Yet Kim hadn't behaved like an adult. He'd locked the door the second they entered the place, pocketed the key. Switched the nearest flashlight on, keeping a hold of her. Moved to switch on some of the others, pulling her with him into the centre of the room.

Easy, easy. He'd pushed her gently into a foldaway chair, and leaned back against the old sink unit. Now they could start talking, exchanging tales. But she'd leaped up, and made for the door with the speed of a house mouse. Screaming, flailing, like a fox being torn apart by a dozen hounds.

Perhaps the shadows made her nervous: the torches took some getting used to, all beams of focused bright. In a few more minutes he'd have switched on the ones at the other end of the room to balance things. He'd also have opened the shutters to let in the burgeoning moonlight. Really, she'd had no need to be afraid.

Indeed, this was the very place he'd come to to banish fear. How many times had he rushed in terror from his tenement house? It was a pilgrimage to safety: down the stairs, through the washing green and up the embankments' slope.

No one could find and beat him there. Or rather, no one tried to. No clothes-conscious adult risked the stinging thistles and staining cuckoo spit. Not once had his mother sought him amongst the pungent wood pulp. His father's belt had never journeyed to that land of rusted nails and fledgling trees.

Of course in those days this outhouse had been just one of many buildings. The whole area was given over to timber factories, cabins, yards: to the housing and storing and cutting and shaping of wood. In those days he'd stand on tiptoe to peer through the window, watching workmen drink their tea and roll their too-thin cigarettes. He'd heard them telling jokes and laughing, seen them rolling dominoes they called bones or playing cards.

No one hit anyone here, no one shouted. Once a workman had come out of a door suddenly and careered into him, and his frightened boy's heart had raced. He'd flinched, backed away, started to raise his right hand to shield himself. But the man had just stared, and said 'This isn't the place for you, son. It's not safe.'

Son.

The one time he'd had to phone his father's work, he'd said 'It's me, dad,' and the familiar voice at the other end had said ' Eh? Who?'

He'd been feeling similarly anonymous the day he rediscovered his beloved outhouse. Esmond had been wheezing and barking all day. Croup, the doctor said, when Jeanette called him out in a lunchtime panic. He'd said there was no cure, but suggested that steam might help.

Jeanette had run and run the hot water. Steam, wheeze, steam, wheeze, steam. Snuffling, screaming, crying, barking, sobbing. Small white limbs throwing off covers, eyes bright with confusion and fear.

Christ, the horror of that helpless screaming. *Been there, done that, for years and years and years.* Buried alive in a cot instead of a coffin. Neighbours patting your head and refusing to see your pain. 'Isn't he getting big?' The mindless comments. Big bruises on small arms. 'He fell down the stairs again.'

'What will you be when you're older?' Frightening questions, when mum, dad and the world said he was stupid, useless, that they'd been given the wrong one at the hospital. They didn't want him – so why would anyone else? He wouldn't treat Esmond like that – never, ever. But he couldn't help him now, put things right. That was the awfulness of childhood, the inability to escape from those around you. Even if people listened you didn't have the words to make them understand.

They can starve and dehydrate me, can ignore me. Was that what the three-year-old was thinking? *Maybe they've injected me with something to make me feel this sick...* I haven't, Esmond, there's no need to keep crying. Steam, wheeze, steam, wheeze, steam. He had to get out of the house, had to drive, feel powerful. You were an adult, in control, when you got behind the wheel of your car.

Familiar streets, new territory, looming and receding. Finally he'd found himself outside his childhood home. Strange, he had no memory of getting there, like a journey repeated on the motorway for the hundredth time. His father had been decanted long ago, of course. The place had gotten less and less habitable. The council had finally moved the occupants into a new scheme several blocks down the road. The new scheme had little gardens and a council gardener who visited regularly. That bastard had really landed on his feet.

David had stared at the past, at its place in the present. He preferred to think of the old man as dead – Otherwise, he might kill the fucker himself. No, it wasn't daddy dearest he wanted to see. Instead he wanted to climb up through the tall weeds of the comforting embankment. Wanted to stand in the shelter of the corrugated buildings, hidden behind their stretching bulk.

He'd gone through the musty disused tenement passage that was commonly known as a close, and up the sloping former washing green. Had kicked his feet through long reeds and thistles, where once there had been short dry garden grass. Then up the weed-strewn embankment to the area behind the washing house – the same washing house which had screened him from danger all those years ago.

It was perfect this place, perfect. The washing house roof blanketed you off from the tenement windows, from swinging belts and staring eyes. The twenty foot high wall which surrounded the timber ground completed the circuit, made you safe from anyone who passed on the other side.

Not that he had to worry much now, on either account. The windows of the tenements had long been made people-less. The area on the other side of the embankment had become a graveyard for cookers and settees.

He reached the top of the slope and stopped, bewildered. Weeds, wood mould and grey squares of concrete stretched out before him: they'd knocked the three main buildings down. Well, maybe knocked wasn't the right word for structures made of corrugated iron. Dismantled seemed a better one somehow. Pushing past bushes and young trees he turned the corner. Ah, memories. The big brick outhouse remained.

Maybe someone was storing things inside it? Only his breathing fast, he began to move cautiously forwards. Closer, closer: the door stood slightly ajar. Turning sideways to squeeze past, he entered. No one had been here for some years. For this decade it was clearly untrammelled ground.

Dust-torn spiders' webs, blown leaf mould. He would bring back a broom and sweep the place out. Not that, at that stage, he'd planned on using it. He simply felt the wrongness of such peacefulness gone to waste.

Outside was a world where people abused and misunderstood each other. Here the timber workers had grouped for their tea breaks, had joked and played. Perhaps he, too, could come here, meet his psyche. Meet the Muse that so often deserted him at home.

At home, Esmond was crying, ill, over-active. At home, Jeanette watched the soaps on the telly and her words-heavy mum called round. Here: no mindless distractions. Here, the potential to bring round who he wanted, when he liked. Jeanette tried hard but she wasn't really in his IQ bracket. He snorted aloud, felt sad.

The city had a Freethinkers Group. Maybe he could join it, find a soul mate. They'd probably want him to manage it if he could find the time. The group could come here and have all-night discussions. He'd need chairs of course, and a barbecue, and plates.

No problem: the DIY shop would sell most of the things he wanted. To raise the money, he'd have to sell some of his compact discs. Luckily there was a thriving market in secondhand goods on the music scene. As he planned out his agenda, his excitement grew.

He already had some spare paint at home which would freshen the place. He examined the window shutters carefully: they'd need some creosote, and new locks. So would the door, which would benefit from some unbreakable reinforcing panels. Not that he planned on doing anything illegal, of course. But if he brought a female Freethinker here and they decided to make love they would need the privacy that locks would bring.

For the next three months he'd come to his Secret House often, growing bolder and bolder. No one saw him, no one heard him. He'd fashioned a thirty feet by thirty feet world where civilised laws no longer applied. He locked his newly-fixed door, let the air and warmth come in through the open just-fixed shutters. He would hear someone coming long before they saw him, could close the windows off from prying eyes.

There was a practical reason for leaving the shutters open while he stayed there, though. Flashlights were expensive. Batteries,

Jeanette would have said if she'd known, didn't just grow on trees.

The chest had though, quite literally. It was a beautiful well-preserved oak. It had been protected with oilskins when he'd found it. Beauty lying in the centre of an outhouse, waiting to be claimed. It contained record books of transactions dating back a hundred and twenty years. Faded prices, promises, old fashioned names.

There was a song there, David had thought when he discovered it – something less inane than lyrics about crass betrayal and unrequited love. As he'd told Jeanette the other day, he'd always dare to be different. You were little more than an echo if you went with the flow.

Kim had gone with the flow when the tide went out. His mind returned with a start to the present. Was it just last night that he'd thrown her over the cliff, watched her fall? His fallen angel, his tamed she-devil. A slight after-ache in his groin spoke volumes about that.

Such loss of control, and he hadn't even been drinking. She'd gone for the door and he'd gone like a bloodhound for her throat. Clasp hands, here comes oblivion. But it hadn't been like it was in the movies, hadn't been pretty and neat. There, the woman said 'Please, no!' then went limp and lightweight. The hero carried her to his getaway car, her skin pale and interesting, limbs gracefully floppy like a doll.

Instead, she'd reached for his face, fingers splayed like talons. A frightening, unseemly, vicious little wretch. He'd kept his head well back, arms pressing hard. She'd started spasming. Cheeks going puffy, eyes like a goitre patient having a fit. Pressing, tightening, panicking, perspiring. How long? How much longer would it take?

And the sound effects, sweet Jesus, the sound effects. Gagging, gasping, tongue obscenely prominent and erect. Sweat had dampened his recently-shampooed hairline. Damn her for causing him such anxiety.

Towards the end he'd heard the sound known as the death rattle – one he'd heard before in the hospital when visiting his grandmother. Then, of course, he hadn't caused it. Still, there was a first time for everything, they said.

Like entering a corpse. Funny, it had been almost as pleasant as normal fucking. OK, so the girl didn't move, but neither did she expect you to make her come. And she didn't ask when you'd be seeing her again. And she didn't force you to maintain her swelling body and ultimately her child.

He looked over now at Esmond, quietly making huge slashing crayon marks on his drawing book. He was a good boy, really. He'd been a good boy himself – not that you'd have known. *She'd* doled out the sneers and slaps and insults. 'I see you've got your nose stuck in a book again,' in her long suffering voice. She was dead now, had died of lung cancer when he'd been sixteen. He'd left home a week later and rarely gone back. Too late now, to show her how wrong she was about him. Too late to show his intelligence, his power.

He'd show the rest of the bitches, though – had already done so. He remembered the girl's gasps – a plea for breath. Soon women everywhere would recognise his creativity. Soon they would study and sing and marvel at his songs.

If he could only find the right woman, bring her to The Secret House. She could be the very first to experience his gifts. He'd have to look for someone sensible, young yet mature, attractive. Someone who would sit at his feet and listen and ask for more.

He smiled, enjoying the images. This time he'd choose someone intelligent who wouldn't make a fuss. If she did, he would have to bolt her in and pull down the shutters. He would have to point out the error of her ways.

CHAPTER THREE

May in Edinburgh was like a battle of the elements as first sun then wind appeared, died down, returned. Wanda liked it though, liked the swirling breeze which puffed out her half-sleeved jacket, its mildness playing through the shoulder length bob-cut of her hair. The other fashion 'n' fabric students favoured much shorter styles. Leave them to their geometric cuts and spike-holding sprays! She preferred tresses that swung with her movements. Hair that a man could run his fingers through, caress and kiss.

Not that she wanted to take things to the opposite extreme and be visually boring. Didn't want hair like Jeanette Frate's. The poor woman's crowning glory was a boyish short back and sides. No hair dye packet would ever boast that shade. Dirty blonde, she supposed that was what you would call it. Dull texture, dull cut, dull shade. Not that she herself spent hours on her hair and makeup. But there was a level of colourlessness in some people's appearance that made her wonder what was going on inside.

Be all you can be. It had been a slogan on the television when she was a child. No one was being all they could be, of course, at least not on this planet. But, despite the occasional lazy week, she, Wanda, was doing her best.

She'd avoided the matriarchal College Halls by finding herself a flat in the private rented sector. She was taking in alterations from the launderette to eke out her grant. She'd done reasonably well in the first two years of her fabric 'n' fashion studies. Had two more years of such studying and scrimping to survive. But after this month she'd be free for the summer holidays. Long weeks of sun-kissed possibility stretched ahead.

Babysitting Jeanette's child would be a particular bonus. Ultra convenient. She could hand back a big bag of alterations, pick up one very small child.

Wanda walked on, reflecting. If she were honest, she wanted to care for Esmond for reasons other than the cash. The one time she'd seen the boy she'd felt a sadness at his near-wordless passivity. Wanted to bring smiles to the pale offspring of an equally pallid mum. Both seemed to be holding back words, feelings. As if the life spark was missing, as if their sense of purpose was deeply asleep.

Wanda grimaced to herself as she started to cross at the green traffic lights. She always thought about things much too deeply. Part of her reason for choosing an artistic rather than the academic course had been an attempt to lighten up.

Be all you can be. Esmond's gran, who had brought him in to the launderette the day they'd met had been more than she *ought* to have been. More sharp, more self-centred, more self-assured. 'I told Jeanette,' she began most sentences. Wanda had disliked her on sight.

As she turned into the road that housed the launderette, Wanda could smell the warm steam. Could envisage Jeanette nodding and smiling. Taking in service washes, explaining to newcomers how the slot machines worked. What did she think about as she stared over the wooden counter? Did she dream of a job – of a life – that was other than this?

She herself wanted to work with people, somehow help them. Strangers were surprised when she said as much. You could see them thinking that fabric and fashion wasn't a form of therapy. But people felt better if they *looked* better. Colour played a part in changing mood.

We get it brighter said the sign on the door of the launderette. It was 4pm. Wanda walked in swinging her alterations bag.

'That's another batch taken care of, Jeanette,' she said long before she reached the counter, in a singing-out voice reminiscent of a Butlins camp. Jeanette did that to you – it was a reflex. You wanted to make her take notice, shake herself, *react*.

'There's more in the back,' Jeanette said neutrally. She was wearing an off-cream overall over her clothes. The last two times they'd met, Wanda had got her talking about her mother, about Esmond. Seemed with Jeanette you had to rebuild the relationship each time. She stared sadly at the pale blue collar sticking out from Jeanette's overall. She dressed like a forty year old yet could only be about twenty two. Jeanette walked into the back shop and came back carrying two more bags.

'Lots of people want stuff hemmed and taken in for the summer.' They looked over as the door opened to admit a portly woman.

Wanda lowered her voice: 'I bet there's a lot more want clothing taken out.'

Jeanette's laugh, clear and genuine, surprised both of them. 'David says things like that,' she admitted. 'He hates people being the slightest bit overweight.'

'Watches what he eats then, does he?'

'No, he doesn't have to. He just stays slim.' She lowered her voice slightly, and glanced towards the window. 'Actually, sometimes I worry that he's *too* thin. You know, if he got ill or something he'd waste away. Matter of fact, you've altered some of his waistbands for him. He always has to get them taken in.'

It was the longest speech Jeanette had yet made without prompting. Wanda felt absurdly privileged and pleased. 'Maybe his job's stressful?' she asked, pushing for information, 'You know, speeds up his metabolism, keeps him thin?'

'I don't think… he's a song writer,' Jeanette said, taking a tissue from her smock pocket. She wiped it distractedly under her nose.

'A *songwriter?*' Somehow she'd imagined a milkman, a security man, or someone who worked for one of those electrical outlets.

'Yes. He's not actually… I mean, it takes years to make any money from it. He works part time in a health food store to make ends meet.'

'Oh, which one?' Curiouser and curiouser. 'I buy muesli and eggs from that shop along the road.'

'It's just called The Health Food Store,' Jeanette said, naming the area. 'David says the owner has the imagination of a dried prune.' She seemed to like talking about David. She began to wave her hands as she talked, shifted her weight from sandalled foot to sandalled foot, played with her hair. Rather like a laboratory monster coming to life, mused Wanda. She choked back a smile, felt guilty for her uncharitable thoughts.

'Does he write in the evenings, then?' she prompted. This time she'd keep the conversation going – really talk.

'No, Mondays and Fridays he stays home to write his songs. Tuesday to Thursday he helps manage the store.' She paused, 'Of course other times he's looking for inspiration. Goes to The Botanic Gardens – things like that.'

'It must be exciting,' Wanda murmured, more to herself than to the older girl. Jeanette jangled her change bag, nodded, looked down. Wanda sighed. This was hard work as always. Did the girl never introduce a new topic by herself? She wondered how many people had resolved to befriend Jeanette then dropped the notion. She was like a New Year Resolution that faded within days. 'What does David write about?'

'Oh, issues which matter. You know.' She clearly hadn't liked that query, was looking away again, arms across her chest.

'I suppose it's a difficult thing to talk about,' Wanda murmured, sending messages of encouragement with her eyes.

A youth walked slowly through the door, tortoise-like due to a heavy duty camping pack. Jeanette looked at him hopefully. The boy swung down the pack, dug into his money belt for silver, put some in the washing powder slot. Seeing that he knew what he was doing Jeanette looked away again. Wanda leaned closer, cleared her throat.

'Does he just write the lyrics or also write his own music?'

'No, he's between partners. There are fewer people can compose the music than can write the words.'

'Maybe he could learn, or…?'

'He's a husband and a father. He already has more than enough to do.'

Ouch. No one, then, could criticise the beloved David. Somehow out of character, this defensive love. This was the woman who had stood by and let her mother criticise her in Wanda's presence for not taking a packed lunch to work.

'He's very good,' Jeanette added as if Wanda had suggested otherwise. Her hands had gone into her pockets, slightly lifting the smock. 'In fact he and Esmond are picking me up tonight – we're going shopping. We try to get enough food to last us all week.'

She made it sound as if Esmond was jointly responsible. Privately, Wanda wondered why David didn't just do the shopping himself in the mornings when it was quiet. Jeanette must be wiped out by the time she'd finished at this place. Why put herself through another two hours of wear and tear? She couldn't be one of those traditional woman's-place-is-in-the-supermarket kind of a woman – not with David acting as part time house husband. Maybe she just liked being with her little family? There were too few people like her nowadays...

Wanda decided to hang around and catch a glimpse of the man. Even if she couldn't find an excuse to stay here she could watch him from the bus shelter across the road. She was mildly curious about the man who had married Jeanette.

As she accepted a coffee from the laundry worker, the student wondered what David would look like. She figured he'd be around five foot two, with glasses and weak grey eyes. He'd have lank brown locks like the before pictures in a shampoo advert. No, make that balding with hair combed over from one side. She suspected he'd be one of those unfortunates who'd started losing his hair before he left secondary school. She bet he would look and sound washed out.

CHAPTER FOUR

Stupid bitch. Wanted herbal tranquillisers and 'something soothing' to sew inside her pillow. He'd sold her a lavender sachet when what she really needed was a good fuck.

David stared out across the counter. You saw it all here – the jumpy ones in for their calming tablets, the weary ones wanting iron tonics and dextrose drinks. Sugar gave quick energy, and the shop packaged it cleverly: maltose, fructose, sucrose. Sugar-based calories by any other name.

'Have you some of that slimming formula they advertised last night on the telly? You know, the natural one with oat bran which fills you up?' The woman facing him would benefit more from life-long liposuction: bust overhanging a Michelin Man sized waist.

'We've got those new bulking tablets,' he said, coming out reluctantly from behind the counter, 'Entirely natural, and additive free.' Christ, some people were a mass of contradictions. She obviously filled her body with all kinds of junk.

The woman left, clutching her package. A young boy squeezed in past her as she blundered through the doorway. 'Have you got some of that body building powder?' His school blazer was thrown across one bony shoulder, too-hopeful face grasshopper thin.

Ah, irony. Women with thick curls seeking controlling herbal hair gels, others with thin locks buying lotions to thicken the hair. Girls bought lemon astringents to keep their grease and acne in check, whilst their mothers rubbed coconut oil into tight, dry skin.

And all the time, he, David, advised them. And they followed his recommendations and spent money and went away. Then praised the manufacturer or the shop itself or Mother Nature. They never, ever gave him a second thought.

No one ever told Mrs Melloway that he'd done a good job. No one ever suggested he was long overdue a promotion or substantial raise.

'Sonny, have you any honeycombs?' He'd give her sonny. A woman wearing a heavy silk headscarf in May. Typical fifty-something bitch, patronising others and probably living off the alimony granted in an bitter eighties divorce. Typical customer, too: shouting and gesticulating as though he were a signpost rather than an expert. An expert who'd picked up the data by himself along the way.

'Just tell the customer you've heard it's good, and they'll buy it,' said Tracey on his first day. She worked on the till in the mornings: he did the till and the salad counter by himself in the quieter afternoons. But he hadn't wanted to be thought of as ignorant, had gotten books from the library on homoeopathic remedies, organic vegetables and the like. Not that it had done him any good – Mrs Melloway his boss still didn't single him out as special. She didn't even ask about his songs.

No respect – that was her trouble. Not that everyone treated him with such indifference – he thought he'd seen admiration in that student's eyes the night before. What was her name? Wanda. Creative, too. Something to do with fashion 'n' fabric, Jeanette had said.

Wanda knew about his song-writing thanks to Jeanette, which made him feel better. He couldn't stand it when people thought he just worked in a store. Stupid cunts – couldn't they see that he was University level? Didn't his obvious creativity shine through?

'Any seaweed tablets, mister? My mum said to get the extra strong variety.' Christ, if there was anything worse than middle class indulgence, it was the working classes latching on to the latest craze. Usually they couldn't pronounce it far less spell it, sent their kids in with notes asking for 'Ekstra Fir-Gin Oil.'

The boy who wanted seaweed pills rolled a five pound note between his fingers as he turned towards the medicinal section. 'Five ninety five for the trial pack's the cheapest we've got,' said David, cheering up.

The boy dug into his purple and yellow baggies. 'I've got a pound coin in the lining.'

You bloody well would. David walked over, using most of his willpower to keep the sarcasm dormant. You never knew who was snooping around.

'Dried kelp, fresh kelp, powdered algae, liquid algae or tablets?' David took a deep breath, 'Seaweed extract, seaweed that's sun dried...'

'Dunno.' said the boy and pointed at a plastic tub with a clear price sticker. 'I'll just take these.'

David was free, once more, to return to his thoughts. Where was he?

Ah, yes, Wanda, with her eyes trained, like a disciple on his face. You couldn't help but feel good about yourself with a girl like that talking to you, nodding. Couldn't help but feel that a soul mate might exist.

What did he write about? Where did he send his work? Who was he influenced by? She'd known what to ask about and when. Would he still speak to the likes of her, she'd queried, smiling, when fame and fortune came his way?

He hugged himself, remembering. They could keep in touch. She could come to the house, have a liqueur or a glass of wine or tea. He'd make supper – no, Jeanette could do that. Wanda could tell him about her mindset, the inspiration behind her work.

But for now he needed a body for The Secret House. Someone subservient who wouldn't panic and run for the door. Why. there were countless women who would welcome what he offered. Sex and solitude, privacy, a home. The House was mellow during daylight now that it was summer. In the evenings he'd keep her warm with his hard cock and soft sure hands.

The shop was empty. Carefully he adjusted his trousers, turned his mind to the sack of walnuts. He had to weigh them out into individual bags. Such a waste of talent, of uniqueness, his IQ reduced to shaking long-shelled nuts onto newly-washed scales.

The scales he'd played through his headphones last night had made him more energised. Jeanette had gone to bed at ten, leaving him ready to rock. In the aftermath of talking with Wanda he felt lonely. How could he best fill the vacant hours? He couldn't fritter away the night on small things, despised the chocolate-eating house-wifes and beer-swilling men he saw all around. Small people leading equally small, often pointless, lives. He, David, was above such petty pleasures. He'd always known he was destined for bigger things.

Big tits. Funny how a surfeit of free time always made him randy. As if it were decreed that leisure time be devoted to his cock. And why not? Sex transcended all cultures, creeds and classes. Creative people like himself needed release much much more. And took it in whatever form it was offered. Soon a mistress at The Secret House, but for now…?

He'd lain back in the armchair and stroked himself. Felt his phallus pushing through his trousers. Imagined what Jeanette would say if she walked in now. Fact was, she'd probably take a vow of silence, but the look she'd give before rushing out of the door would say it all.

Squeezing, sliding: he couldn't quite get there with his much-used graphic images. He tried and failed to conjure up a more thrilling scene. Maybe he should go to The Secret House? He'd be closer to the memory of Kim's biteable nipples, the final movements of those small convulsing breasts. And her backside, bared and ready for his inspection. And the roughly triangular shape of her dark brown bush…

No, no. Trying too hard, he throbbed and leaked, unsated. He'd have to let his fingers do the walking once again. Across the Phone Directory rather than across his cock, though. Was it the fact that another did the work which made him feel such lust? *A girl's* imagination working overtime, *a girl's* promised mouth working towards a definite end…

Which girl's mouth, though? He got the list out from his desk tray with anticipation. Jeanette didn't know about this tray. It slotted in above one of the drawers in his writing bureau. He kept it locked, kept the key in his portfolio folder at all times. His Secret List. His Secret House. Men had to have their secrets. Men had to be have hidden moments if they were ever to control their own lives.

The flat, the street, the very world seemed quiet. Holding its breath as he, David, decided who he'd have. Mandy with her huge mammaries, an endless milk round? Or Debbie Demure, who aimed her tongue to please? Already hard again, he settled for Nancy, who nursed more than hurt fingers. SRN stood for Sucking Raving Nympho – or so the advert said.

Silly, really. He could have been much more creative. There was a place in this line of business for the more sophisticated entrepreneur. If he hadn't already been so busy he could research the situation. One day, when his songs brought in funding, he might.

The only thing that needed setting up now though was his penis. He cradled the phone at his left shoulder as he dialled. He'd need his right hand – and wrist action – free for other things any second now. As soon as her promises began to filter down the phone line, he squeezed and stroked.

'I'd like you to take my uniform off.'

In his head, he unbuttoned and unzipped her.

'You'd slide down my nursing dress, and pull off my panties. I'd get hot just watching you. I love doing it with men. I love…'

He'd been worried for a moment she was going to tell him she also loved doing it with women. Another call, to a *Guess What I've Been Up To?* line had gone off at a tangent like that. Stupid bitches. He'd hung up in disgust. Men wanted women to themselves, in blissful private. They didn't want to share them with another cunt. Men wanted women who cared enough to try hard. Women who were clean and encouraging and hot and tight and wet…

Like Nancy the Nurse. God, yes, he'd do it to her. She wouldn't want the others after she'd been fucked by him.

'Take your pants off' she said, and David unzipped himself.

'Imagine I've got your hardness in my hand…'

He could imagine her dark hair swishing silkily against his shaft.

'…and my long, blonde hair is brushing against my tits…'

Blonde hair, was it? He'd been picturing a brunette pageboy cut. That jarred.

'I've still got my nursing cap on, waiting for you to instruct me…'

He'd have her cap off and a whole lot more besides. He imagined tearing open her bra and pulling off her G-string, pushing her stockinged legs far apart on a sperm-smeared bed. When he was rich he'd keep women like this in a harem. When he was rich he'd have sex as he liked it all the time.

Screwing them, squeezing them, sucking them, buggering them…
'*You slide right up me…*'

He came, body bent forward, hand catching his every squirt. Hung up on Nancy mid-sentence, got a tissue, scrubbed hard.

David blinked, remembering the recent session. He looked blankly at the empty health shop then looked down dazedly at himself. He was hugely and visibly hard again. What if a female customer walked in and he had to come out from behind the counter? He could offer her a health drink with a difference, that was for sure.

This time he'd find the right woman – well, girl, preferably. Someone unformed who could be guided, moulded, trained. He'd look for quiet, raw potential, sexuality. Nothing blatant, more a prospective untapped need. As he weighed and bagged the walnuts, David watched and waited. Some day soon the right customer would come along.

CHAPTER FIVE

U p, down, up, down, up. Jeanette stared at the buttocks all around her. Were other women sizing her up the same way? She did another press up, found her eyes trained on a bottom in tight pink leggings. Wanda had said her jeans would do just fine. Wanda had also said that no one cared how you dressed here. Now, faced with such fashionable class mates, she wasn't so sure.

Wanda had said a lot of things, like how women needed time out from being mothers. Wanda said that women had to do things for themselves. Like making your thighs ache? Like tightening the muscles of your shoulders? Jeanette snorted wryly as her knees pressed more deeply into the mat.

Up, down, up, down... She urged her willpower to come forward and help her continue. The teacher had said newcomers should go at their own pace. But she didn't want to be singled out, made different. She'd feel so self conscious if she gave up before the rest.

'Now we'll do some running on the spot,' said the teacher. The class spread out immediately like a blown dandelion clock. Ah, so there were others like her who preferred a quiet corner at the back of the spacious room.

'All right?' Wanda came over looking slightly dishevelled.

'A bit out of breath.' Jeanette said. She wished she could think of something witty or at least interesting to keep the conversation going. Wanda would soon get bored with her, find a better friend.

Wanda was the friendly, chatty type, determined to get the most out of everything. Why were some people born so clever, so attractive, so *right*? They got an education, a good job, a social circle.

Whereas she... Well, it was better than she'd ever hoped for, but she sometimes felt there was something missing from her life.

Maybe if she had more to contribute? Jeanette quickly bent and retied one training shoe to fill the silence. Even if Wanda never asked her back to the class, she'd have something to tell David. He wasn't the only one who could go out at night.

'Now for some leg work,' The teacher restarted the cassette tape and the women began to kick their legs out in a can-can, lifting their arms to match. Such co-ordination, such grace. Jeanette did what she could, even though her lungs burned. She wondered how Esmond was getting on downstairs.

Ninety pence for the creche – it was a bargain. Obviously subsidised, which was just as well. Even with their low rent it wasn't easy balancing the budget. When the area was upgraded the rents would go through the newly-refurbished roof.

'You're doing OK.' Wanda again, skipping unselfconsciously over. So what if she was just being polite? Jeanette's mum had been so protective that she hadn't had a chance to make mates at school, far less find a best friend like everyone else.

It had been: 'Who's that girl with the long hair you were talking to? She might have nits.'

She'd been similarly forbidden to talk to the one girl in the class whose mother wasn't married, to the twins who lived in a rundown part of the town. Girls who swore were to be avoided, as were those who wore makeup and giggled and joked with boys.

She'd have ignored the list, if her mother hadn't picked her up from school all the time. Right through Primary she'd done it, eyes everywhere, seeing all. 'Mum, you don't have to come anymore,' she'd begged, hating the other girls' laughter.

'What with strange men hanging around, and a main road to cross and all?' You couldn't reason with a mother like that. There were germs lurking in the school lunches, sex attackers inhabiting every park and side street. All of them after little Jeanette, all desperate to molest her with their pricks.

Dirty word – Mum would have gone all mottled pink if she'd heard her talking so dirty. But David ignored her mother's list of life-long banned words. David said that language was there to be used, that we should be proud of our bodies. That we should call things by their proper names.

David said a lot more, yet undressed alone whenever possible. She knew he considered himself to be too thin. He looked fine with his clothes on, though, especially when wearing his off-white summer slacks.

The song ended, and was replaced by a slow, haunting Gaelic one.

'Now for some thigh stretches' said the teacher, splaying her legs out at the sides. Grimacing slightly, Jeanette copied her, flexing her ankles. Immediately her legs felt slimmer, longer, more *alive*. There was something compelling about lengthening yourself out like this, really concentrating on your body, each tiny muscle pushing to reach its goal. Straightening again, Jeanette was amazed at her own daring. She'd faced strangers, new movements, and survived. She'd been doubtful when Wanda had suggested it. She hadn't exercised for years, was used to work and home.

Home, where she watched TV, and knitted, the demands of hand and eye co-ordination negating the need for conversation. Not that David actually sat beside her much. He preferred to relax on the floor with his headphones on, his eyes flickering in rhythm with the buzzing hum. Sometimes she loved the peace, security. Other days she felt like his mum.

But no, his mother was dead – and he'd hated her. He didn't hate Jeanette – he just couldn't show much love. He paid her compliments, though, in little ways. What had he said recently? 'Not many women your age can knit like that.' She'd been making him a jumper, a thin lemon V-neck to see him through the summer. 'You could take orders from other people if you wanted,' he'd added, fingering up a sleeve.

'How do you mean?' she'd asked, knowing he loved to explain things.

'Bring in some money, charge for wool and your time.'

She'd been so pleased that she'd wanted to hug him. But you didn't hug a man like David – he was always too remote. Instead, she'd returned to her needles with renewed fervour, clicking, clicking against the background of the news. Another young girl missing in Scotland. Where did they run to? It happened all the time.

Stretching, contracting. They were on to the cool down, now. Maybe she should have told David where they were going? He'd have happily picked them up in the car.

It was about time she benefited from it – she contributed to its petrol costs most weeks. It wasn't even as if she could drive. David was too busy to teach her and the idea didn't really appeal.

She wasn't sure why he insisted they keep the thing. When Esmond had been a baby it made bringing all the bulky goods home very easy. He'd gone out time after time to buy Esmond nappies and milk and teething rings and toys. Now, though, Esmond could walk for reasonable distances, and David himself often walked to work. It saved all the hassles of parking, for one thing, saved petrol money, kept him fit.

Mainly he drove around at night, seeking inspiration. Surely he could get that inspiration if he walked? It was safer to avoid Princess Street and The Tollcross areas of the city in the wee small hours, but the area they lived in had always been trouble free. He could even pace about on the little patch of lawn outside if he wanted privacy. People went to bed early around here. No one would see.

She wished there was an easy way to approach the subject. David was sensitive, involved in a difficult line of work. Sometimes, when he got a rejection letter, she almost wept for him. Not that he told her – but she saw the dark, tensing-in of his face. At moments like this his features looked thinner and younger. Yet he kept the hurt within, his pain unshared. He was a brave man, a masculine man, one of the old school. Would her dad have been like that if he had lived?

A photo of a man with a bonnet, leaning against a tree in the local park. That was her sole reminder of her father. Oh, she'd seen the wedding photos, but they were all starched clothes and Brylcream, they didn't give an impression of the everyday man. The inner man whose inner workings had suddenly failed him. Coronary Heart Disease, the silent killer, stalking within. According to her mother, he'd complained of a pain earlier that last day in his upper arm.

'We didn't know then what we know now,' she'd said again and again. How often had she said that in the twenty years since he'd left her widowed? 'He just went out for a paper and never came back.' So she, Jeanette, had rarely been allowed out thereafter, to play or to study in an unknown, alien world. Doomed at eighteen months old to a life of being tracked closely. Doomed to years and years of little free will, restricted choice.

Her mother had even chosen the Health Food Store job for her. She'd seen the card in the shop window, gone in and fixed up an interview. Jeanette had come home from school that night and her mother had run her a bath and explained about the job. Helped her choose a suitable outfit. Walked her along, come back half an hour later to see how she'd was getting on. Ah, irony, sending her to work with the beautiful David. Sending her to seduction on a batchelor bed.

People were clapping, smiling. Jeanette looked up, blushing – everyone else had scrambled to their feet. She realised they weren't looking at her, but at the teacher. 'See you next week, girls,' the woman said.

The exercisers began to cross to the sides of the room, collecting their belongings. Jeanette picked up her jacket and bag. When she turned round, Wanda was standing beside her. *Please don't let her suggest they go for coffee or for a drink.* She'd told the student everything she could think of on the way to the class. About David, about Esmond and her mother, the launderette.

'We can get a shower downstairs, Wanda said easily. 'Much more hot water than the ancient thing installed in my flat.'

Jeanette didn't want a communal shower. Still, she followed the younger girl out of the exercise room. At least this way there was more chance of David getting home first and noticing her absence. He was due to leave the Health Food Store at five-thirty tonight.

Would he be curious, worried, no longer complacent? He was always so sure of finding her at the kitchen sink. For a moment she felt childish at this tiny piece of game-playing. But wasn't he the one who was always saying that married people should still lead individual lives? He'd probably phone her mother, who'd say she'd handed Esmond over to Jeanette at the launderette as usual. She'd just let Mrs Landrew assume she was taking Esmond home for his tea.

Tea for the three and a half year old had been chips from the chip-shop, with she and Wanda sneaking a few to keep them going. Then they'd gone straight to the Community Centre, and got Esmond registered and settled in the downstairs creche.

They went there now. Esmond was at the far side of the room, kneeling before a two-tier garage. A women was showing him how the little cars were hoisted up and down by the ramp. Relieved, Jeanette backed away again. She wanted to be a good mother, raise a happy child.

She walked along the corridor towards the changing-rooms following Wanda. 'I'll just wait by the basins while you have your shower.'

'No, listen – there's a coffee bar.'

'Oh, I don't know…' She hated to sit alone.

Hated to sit with strangers also, but that's what happened. Wanda got them both coffees from the serving hatch and she relaxed. They were swiftly joined by two other women. Much juggling of crockery, smiles all round. The others said what a good class it had been and she agreed with them. Then picked up her coffee cup, looked across the room, away.

'Have you been to this place before?' one of the others asked. She seemed to be a regular, nodding to everyone. She wore an expensive-looking grey short-sleeved exercise tunic and matching pants.

'I have, but Jeanette's new…' Wanda began talking for both of them. Jeanette enjoyed the prickling warmth of the coffee's steam playing over her face. 'Time for that shower,' said Wanda, smiling at everyone. 'Back in five minutes,' she'd called over her shoulder as she walked away.

Deserted, left amongst strangers.

'I'll have my shower when I get back,' Jeanette muttered, feeling lost.

'Same here – I hate bathing in public,' said the woman next to her. Unlike her friend, she wore a black, baggy T-shirt and grass-stained jeans.

'This is the first exercise I've had since school' Jeanette added. She set down her cup, but still held it in both hands. 'Actually – no, there was this class once…' Smiling, she named the upmarket gym. As she described all the mirrors and posturing, the bejeanned woman started laughing and nodding. Her friend – who probably loved such places. – managed a small, polite smile. 'I don't think they had a creche there.' Jeanette ended breathlessly.

'Oh, you have children?' the friendlier woman said.

This was safe territory – known territory. 'One child.'

'Boy or a girl?'

'A boy. Esmond.'

'Desmond?'

'No, Esmond. My husband's idea. He wanted something a bit different. I think he got it from a book.'

'Yes – nice to get away from all those Johns and Williams,' said the nicer woman, 'Does your husband have an unusual name?'

'No. Well our surname – Frate. I suppose that's quite unusual.'

'I certainly haven't heard of it before,' the woman in the matching exercise gear said.

An awkward silence. Could she tell them about the launderette? Not really – it didn't follow naturally on from a conversation about names. Her own maiden name was quite ordinary. So was Wanda's. What was it? Johnson – no, James. Wanda James. Wanda, come back, come back and rescue me. The other women determinedly sipped their coffee as the seconds ticked by.

'David writes songs – I suppose that's why names and words are important to him. He says most of us don't use language well.' God, had she really said that? She was never, ever first to mention David's songs. The woman she'd begun to like leaned forward.

'What does he write about?'

Clever things quite beyond what she, Jeanette, could deal with.

'Oh, freedom, individual rights… important themes.'

The neater one put her head to one side and studied her.

'And does he sell many of them?'

She felt the blush begin: 'They're under consideration. The… process is slow.'

Another pause. Another.

Wanda, come and rescue me. 'He… it's a difficult thing to do. Something like house or hip hop comes along – helps push out the more traditional stuff.'

'People jumping on the bandwagon?' her new friend queried.

'Uh huh.' That was what David said: 'It's selling out if you go with the flow.'

This time Wanda did indeed appear, hair still damp in places, fringe like thin ropes across her head. Still, you could get away with that in nice weather when you looked like Wanda. Jeanette's own hair was unexciting even when newly dried.

'Fit for the road?' asked Wanda, smiling at the three of them.

'Fit to drop,' said Jeanette. She felt a sense of connection with the kindly student: she was just so sensitive, so nice. She'd seen tonight as something to get through to impress David, but had ended up enjoying the exercises, had held her ground. 'Time to collect my little boy,' she added brightly. She wondered if the other women wished they had a cosy little family like hers.

Walking home, she decided to join the Centre. She could afford to go to the keep fit class every week providing she stopped buying chocolate bars from the launderette's confectionery machine. It was good for Esmond to mix with other children. Good for her to be something other than a working wife.

She grinned as Wanda pointed out her favourite colours of car to Esmond. If the student still wanted to babysit, she could. Maybe once a week at first till the three-year-old got to know her, got used to seeing less of his gran. Wanda was young, energetic, had fresh ideas. David liked Wanda, and David was usually right. As they neared the flat, Jeanette looked forward to seeing him. She wondered if his day had been as thrilling as hers.

CHAPTER SIX

The moment she walked in, he knew she was exactly what he wanted. She came through the door in stages as if her legs were reluctant to follow her head. Not so much shy as self conscious. There was a difference, if you thought about it long enough.

He'd been thinking about it for months now, watching, waiting. May had rained itself out and June had filtered in. June with a splairge of colour, as Robert Burns had written. People rushing to tend gardens and window boxes in every corner of the town.

He'd despaired, then, of finding the right sexually-available woman. He wanted her now, at this, the absolutely perfect time. Sunshine begged mankind to take a lover. People wanted to pair off in summer, the way they did at parties on Christmas Eve.

May, June... with Jeanette wittering on about creches and keep fit classes. In July he'd seen her, his ideal conquest, began to make small talk over the cash register each week. July was an awkward time – contained Jeanette's twenty third birthday. He'd had to find a card without a verse, sign his name.

'*Thinking of you on your special day.*'

That was the wording. He wished he could honestly buy a card with lines of love. Wished he could take her out somewhere, see other men's envious glances. But no one looked twice at Jeanette.

Instead, as usual, he'd bought perfume which she dabbed on her wrists to please him. Dabbed behind plain ears – she never would agree to get them pierced. He bought her chocolates she'd share with Esmond when he wasn't looking, gave her an awkward, geared-up-for peck on the cheek.

Cheeks, cheeks: his potential new mistress had pale cheeks which would suddenly flush with colour. Buttock cheeks hidden beneath cotton knee-length skirts. He imagined they'd be slim, though: small, white globes, curving upwards. After all, she didn't buy very much food. Not one of life's hedonists, not a gourmet: just someone who ate enough to stave off boredom, to survive.

In August, still keeping it casual, he asked her name. Pauline. *Pauline.* Slowly, he got to know her, giving and getting data when other customers weren't around. Even his fellow staff didn't pose too much of a problem. He was so distant when Tracey was with him on the morning shift that Pauline had soon switched her visit to the afternoons. And Mrs Melloway was usually closeted away with her phone inside her office or out chatting with some salesman about rising profits from failing health.

Yes, his chosen one had soon got the message, avoiding the shop during busy periods. Good girl, she left as soon as a queue began to form. She'd been keen enough, though, to persevere with their relationship, popping in twice a week during the off-peak hours when he had plenty of time.

Always time for you, darling.

One day he'd prove it. This had to be a sophisticated human robbery – Kim had been the equivalent of a smash 'n' grab.

Slowly, slowly. After finding out her name he'd began to query her connections.

'Come from a healthy family, do you?'

Jokey, flirty – small talk could lead to larger things.

Surprise, surprise, she was estranged from Mummy and Daddy. She had that look about her, you could usually tell. Maybe Daddy had gotten too close before she'd put distance between them. Maybe Mummy had turned her face into the pillow and gone conveniently deaf.

No matter. The main thing was no parents would come looking for her. No brothers or sisters. And aunts and uncles (didn't he know it) wouldn't help. Safe on that score, then: now for workmates. He had to tread easy, space the pointed questions out. Lots of chat about the music the shop radio played, about what had been on TV the previous night.

A good sign. that – she always watched several programmes. No hectic social life, no special dates. Just me, myself and I in a bedsit.

'This your local?' he'd joked on her third visit, and held his breath.

'Sort of,' she'd said, and volunteered that she lived in the big house that had been turned into bedsits along the main road. That was the key, really – humour. He had to keep reminding himself to smile.

His mother had smiled, the cow, at acquaintances, neighbours. Smiled and smiled and gone home and watched him being beaten red and black. Smiles were for liars or for weaklings. He'd be a liar for a while, but at least he'd know it, no hypocrisy there.

His unhypocritical Pauline was broke – she spent so little. She'd stayed in court shoes instead of moving on to sandals when the days were hot. And her hair was slightly frayed, like she'd done her own trimming. And she came in mostly for wheatgerm and pulses for soup. One day he'd asked why, learning, assessing. She'd shrugged, looked awkward: 'Because it fills you up.'

He'd fill her up, he thought cynically. He gave her copies of the free health magazines that the shop offered, suggested answers for the prize-winning competitions they contained. 'Makes a change to get something through the post which isn't a bill, eh?' He always slipped slightly into the working class idiom when he spoke to her. The working classes feared and loathed a middle class accent and she sounded less educated than he.

'Well, I do get my giro,' she'd said. Bingo. Unemployed and lonely and single. She must be around eighteen or nineteen. Hard to tell, really: shyness kept the face soft and young. And the body? Praise God, a soft, young body. One waiting, like a party hall, for an influx of fun.

He bet she already lived for Tuesday to Thursday when he worked here. Give her her due, though, she only came in two days out of his three. Nice that she had a little pride, a little willpower. He hadn't decided whether to let her keep it or not. On the one hand, he wanted someone amenable. On the other, it was a challenge, taming fire.

Fired up. Christ, he was, when he thought about it. She and he together, forever, alone. She'd become so dependent on him, so damn grateful. He'd feel so special – her recreator, her All.

'Can you restock the smaller fridge with those yoghurts, David?' The boss lady giving the orders. He wondered what she'd do if he said no.

Soya yoghurt, goats' yoghurt, sheep's yoghurt... did nobody eat the cows' milk variety anymore? Lactobacillus Acidophilus cultures springing up every bloody where. And fromage frais with every type of fruit Man had discovered. He'd brought some home for Esmond months ago. He wanted his son to try different things... well... have the option. No pressure on *his* child. No: 'You'll eat this before you have anything else tonight.'

Cunt. The anger was there as though it were yesterday. Strange that it hadn't ameliorated with time. But then nothing had changed – they still hadn't apologised. Thick skinned bastards that they were, they still probably hadn't admitted they'd done him wrong. Well, *she* might have – being that she was in Hades or Purgatory or wherever they put the souls of women who didn't treat their offspring right.

His dad, the fucker, had always been friendless. He'd be in shit creek now: he'd relied so much on his wife. At least – at last. – he was suffering, increasingly an outcast. He'd retire soon to years of solitary confinement, and probably go mad.

But *she'd* laughed and talked and first footed the neighbours. She'd enjoyed life sometimes while he, David, begged and screamed.

He had to go past it, beyond it. Find people who loved and admired him *now* for who he was. Like Pauline, who smiled at his jokes long before he reached the punchline. Pauline with her brown hair, brown dress and sad, but now hopeful, brown eyes.

The kind of girl nobody ever noticed. The kind of girl few people would ask out. Strategy was everything, from first remark to conclusion. Like a song, penned from the opening notes to the orchestrated end.

God, but he'd enjoy the chorus, the repetition. When he played with her nipples, her vulva, she'd sing like a bird. He'd be gentle, though, providing she deserved it. Kind and considerate, a sensitive lover, a friend. He watched the door with constant peripheral vision. When she came in he wanted her to think she'd seen him first.

Finishing the yoghurt stacking, he walked back behind the counter.

'David, can you just weigh out those carob drops?'

He walked over to the scales, felt his chinos rubbing against the counter. Looked down, winced as he saw they were beginning to wear below the waist. He'd buy new ones. Clothes didn't make the man, but they made a difference. He had no time for men in polyester trousers or those ugly green windcheaters things.

Pauline looked equally drab at the moment, but he'd soon change her. The Health Food Store sold cosmetics which hadn't been tested on animals – he could make up a little animal all of his own. He'd already taken some foundation to cover up the thin scratches Kim had inflicted on his lower arms. He could brighten Pauline with some pale green eye-shadow, mid pink gloss for her lips. Her face was a bit white at the moment, sort of pale without the interesting. Bedsits did that to you: you literally sat up in bed to watch TV.

No matter. He'd take her outside on the embankment for a suntan. She'd have to prove that she could behave herself first. Her reward: long hours outdoors, with him, in the late summer heat.

He stirred the catering carton of vegetable salad. When he'd got round to buying that barbecue they could cook king prawns and noisette lamb chops. No one lived near enough to smell the cooking. No one even lived near enough to see the smoke…

Forget barbecues for now – he must concentrate on buying trousers. Where would he go for them? They'd have to be long-last-ing, off-the-peg. He watched the clock as he served, stirred further cartons. Lunchtime always took ages to tick round.

Peering through the window, he could see that the tailor's shop was empty. He preferred small shops like this to the busier ones in town. Walked in, past leather and chambray bootcuts. Tried on a pair of cream cotton trousers. He'd get Wanda to alter the waistband. Elsewhere, they were an impressive, debonair fit.

'I'll take them.'

'You what?' the female counter clerk said, mouth gaping, eyes staring.

'I said I'll take the trousers.'

Another stare. 'Oh. Right.'

He felt his face begin to tauten across the jawline as she stuffed his purchase carelessly into a bag. Bitch. Her likes had mocked and spurned him at school, at university. Now the fair sex patronised him most days in the store.

He'd show them. He'd feel them as well. She'd lose that impudent expression with eight inches of cock rammed down her gullet. He pressed hard as he signed the credit slip, imagining the pen was a tattoo needle penetrating her flesh.

As he walked back to the health store, he mentally teamed his new trousers with every jacket he owned, and then with his car coat. Brown and cream could look so expensive if you twinned them right. He hoped Pauline would appreciate him and his varied wardrobe. It would be easier for her if she did.

CHAPTER SEVEN

'Would you like some juice, Esmond?'
Esmond looked up from his drawing. 'Juice,' he said.
Wanda went over to her tiny fridge and found a bottle which she'd bought on special at the supermarket. Saw belatedly that it contained artificial colour and preservative. Quickly she put it back on the top shelf and closed the door. She couldn't give the son of a Health Store manager additives!

'Let's have milk or water instead,' she murmured bringing him two plastic tumblers. She knelt beside Esmond and studied his crayoning, a red fire engine with a blue blob of fireman at its side. The boy was so self absorbed, so withdrawn despite her efforts. Had she been the same as a very young child? She could remember herself at six or eight wishing that her mother was trendier. She could remember wishing that they did more with their day to day lives.

Esmond didn't get the chance to do much with his little life. He didn't seem to go to the cinema or the park or anything. Just to his gran's house when David worked at the store. The creche was obviously helping to expand his horizons. That morning he'd mentioned one of the other children by name.

'Shall we give the fireman a yellow hat?' Esmond looked up then down. Strange that he was so much like his mother. You'd think his father's genes would be stronger, would dominate. David's penetrating eyes, white teeth and gloss black hair looked indomitable. He made a nice change from all those pony-tailed students she met at college with their triple earstuds and hooded tops.

David had that casual flair that helped enhance both the well-cut clothes and the man inside them. She hoped that she'd find the time to get to know him better: during the two short conversations they'd had she'd tuned in like a disciple to his strong, sure voice. As he drove them all from the launderette her gaze had swept from the pristine casualness of his trousers to what the romantic novels her mum read called his lean and hungry thighs…

And they *must* be hungry – married to a plain Jane like Jeanette. Unless she performed tricks of the tongue and torso that Wanda couldn't foresee. No, these small teeth looked as if they stopped at nibbling biscuits and spineless white rolls.

Maybe he had a hauntingly beautiful mistress hidden away somewhere? Maybe he stayed with Jeanette because he couldn't bear to leave his child? Something Jeanette had said suggested she'd been pregnant when they married. Poor David. A lifetime of boring sex for one drunken night.

Be all you can be.

Damn her thoughts, for being so vicious, so – let's face it – *jealous*. To see the Frate's marriage in terms of mere lust was unkind. Jeanette was a hard worker, a good listener. With David only working part time, she was probably his patron of the arts.

That was another uncharitable thought – what was wrong with her these days? Surely David didn't just stay with his young wife for the cash? There were more beautiful women around who'd be happy to provide the readies. Just thinking of him brought a low, pelvic ache.

Enough. She'd only seen the man twice, this was a flight of fancy. Determinedly Wanda picked up a fresh sheet of paper and pencil and began to write out a little story Esmond might like. She could read it out in different voices. Maybe leave sections where he had to guess out loud what happened next.

Yes, they both needed fun, diversions. She'd been too much alone these past few weeks. Roll on September and third year practicals. Leisure time could make you act strangely if it went on too long. So could celibacy. Why was it so difficult to find someone that she liked, *wanted*? Few of her contemporaries at College appealed to her that way. Somehow she always felt older, wiser, *different*. She wanted someone established, dark and strong…

Wanda closed her eyes and pictured her Adonis. The image strengthened, intensified. *Sorry, Jeanette.* Not that she'd ever give in to such lust – she hated adultery. Cheating and lying and hurting others wasn't for her.

Nice to dream, though, of what she and David would do together. She imagined kissing him, caressing him, pulling those crisp, pressed trousers off and stroking the hirsute flesh and heavy balls beneath. Lucky that she wasn't guiltily religious. Some faiths believed that the thought was as bad as the deed.

CHAPTER EIGHT

David sat at his desk, and contemplated his latest erection. Jeanette, thank goodness, had already left for work. He'd have to leave too, in twenty minutes. Some things, however, just wouldn't wait.

Wouldn't wait for a dip in his libido. He'd brought himself off last night, had climaxed strongly. Had done so again, beneath the blankets, during the twilight hours. This latest desire had arisen – and remained risen – after he'd bathed and dressed. It knew that Pauline was ready for him, and waiting, that it was almost time.

Time, now, to dial the Three Way Pleasure phone line. He'd enjoyed that one, when he'd called it before. He dialled, listened, started tickling, teasing. Got a cushion and rubbed himself against it, breathing hard.

Ah, there was respect in the voices which recorded the sex lines. Broke actresses, probably, who did it right or didn't get paid. One day they'd all have video phones so he could see them. He was a normal man, and men liked to look.

Not that hearing was bad – providing you used your imagination. Good voices – breathless, husky, sweet as coconut milk. Not that they went far enough, damn the legislation. Gave soft innuendo when he wanted hard – brick hard – talk. He wanted women, pliable women. Young flesh which did everything on demand.

There was nowhere to go locally that he knew of. No palatial building offering service with a smile. Oh, there were strange ads from masseuse parlours in the papers. But it wasn't clear that you paid for getting more than your back and shoulders rubbed.

You paid a fortune for this sex chat he thought, cradling the receiver against his shoulder. Sometimes he thought it was the secretiveness that got him off. Nice wife and child leave for work and granny respectively. Nice husband phones dirty talk line and strokes himself and shoots. It didn't take much these days, with his plans-for-a-playmate almost ready. Didn't take much to send his semen to the skies. Literally, according to Jeanette. She'd said it was what she'd heard when she was little. *Every time you masturbate you kill lots of babies.* That's what the boy next door to her had been told by his mum.

She'd shyly told David about it just after they married. He'd been watching a late night programme about religious systems at the time. She'd laughed as she said it but sounded fearful. 'When a man masturbates he destroys potential babies. D'you think a woman does the same?'

Damn all women, with their endless superstitions. Damn the one who'd gone to her Church of Scotland Communion then watched him being thrashed. He'd never, ever preach one way of life and live another. Wouldn't pass on such thoughtless rubbish to his wide-eyed child.

'*Imagine you're sliding inside me, I'm so wet for you...*'

As the phone sex continued, David sucked his fingers and gently rubbed himself. Any minute now, any second: juices building, leaking from the tip.

Each act of masturbation kills lots of babies.

David jerked faster, harder. He was about to kill some more.

'Sorry I'm late.' Trying to curve his mouth into a smile, he hurried to stand beside his boss at the counter.

'Happens to the best of us,' said Mrs Melloway. But her tone was cool and her smile was hard and false.

'Jeanette was ill,' he lied wearily, 'I had to go to the chemist to get her something. I won't be late again.'

'The gentleman here wants two bhagees and eight falafals.'

Silently David put the slightly greasy snacks into a bag.

He didn't want to lose this job and further undermine his track record. Those last few years, he'd lost Brownie points through moving around. Not that it had always been that way – once he'd been quite settled, at least on paper. After dropping out of University, he'd stayed with the Post Office for two long years.

Then, when his hands had balked at stamping pension books, he'd moved on to selling furniture. Was a cut above your average salesman who was lucky to have a certificate to his name. He'd made bonus after bonus selling lifetime-guarantee beds that OAPs would shortly die in, and telling incompatible couples that the latest coffee table would change their lives.

It had changed his after a while; he'd felt more and more restless. Same sales staff, same furnishings, same white emulsioned walls. He'd moved on to doing bar work, thinking what he was lacking in was freedom. He'd had the days to himself, worked nights in the more upmarket clubs.

Isolated. Lonely. When he'd worked in the furniture store he'd had a social life. Well, he'd gone down the pub for a jar or two after work. Oh, they thought he was different because he preferred orange juice. But he'd been part of something, for a few years, nonetheless.

The club staff had been different, avoided the bar scene. They didn't want to sit on the other side of the counter on their precious days off. They tended to form cliques, visit each others houses. Day after day he'd sat in his bedsit, alone. Alone with his experiences, with thoughts that needed telling. Then the songs had began growing in his head.

'Paint It Black' – that had to be his all-time favourite. Jagger mouthing sex appeal, trapping darkness in a rhythm as sweet as light. To write something like that, only more complex... Something which demystified life's drives.

Someone had to educate mankind about the important things. He, David, could do it, could succeed. Attitudes, upbringing – he could make the wrongs of the future right, or prevent their happening. Noel Coward wasn't the only one who'd noted the potency that cheap music had.

Not that his music would be cheap – it would be priceless. Bought by the masses, but only fully deciphered by the few. How many mums and dads had hummed along to 'Lucy In The Sky With

Diamonds', thinking it quite tuneful? Only their sons and daughters knew it was about LSD.

He hoped that Mrs Melloway would buzz off soon, leave him to manage his kingdom. She seemed to have got the taste for serving – he'd like to teach her all about taste. He watched closely as she used her generous smile on the customers. She, who'd told him to put as little filling as possible in the rolls. Small-minded people leading small, petty lives, the living dead. At least Pauline Clark's life was about to change and expand.

And how. He kept watching, waiting. Serving sauerkraut when he wanted to ensnare. Soon, soon… That morning he'd transferred the handcuffs from his desk tray to the inner pocket of his jacket. He'd liked the cold feel of metal in his hand.

He'd ordered the cuffs through an American True Crime magazine. Some San Francisco box number sending brown paper parcels round the world. He'd put the magazine with his girlie ones in the bedside cabinet. Jeanette knew about the girlie mags but she'd never look.

Prude, prude. The few times they'd done it had been… uneventful. He'd felt awkward, ill at ease after their one night stand. Usually he picked up girls at the end of discos. The ones who hadn't gotten off with anyone were glad of a bit of attention after the dance. They'd have sex on the back seat of his car or in their bedsits. He didn't take them to his place in case they wanted to spend the night.

Best to keep it quick and easy and pleasing. No point in weaving ties which might cruelly bind. Jeanette had been an exception there – he'd been drinking. Had impulsively seduced the quiet girl who served beside him at the Health Store every day.

He hadn't even fancied her, not especially. Merely wondered about the body beneath the overalls as a matter of course. He hadn't lusted after her, hadn't fantasized. Then Mrs Melloway's birthday had come round and she'd taken them all out for a meal. According to Tracey, Mr Melloway was out of the country on business and the poor cow hadn't wanted to celebrate alone.

Who said there was safety in numbers? Eight of them had gone out to a vegetarian Indian restaurant. He'd felt dislocated, uncertain, unused to such a crowd. He'd have a glass of spirits before the food came, he'd decided, something to take away the self-consciousness that made him feel left out.

The first gin had gone down well, so he'd had a second. The teenage Saturday girls, who'd clearly had a few drinks at home before coming out, were already high. Mrs Melloway had insisted the schoolgirls all go home by the last bus, however. Terrified she'd have to pay for a taxi, David had thought.

That left himself, Jeanette and Mrs M to continue drinking. They'd gone on to the casino – she'd signed them both in. The older woman had been unusually benevolent. Jeanette had looked at him knowingly, and smiled. He and she against the wicked capitalist. He and she understanding the way things really were.

And suddenly he'd wanted to fuck her across the table, in view of the croupiers. Wanted to pull off that plain grey skirt and dull blue blouse. He'd bought her a couple of vodkas; it had been simple. Waited till the older woman looked tired then called for a cab to take them all home. Heartbeat speeding – *we're getting there* – he'd given the taxi driver instructions, making sure Mrs M was dropped off first.

Then they'd been driven on to his flat for a coffee, Jeanette leaning heavily against his side.

'We shouldn't,' she'd said at one stage as he undressed her. But she hadn't sounded convinced and he'd continued to slide down her skirt.

'I've never...' she'd slurred. That had clinched it. He'd gone throbbingly, hurtingly hard. A virgin – a tight, hot, novelty tunnel after the slack-walled disco Queens. A virgin ready to give up her modesty to him on their first ever evening together, clearly appreciating his masculine delights. He hadn't thought for a moment about contraception. The women he usually slept with could well take care of themselves.

But Jeanette couldn't – or didn't. She'd thought she was going out for a vegetable biryani, not a hymen-tearing time. He'd smiled his false smile and spoken softly to her in the days that followed. Taken her to the cinema, the theatre, to the pub. Planning to gradually taper off the outings, let her down slowly. What was the saying? Never shit in your own nest.

It was so true: it complicated things, made subterfuge essential.

He couldn't just ignore her on the post-coital day. She'd make a scene and Mrs Melloway liked to run an orderly shop. After each date he'd taken her to his bed but the couplings had been dry, tense, awkward. She continued to dress plainly, could hardly bear to look at her own body unless she was drunk. When sober she didn't have much to say for herself, but she listened.

The most startling thing she'd ever said was: 'I've had a pregnancy test.'

Positive. She'd been crying when she told him. He'd wondered about denying it then realised he had to think of the kid. *His* kid, which deserved every chance available. His kid, which he wouldn't have shouted at by some harassed single mum.

So he'd married her three months after taking her virginity. She'd been eighteen, he was thirty one. Over thirty was a good age to marry. You knew who you were, what you wanted to be. A songwriter, that's what, with international status. Now all he had to do was find a way...

With his mother-in-law interfering and Esmond having sore throats and Jeanette making small talk, it was really hard to write anything. No wonder he was often driven out to The Secret House these days. He'd soon be spending even more time there. More energy. More sexuality. With a new woman-world to caress and conquer, his creativity would unfold.

It was about to – Pauline had just walked in. Damn Mrs Melloway, damn her. She had to finish serving this customer, had to leave so that he and his almost-mistress could talk. Pauline had her head dipped, was moving over to the freezer. She never bought the vegetarian chilli or frozen lentil roasts. Cost too much, they did, in their fancy packaging. Perhaps he'd steal some for her when she was truly, irrevocably his.

She was staring into the fridges for show now – looking much too intently. In a moment she'd move over to the shelves of bean-filled tins, meet his gaze.

She met his gaze. And smiled. He smiled back, rolled his eyes sideways at his boss. Pauline laughed, a hollow sound, uncertain, which seemed to go on and on. Mrs Melloway glanced over. David froze.

I don't know her, don't know her.

The phone trilled startlingly through the shop.

'I'll get that,' said Mrs Melloway, hurrying into the back. David served the next customer then glanced round to check that the boss hadn't returned.

'We got in some vouchers off those pasta meals.' He turned to Pauline. Handed them over, let their fingers brush, smiled some more. 'I thought you might like to try them for a change.' Subtle that: showing her he'd noticed what she'd bought from him so far. Making her feel special, feel that he cared.

'Great. Thanks.' She'd never been big on conversation. But the way she looked at him made him feel great.

'I...'

'You...' To his embarrassment, they both began speaking in an eager voice at once. He hated that: it was the equivalent of getting off the bus and dancing a pas de bas with a stranger. 'You first,' he said with hard-won gentleness.

'I was wondering about that frozen yoghurt. Is it good for you, do you think?' Scraping the bottom of the barrel for conversation. He felt a moments irritation at her boring, predictable life.

'We haven't had any in yet. I could ask for you.'

He waved his hand vaguely in the direction of the back of the shop. 'Oh, no, no. It's not important – I just fancied a change.'

A brief silence while they stared from opposite sides of the counter at the salads. He dredged up a new subject: 'What did you have for tea last night?'

'Oh, stovies. Without meat, you know.' She obviously thought he was vegetarian, perhaps because of his leanness. No matter: it was good that she was anxious to please.

He forced himself not to breathe deeply: people noticed those things and it made them edgy. Two months of foreplay. Two months too long for his aching groin and Muse. You couldn't stay at the same stage forever, waiting for perfection. You had to make things as safe as possible, then take a chance. 'Talking of meals, have you ever tried vegetarian chilli?'

'I might have years ago... Mum got in those frozen convenience meals a couple of times.'

'No, I mean the real thing – from a Mexican restaurant?'

She knew what was coming, already she'd started to blush.

'I don't think so.' She passed her clutch bag from hand to hand then looked up at him timidly.

'Would you like to?'

'Yes. Yes… I would.'

He had to hurry before Mrs Melloway came back to stand beside him. She knew he was married, had employed Jeanette, for goodness sake, and still asked how she was. And Tracey, who only lived down the road, might pop in for some halva bars for her sugar-mad kids.

He leaned forward, urgent but orderly: 'Look, I'll have to go now. I help with the accounts this time of the month.'

'Oh, I see.' She was looking confused, maybe thought he was backing out of it.

He smiled: 'I'm stocktaking tonight, so I'll be working late.' She nodded, frowned slightly. 'But I'm always ravenous by the time I'm finished. If you can meet me at a quarter to ten…?'

'Where?' The word came out in a rush. pathetically eager. He ought to be flattered. Just a few more minutes and he'd be home and dry. Well, home and wet, really. Leaking from the tip, then spurting like champagne over each inch of her.

'Just outside here would suit me fine.'

'Quarter to ten, you said?'

'You got it. Quarter to ten.'

She was still standing, smiling shyly. *Go*, he was screaming. *Go, bitch, go bitch, go.* He could hear the ting as Mrs Melloway set the phone down.

'I won't eat much tea, then,' Pauline said.

'Oh… right.' He backed away towards the door that led to the staff room. 'I have to go, Pauline. I'll look forward to tonight.'

He'd done it – or was about to. Had arranged their date, remained unseen, unheard. Tonight, oh sweet jesus, was going to be the night he'd planned and dreamed about. Food, drink – everything was ready at The Secret House. The foods were dried, of course, had a reasonable shelf life. He hadn't been sure he'd be able to arrange her residency for this week.

Mind over matter, that was how the saying went. *His* mind over *her* matter, his cock deep in her hole. God, but she was going to get the meal to end all meals this evening. The fare he'd offer would be hotter than chilli beans.

The next bit, of course, was the most difficult. It was hard to determine in advance when it would be dark. He'd have liked to have suggested a later meeting time, but she might have grown suspicious. It was vital to maintain her trust.

He'd put the Escort in for a service, which complicated matters. Jeanette had fretted about the engine's rattle when he'd driven them to and from The Cameron Toll Shopping Centre the previous week. Not that Pauline would have gone willingly into the vehicle anyway. A few weeks ago he'd suggested taking her to the wholesalers with him so she could look around. Not that he'd have done it – testing, testing. He'd have found an excuse to back out on the day. She'd asked how they'd get there, and he'd said he would drive her, She hadn't said no, just shrugged, looked awkward, frowned.

Walk this way. Providing he kept them to the quieter streets they'd not be noticed. She'd enjoy the exercise. It would be her last journey in the outside world for some time, He'd planned their route to avoid the fish 'n' chip shops which spilt tell-tale light and customers onto the late night streets.

Streetwise to the last, he'd stand at the bus stop while he waited to meet her. It was two doors away from the Health Store, absolutely ideal. She'd walk up to him there, start to chat, linger for a moment. Two people at a bus stop making small talk about when the buses were due.

If he was ever questioned he could say that was the first and the last time he'd seen her. 'Yes, officer, she was chatty – lonely, I think. The bus didn't come, so we walked along the road together. I went into the pub for a refreshing orange juice. I don't know where the lady went after that.' Foolproof – well, as good as it could be. Undiscovered brilliance against the dull background of the world.

'Just going to the gents,' David said, as he passed Mrs Melloway on the stair. His shaft was swelling; he was going to have to pleasure it again.

CHAPTER NINE

A lemon dress, white handbag, white cardigan. Pauline was brightly dressed for once and he wanted to damn her to the skies. Where was the brown jacket and skirt he could walk alongside unnoticed? Close-fitting clothes had replaced her shapeless look. He tried to think his mood lighter as she walked up to him at the bus stop. Easy, easy. He forced an encouraging smile.

'Thinking of going home?' she asked shyly.

'No, my car's in for a service.' Did that sound blunt? He concentrated on relaxing the tiny muscles in his face. Then he made his hands unclench and gestured at the bus stop's board. 'I was just checking what time the morning bus would get me in for work.' A pause. He remembered the protocol: 'You look nice.'

Too nice. Three teenage boys looked her over as they sauntered past. She was attracting admiration, attention: the skulking caterpillar had become, if not a butterfly, at least a moth.

'Let's walk.'

She asked him how long he'd worked in the shop as they turned into the next road. He answered, asked her about what she'd like to do. Half listened to her dream-filled answer, knowing that all the time they were moving slowly towards The House.

'Of course we have some less wholesome customers…'

Making her laugh. Walking, talking, keeping her in his thrall. He told her of his favourite restaurant meals, couldn't really afford them. He'd studied the menus in the windows last week.

'I don't really get out much' she said, her steps unrhythmic.

He smiled at her. 'I know what it's like, on the dole.'

'So how did you...?'

He went on to tell her about the weeks on a giro after quitting university. She'd appreciate he was a free spirit, beyond the rules.

'So why did you leave the college?' she asked, frowning.

Less educated people always called university that. He felt a rush of contempt, bordering on hatred. It was hard to explain to someone like her.

He tried, anyway, dredged up the memories: 'Because they were inflexible, said that you couldn't write that Eliot was better than Keats.' He glanced sideways but she still looked uncertain. 'Then if your essay was passionate, they'd accuse you of writing a polemic.'

She nodded, said nothing.

'I didn't so much drop out as move on.'

'I wanted to stay on at school, but...' Her small features were sad, she sounded wistful, 'Well, Dad and I... you know... didn't get on.'

He knew. He felt a moments connection, thought perhaps they could have a future. He could teach her about people, about life.

They walked on and he looked at passers by with peripheral vision, wondering if they were noticing him with her.

'Is it far now?'

Nearer than you think, baby. He checked his watch, found they'd been walking for forty minutes. They'd covered quite a distance, moving smartly: the shoulder carrying the white bag was beginning to look hunched. 'Hey, I thought you were the health freak,' he murmured, ruffling her hair briefly, 'We could have taken the bus.'

'Oh, I'm not complaining,' she said quickly, half-shying away from the contact. 'It's a nice night for a walk.'

Walking, talking. She began listing the jobs she'd like to do, her lack of experience. He felt his heart began to beat faster, harder. The risky part was fast approaching, the twilight zone when they switched to a dingier part of town.

At first she didn't notice – or didn't say anything.

'If only everything wasn't part time nowadays,' she said. Normally he'd have corrected her, said 'Not *everything*.' Being accurate about language was partly what good songwriting was about. Instead, he said 'Mmm', hand on back again.

Two more minutes till he found her a full time job.

'You mean the restaurant's near here?' The first warning sign: his scalp prickled.

'That's right – ethnic,' he said. She was slowing down slightly, looking doubtful. 'The best restaurants are in the most unlikely places,' he added, trying to sound assured. Aware that his words had tumbled out in a rush, he tried to slow his breathing. He must keep her with him – she mustn't escape – not now.

He reached for her hand, found it, held it. Was his own palm as damp to the touch as hers? She was completely in profile, studying the street ahead of her. 'This way,' he said, urging her towards the kerb. 'Almost there,' he said truthfully as they crossed over. Now they were one street away from where he used to live.

A black dog crossed towards them, head dipped strangely. As it neared he could see its spine arching whitely from its coat.

'David, I don't like it here.'

'I'll protect you.' He fancied he could feel a pulse beating in her wrist.

Almost, almost. A figure came towards them out of the cooling grey-blackness. Difficult to tell from a distance which gender it was.

'We could ask them where the restaurant is,' Pauline said, tilting her face towards him.

'I know where it is – I've been there before.' He tried to smile but his jaw ached, making movement difficult. 'This way cuts down our journey. You said you'd been walking too long.'

The man was level with them now, level with a streetlight. He looked thirty-something. Around here, that meant he was nineteen. A three day old beard failed to cover his angry acne, green parka turned grey through unlaundered years.

Pass by, mate, pass by. Even if she asked for directions, this waster wouldn't remember. He wouldn't come forward if she was reported missing at a later date. Let's face it, his kind didn't give a flying fuck about anyone. Hey, that had potential. Flying fuck. Maybe he could suspend her with ropes.

Pauline hesitated slightly, but the man walked on. *Not into nuances of body language, darling – try putting a hungry pitbull in his way*. She hadn't had the guts to stop a stranger, the little idiot. The British would die rather than make a fuss.

Not that he wanted to eliminate her, like he had her predecessor. That had been an accident, a stupid mistake. No, he wanted Pauline to be here for him, to want him. To need him – ah, language. – to knead, and knead and knead.

How long now since that little runaway had disobeyed him? This was August: he'd found her sometime in May. Over three months: three months of forward planning. This time he'd anticipate a struggle, prevent her flight. He didn't want to knock her out – wanted her conscious. Maybe he'd tie her up as soon as they got through the door.

She'd gone quiet now. Did she sense that his mood was changing? Did she guess what was coming, even *know*? He'd steered her to the inside earlier, acting the gentleman. It meant she was nearer the tenement, nearer The House.

He glanced back: there was no one in the vicinity. When he let go her hand, she looked queryingly up at him, half-smiled. *Go for it.* He flexed his shoulder, inhaled, shoved hard. Too hard. He winced as she shot forward, battering herself against the wall at the side of the tenement, flailing back. He caught her in mid-fall, blocked her off from the pavement with his body, pushed her into the passageway till she was safely out of sight.

After that the worst part was over. Simple to half drag, half carry her along the close. Then out into the 'backies' as his parents had called the back washing green, up the weed-strewn embankment to his Secret House.

She was sagging against him, moaning. *Save it, baby.* She'd hit her head on the door and must be slightly concussed. Still, he held her tightly around the neck as he unlocked the entrance to his hideaway. She might be faking semi-consciousness, might try at any moment to escape.

She wouldn't escape – not ever, maybe. Unless he stopped desiring her when she grew old. He'd always preferred younger quieter women. They had a tendency to look up to you, listen to what you said.

Pauline wasn't listening to anything, except her own whimpering. He mimicked her softly as he let her slump to the floor. Then he locked them both in, checked the shutters were securely hooked down. Humming softly, he turned on the flashlights till the interior grew bright.

Welcome to my world.

He squatted by her side and started to lift her dress up. Watched as, eyelids fluttering, she tried to brush it down. Again she reminded him of a dying moth, caught against the net curtain in the kitchen, its struggle half hearted, almost limp.

He was far from limp himself – he felt rampant. His prick bulged against the oatmeal cloth across his crotch. He got her arms out of her jacket sleeves with difficulty. He had to roll her onto one side then the other, pulling hard. To get the garment off fully he had to lift her upper body. Trembling at the warm contact, he supported her at the waist. She whimpered some more, flexed her fingers slightly. Still she stayed gently, reassuringly asleep.

With the skirt part of her dress up he could see her panties. High, creamy creations, made of cotton which reached up to her waist. They had known many washes, were purely practical. She hadn't intended to sleep with him tonight.

He snorted, remembering the phonelines. Women who intended to take a lover dressed up in black and red lace. Suspender belts, peephole bras, open crotch panties. Some wore strawberry love gel on their labias for male lips to remove. Even his most demure one night stand had worn ivory silk briefs which she'd tried for long moments to hold onto. He'd preferred her shy hesitation: it made him feel more in charge.

He was in charge now. Swiftly he unbuttoned Pauline's dress bodice. More cream cotton here: he gazed down at the sweat-stains on the band of her bra. These were the things women wore in a long-term relationship They were also the things women wore when they undressed alone. Maybe the two became interchangeable after a while. Take himself and Jeanette...

Pauline opened her eyes, startling him. Stared unfocusedly for a moment, parted her lips. He waited for her to ask what had happened. Where was she? How had she got here? The usual classic lines. He thought up the answers as he watched her. Saw fear change the size of her pupils. She obviously knew.

He drummed his fingers on the ground, felt suddenly awkward.

She was unschooled in this, she didn't understand. In the next few days she'd realise how special he was, would even bless him. For now he must be realistic enough to expect escape bids, questions, tears.

'It's all right,' he said, as her mouth trembled. He watched in fascination as she lifted her naked arms and laid them over her bra-clad breasts. 'I've got in food, juice. I write songs, I don't just work at the Health Food Store. I've got some with me that you can read.'

She was just staring, staring. Christ, she was as bad as that cold bitch at the tailors with her unsettling gaze.

'Say something,' he ordered, surprised when it came out angry.

She flinched, made a snorting sound: 'I've hurt my head.' Not *you've* hurt my head – that was encouraging. She obviously didn't bear him ill will.

Which made sense, really, when you thought about it. If it wasn't for him she'd be watching something boring on TV. At least for once her adrenalin was going. For once she didn't know what was going to happen next. He did, though – an exchange of bodily fluids. He reached for one of the arms which shielded her breasts.

'My head hurts,' she said again, eyes widening.

'No problem,' he said, edging away. He stood up slowly, always watching her. Moved sideways to the cupboard under the sink. He could have made the journey still squatting, but that would have made him vulnerable. She could then throw herself at his undefended back. From there it would be a simple matter for her to stretch her nails forward. He had a horror of something happening to his eyes.

Black eyes. He'd received one of them after Mum had found a girlie magazine in his schoolbag and told his father. Too late, she'd screamed for him not to hit David's head. When the skin puffed up she'd been livid and said they'd have to keep him indoors now. 'What would his teachers think?' she'd asked. As her high tense voice formed the words she'd glared red-facedly at both of them. As if he'd been at fault for somehow running into his fathers fist.

Fists – he unballed his hands again with difficulty. He was safe now, he had to keep focused, calm. He blinked, found himself staring into the sink cupboard. It looked different. Of course, it was the one at The Secret House. What was he here for? Painkillers. He had to keep a grip.

Still, he felt pleased with himself in general. Fancy having painkillers. He'd put them there after a day outside on the embankment had brought on a sun-sore head. He'd also brought long-life orange juice and crackers, put chocolate bars in plastic boxes to protect them from the ravages of time. He'd similarly have to shield such food from determined ants and spiders, from handcuffed women, from the shuttered-in force of the heat.

Some of the storage boxes at the Store had been surplus to requirements: he'd syphoned off sultanas here, and currants there. A dozen dried prunes was small extra payment for all the work he put in. He wouldn't have had to steal these figs if Mrs M had paid him right.

Feeding Pauline simply wouldn't be a problem. Huge trays of pizza came into the store every day. Usually he was the one who cut it into squares for the customers: he could trim off a centimetre all round. That alone would last her a meal or two. And there was always a crumbling pastry left over from lunchtime, a drying salad roll that the staff were allowed to take home…

But for now the lady had a headache, and he would see to it. Paracetomol, stashed away under the sink three weeks before. Take one or two. He decided to just make it one. After all, he wanted her to be a little lively. He didn't want to fuck a corpse again.

When he brought the tablet over, he found she'd struggled up into a sitting position. Careful, careful – he hadn't heard her move. Already she had pulled the top part of her dress back on, and was trying to refasten the buttons of the bodice. Bad girl. He slapped her hand away and watched her mouth form an uncertain 'Oh.'

He handed her the tablet and she let it drop to the ground through spreading fingers.

'No, take it. It's paracetomol. For your head.' She began to edge away from him on her haunches. 'You said you had a headache,' he said patiently. He fetched the bottle and brought it to her: 'See?'

Dumbly, she shook her head. This was crazy. He wanted someone to appreciate him, not to complain. Disobedient, too – she'd have to be taught a lesson. If The Maestro brings you tablets, you swallow, fast.

Cock pulsing, he went over into the corner and dragged the trunk into the centre. When he turned around the little fool was backing further and further away. Till her back hit the wall, and she started to move sideways. Came up against the door, saw the fast-held lock. She began to cry then, to get it out of her system. He watched her crumple – he could afford to wait.

Quarter to eleven. Some of the clubs stayed open till two in the morning. He couldn't stay out much later. The car was in for repair so he couldn't give his usual excuse of just driving around. Still, three hours or so was ample time for the punishment which awaited her. Excessive time, really, in which to teach a young girl new tricks. Then he'd walk back to one of the busier areas, hail a taxi. If he felt truly energised he'd stride all the way home.

She stared at him as she sobbed, trembled, whimpered. Gradually, as he made no move towards her, she calmed down.

'You should have taken the painkiller when I brought it to you,' he said quietly. 'I'm your host, here, and you must always do what you're told.'

'I'll take it.' Her voice sounded different – higher. They both looked at the tablet, abandoned on the grey expanse of the floor. *My move.* She began to edge nearer the pill, but he pre-empted her, walked over and ground it beneath his foot. He'd seen it done in a film to thwart a cocaine addict. It had the same effect here – Pauline started to cry.

'Stop crying or I'll really give you something to cry about.' He felt a moment's revulsion – his father had said that to him. The old man, though, had lashed out without a reason. He, David, was giving this Pauline every chance. She brought one hand to her mouth, exposing one full bra cup. Noticed belatedly, and tried to cover both breasts with one arm.

No chance. It wouldn't be her breasts she'd want to cover in a moment. He jerked his head towards the trunk, gestured with his head.

'Bend over that, now.' Her eyes widened, unblinking. Deja vu – memories of that brainless runaway Kim. 'It'll be worse if I have to come and fetch you,' he said evenly, but the disappointment was nagging away, deep down.

No respect, no sense of his superiority. He bent over her and she went into an ungainly ball. Then uncoiled suddenly, surprising him.

Her flailing foot struck him in the stomach, an ineffectual blow. Shit. He grabbed the foot, held it, moved it sideways, kept holding it there, out of harm's way.

After that, it was easy to crouch to one side of her. He got hold of her nearest arm and twisted it all the way back. 'Put the other one back or I'll break this one,' he threatened. She cried out, writhing. He pushed further, and she did what she was asked.

He put the handcuffs on, scraping her wrists slightly. With her legs out in front of her, she could only twist from side to side. And shriek a lot – but no one could hear her. For your eyes only. Only *she* heard the swish as he pulled his belt free of its loops.

He edged behind her and forced his hands under her armpits, in one movement lifting her up and pushing her forward. She fell awkwardly, almost diagonally over the waiting wood. He lunged after her, and got her into position, keeping a knee on her back so she couldn't move.

He had practiced the next bit on himself, so it was easy. He reached for the iron hoop he'd embedded in the foot of the trunk. He'd bought a strong metal clip which fastened the loop to the hand-cuffs. It was amazing what you could do with a little DIY. Finally he got hold of the two leather straps he'd bought several weeks before. He'd secured them with heavy duty staples to opposite sides of the lid. Taking his time about it, he rubbed them between his fingers. She wasn't going anywhere – she could wait.

It was nice, for once, to be the powerful one. Grunting slightly, he brought the straps together and buckled them over her slim white back. Buckled them so that she couldn't escape, but could tease him with the occasional wriggle. She'd gone very quiet now: the calm before the storm. Forget the mundane. His mind went beyond every-thing but his cock as he pulled down her panties. She kicked against the trunk a little, and he said 'Don't,' twice, in a reasonable voice.

She went for an encore – testing, testing. Experimentally, he brought the belt down on her thighs. At that, her mouth made a lot of noise, but her legs went quiet. Just the toes drumming against the concrete, out of control.

She was learning – but very slowly. He told her to ask nicely for each stroke. She kept getting the words wrong, though, said 'Oh, please,' a lot. Sometimes, when his arm came down hard, she just screamed. He was, he thought exultantly, taking her mind off her headache. Training a new disciple was top to toe fun.

Not that he didn't take his duties seriously: there was much work ahead. She had to learn to honour and obey him. He'd want her to show desire, control. Maybe she could tell him what women looked for in quality music. But he didn't want criticism – she had to know her place. She was his servitor, an underling. If she did well, he'd treat her right.

Maybe he'd make her sit a test, maybe several. He looked at the red raised weals on taut white skin. If you wet flesh, it takes a belt much harder. He pictured pouring the mineral water over her tethered haunches, jerked hard then came. Time later, then, for proper lovemaking. She'd enjoy it more, anyway, with her punishment over for the day. There was just two hours left of their first night together, two hours of her inaugural training. He hoped she'd learn due deference so that he could put away his belt.

CHAPTER TEN

Wanda relaxed as the video about getting what you wanted finished, signalling the end of her first Assertiveness Training class. She'd talked stiltedly about feeling older than most of the other fabric 'n' fashion students despite being the exact same age.

'That's it till next week, but if anyone wants a private word, I'll be over there by the coffee machine,' Marie the facilitator said.

Wanda hurried over, aware of the class's eyes following her. 'I… em… have this friend who didn't book up in time.'

'That needn't be a problem,' said the older woman. She flicked her shoulder length hair back. Wanda stared at the incredibly heavy tresses. She'd look so much better with a less severe parting and a trim…

'So she could come next Friday?' This was encouraging.

'Yes. I don't see why not.' Marie was a casual person, not very animated. Was that what Assertiveness did to you? 'I'll tell them at the General Office that someone else will be along to book. She'll only have to pay for nine classes instead of ten.'

'Well, it's… not definite yet.'

'Oh?' Marie looked like a bloodhound, sensing the kill.

'She – her name's Jeanette, she's a new friend of mine.' She stopped, wondering if it was ethical to talk about a potential class-mate, 'We started going to the keep fit here together a few weeks ago. It's made her a bit more outgoing, but she'd really benefit from this.'

'Only if she wants to.'

'I know. I've mentioned it to her and I think she does – deep down.'

Marie flicked through some papers in her folder, brought out a leaflet. 'Give her this – it explains the basics. I'll write my number on the back.'

'Oh, she'd never phone you.' It was impossible to imagine Jeanette on the telephone. She found it hard enough to talk face to face.

'Really?'

'Mm. She's awkward with strangers.'

'A loner?'

'No. She has a husband. He's brilliant. Helps looks after their little boy.'

'Doesn't sound as if she's doing too badly,' the older woman murmured.

'She's not,' Wanda said, feeling proud that she was taking steps to help Jeanette. 'She knits these amazing jumpers. I keep telling her to take in orders. If the classes could make her believe in herself…'

'So she mainly needs confidence building?'

'I think so. It would help if she realised how many women would like to be in her shoes.'

CHAPTER ELEVEN

S hoes, David decided, were unnecessary. She wasn't going to be walking anywhere. Roughly he removed the white plastic sling-backs beloved of chain stores sales and huts on the beach. Ravers wore them to go whoring. They made her look tawdry, like all the rest.

Rest and be thankful. She whimpered as he lifted up her feet, gaze set like a rabbit's was when faced with a hypnotising weasel. She still wore the handcuffs, but differently: he'd freed her arms from behind her back and recuffed them at the front. He didn't want to cut off her circulation for no good reason. He didn't want to be unnecessarily unkind.

The little toe of her left foot looked swollen, rubbed, sore.

Rubbed. Sore.

He'd had to make her both last night. Now it was Friday evening and they could relax together. Now she could learn from him throughout the coming weekend.

Jeanette thought he was at a song writing conference in Glasgow. He'd promised to be back by Sunday, in time for tea. He'd driven the car to a long-stay car park in an unfamiliar area. No way was he leaving it like a beacon outside a derelict street.

Then he'd walked here, plotting, planning. Packed enough food to feed them both till Sunday night. Brought his briefcase filled with his songs, a book, a newspaper. And body lotion, stolen from the store.

Everything taken care of – everything. He smiled at Pauline, brought the soothing bottle from his case. After beating her last night, he'd untied her, removed the cuffs for a while to permit full movement. He'd been gentle, said she was free to walk around. He'd come at least twice whilst using the belt, so felt satisfyingly empty. He didn't want to touch her after that. With the anger drained from his system they could begin their relationship. Surely from now on she'd be anxious to please?

Yes, he'd been kind, but she'd gone into the corner as fast as her hands and knees would carry her. Like a dog that expects a kicking. Like a spider that's been torn from its web. Snuffling, nose running, hands trying to cover everything. She couldn't stay like that all night.

She'd screamed when he came towards her, when he only wanted her to put her dress on. He'd explained as much, reminding her of the unpredictability of August nights. It was important that she keep her limbs warm for him. It was important she take care of herself.

She'd struggled for long, long minutes to shrug on the lemon cotton. He'd decided not to give her back her underwear: it would take too much time. Instead he'd put it away – sad bra and briefs – in a carrier bag, one of several he kept in the cupboard below the sink. Later, if they went out on the embankment, she could wear them. For now, she should be ready for him at all times.

Next, he'd cuffed her arms at the front, and tied her legs loosely at the ankle. Then he'd covered her with a blanket, and an old quilt he'd told Jeanette he'd put out for the dustbin men. She'd winced when he kissed her forehead. She hadn't said anything when he'd bade her goodnight.

That had been around one-thirty am on Friday morning. He'd returned, nine hours later, wondering what he would find. He'd half expected her to have died, or somehow been taken from him. He'd feared similarly for a stray kitten he'd been foolish enough to love as a child. Mum had held him back as a neighbour took it to the animal pound. Strange, how he'd known from the start that something bad would happen. He'd held his breath each time he opened the cellar door. As he had this morning as he opened the Secret House door. He'd pictured her lying, flat out, face blueish-white and strangely waxy. He'd see an arm, as pale as lily-of-the-valley. Lips that would never smile or laugh at his jokes again.

Instead, the first thing that had hit him was the smell, the heavy sweetness. Christ. How could he have forgotten she'd have to shit? When he'd been here all day he'd had to go outside to the covering woodmould. Pauline hadn't had the opportunity, poor cow.

She was rocking back and forward, obviously expecting punishment. She'd been quite thoughtful, really: defecated near the door. The area was easy to sweep, and she'd left her blanket unsullied. She'd squatted cleanly: he'd been right not to put her pants back on.

Disinfectant. He had some left over from his initial cleaning sessions. He found it in the cardboard box by the wall across from the windows, whose shutters were still tight-closed. No way could you open them without tools, wearing handcuffs, though scratches in the woodwork indicated that she'd tried.

He opened the door wider, fetched the large, gleaming shovel. Got the mop, an old one he'd taken from his everyday house. He'd told Jeanette it was time to invest in a new one. The thing was functional, if somewhat bare.

The shovel, from a garden centre, had cost him dear, though. He'd bought it after throwing that dead teenage runaway over the cliff. There was prime burial ground all around him. It had been madness to transport a body all the way to a neighbouring town's beach.

'Clean it up,' he said, setting down the cleaning materials. There was very little faeces there. Just proved she had indeed eaten lightly, been working up an appetite for her restaurant meal. She stared, trembled. 'I'm not angry. Just clean it up.' He backed away till he was no longer blocking her view to the doorway. She began to edge herself forward on her buttocks, and he remembered how she was cuffed and bound. 'I'll undo your ankles,' he said, advancing towards her. She watched, unblinking as he approached, removed the rope. She cried out as it came free, drummed her feet up and down. Despite the looseness of the binding, the ropes had left faint pink lines.

When she struggled forward and used the shovel, he felt he almost loved her. She was doing what he wanted, earning his respect. She looked at him before taking the shovel outside, and he nodded. If she saw how remote they were she was less likely to try and attract attention when he wasn't there. He hadn't gagged her last night, figuring it was too risky. People had choked to death playing bondage games in the safety of their suburban homes.

Still, he followed her, watched her dig a little hole and dispose of the waste matter. Either her ankles or her pride was hurt, for she hadn't attempted to run. Helpfully he poured disinfectant over the damp patch of flooring, watched as she shuffled back in and picked up the cloth. When she was finished he explained that he would clean her extremities. Again she watched numbly as he poured disinfectant over her hands.

Lucky he'd stolen that sparkling mineral water. He fetched some from under the sink and wet a large new handkerchief. Knelt and washed her face, her disinfected palms. They'd have to keep washing themselves like this for the rest of the weekend.. On Monday he'd bring gallon containers of tap water in the car.

Somehow, in his fantasies, she'd always been soft and silky. Now he was going to have to buy a bucket she could use as a commode. Letting her out to empty it each day was risky, at least at this stage. If a tramp or curious child was to appear... Yet if he disposed of her wastes himself it made him little better than a menial. It was hardly the kind of task which inspired you to write songs.

Ah, his songs, his songs. He looked longingly towards his briefcase, and Pauline followed his gaze then stiffened. He'd have to start up a general conversation, work round to the subject. Only children could begin with the topic they most wanted to discuss.

'Did you sleep all right?' His eyes were level with hers. He could hear her breathing. She nodded, her mouth looked strangely pursed. 'Later, in the winter, I'll get you a paraffin heater.' She nodded jerkily, exhaled in an extended, trembling sigh. And urinated, like a puppy, water rivering out from under her across the floor.

He watched in fascination – Christ, he'd often done that. For years and years his bedroom had smelt of fear. Fear made your shit lighter, looser. Put pressure on your bladder five minutes after you'd been to the loo. Always, there would be that moment of ease as he surfaced from dreaming. Then he'd remember his father's kicks and his mother's collusion and the tummy-tightening terror would begin.

'It's all right,' he said, as her hands covered her mouth, the metal cuffs clanking, 'I'm not going to hurt you. I understand.' In time she'd find out he was reasonable. She'd recognise his talent, and be awed.

But for now he had to take care of more practical things. He'd had to beat her quite hard last night, when she'd disobeyed him. 'Let's have a look at you,' he said gently, taking her wrists in his. She quivered, head down, made a sound like a fighting cat does. He patted her hand, saw the torn nails where she'd clawed at the shutters in vain. 'I'm not going to hurt you. Don't be awkward. I'm here to make things right.'

Glad of his superior height, he stood up and pulled her forward. Got her into the centre of the room, pushed her down. Once she was on her belly all of the air seemed to go out of her and it was relatively easy to hold her flat. Despite the awkwardness of the cuffs, she twisted her head round. Began to whimper when he lifted up her dress.

Jesus. She must bruise easy. He touched the warm expanse, and she grunted, flinched. She did that a lot – predictable. He hoped there was more to her than met the eye. Though he'd like to see less, at the moment. He stared, disgusted at the puffy expanse of flesh.

He wanted soft, white hemispheres to stroke, the kind you saw in magazines. The kind the girls on the phones lines said they had. Still, he had to do the best he could with what was available. He had brought along the body lotion for that very task.

Smooth, silky, superior. He wanted his new woman to have perfect skin. This mixture contained coconut oils, was nicely scented. People everywhere were crying out for such a massage. Health Store shampoos, tropical oil conditioners... she'd have to use cold water, of course, but that drawback aside, she could have everything. For special treats he could set up a mini bath tub, bring hot water in containers from his flat.

What was it they called it? A whore's bath. Meant you soaped yourself down without benefit of bath or shower. His little whore, exclusive only to him. Though he suspected that when he took her he'd find that he wasn't really her first. He'd be the first who mattered, though, and that was what counted. He'd be her last, she'd get used to only him.

She'd respect him for the creative things he most deserved respect for. He didn't need *male* respect, for they respected the wrong things. He was above all their macho sport, their lager drinking, computer programmes and gaming hall machines and darts.

Not that the university crowd had been like that, but he'd still found them wanting. They were so unrelentingly communal, in and out of each others rooms. They had filled up their lives with trivial interaction. Their essays had been conventional, yes-man works.

No more of such rigours, no more. Now he had his wife, his mistress, a part-time job which gave him perks and brought in regular money. He had his talent for lyrics, his phone girls, his Secret House.

As he practiced his Song Writer Of The Year Award acceptance speech, David poured some of the body lotion into his palms. Firmly he began kneading the dull purple buttocks before him. He'd work hard to make them shiny and bright. Life was full of possibilities, getting better and better. He just couldn't understand why Pauline was crying again.

CHAPTER TWELVE

'It's dangerous,' said Mrs Landrew. There was a break in the conversation as Jeanette greeted a new customer and accepted a service wash.

She turned back to her mother, her voice even: 'I don't see why.'

'Seems obvious to me.' The older woman wasn't used to questioning.

'But Mum, I like it – feel happier afterwards. It's fun.'

'Exactly. Women get hooked on this sort of thing – exercise addiction. My magazine said…'

Keeping her features neutral, Jeanette tuned out. The monologue would take several minutes, and she wasn't expected to contribute. She sighed. She had never really known fun until now.

'Mum…' She must have sounded different, for the greying brown head jerked suspiciously, 'Maybe you could come along with me sometime? I mean, Wanda can't always make it. It would just be us.' That was a lie, but a necessary one – her mother hated students. Hated men who worked in health food stores part time…

'Me? At that place? People break bones at those classes. They've had to set up this clinic for sports injuries, the freesheet said. I'm not taking chances. Always looked after myself.' She looked round the launderette as if to gain support from the three seated customers. 'After the way your dad died, it's no wonder I worry about health.'

More difficult territory. Jeanette looked at the counter, discarded thought after thought. If she said that exercise made you fitter, her mother would take it as personal. She'd assume she was being criticised for not taking her dad on regular walks.

'Esmond likes the creche,' she said instead. Her mother opened her mouth again. 'It's supervised,' she continued hurriedly, 'the children there are all well-behaved.'

'Passed about like a parcel, the poor wee morsel. He was fine with me. Don't know why you had to start giving him to that Wanda every Wednesday, when he has a family of his own.'

But Mum, Mum, you complained you had to babysit too much. You said you were being taken for granted, that you'd already done your bit.

Such hard eyes. Her mother must have been hurt very much to see the world through such hard eyes. Maybe if her husband hadn't died so early? She'd always respected men more than women so maybe if she'd given birth to a son…?

'She… Wanda wanted the experience. She'll be designing kids' clothing soon.' She swallowed, tapped her pen against the counter, 'It helps to see what kids prefer, where their clothes wear out.' Why had she said that? It was utter rubbish. Wanda had been designing evening dresses for some vaguely-promised show. Still, she could hardly tell her mother that David didn't like her, could hardly say that they were tired of being criticised for swapping working roles. It wasn't even as if she, Jeanette, was an especially feminist working mother. She still looked to David for approval, for praise.

A silence. Mrs Landrew took an unusual interest in the posters on the wall behind the counter. Then: 'She doesn't change his outfits, does she? You can't be too careful nowadays.'

Jeanette blinked, thoughts racing. Can't be too careful? What was her mother hinting at now? 'He just wears his dungarees or his shorts and T-shirt, Mum. I give her his little shell suit in case it gets cooler in the afternoon.'

'Only, it's not just men who… *do things* to kids nowadays – it's women as well. My magazine said so. Couples are often the worst.'

'He's fine, Mum.' There was no point getting upset, in getting defensive. Her mother had been treated badly by life. Anyway, Jeanette had never experienced much anger. Rage was something that happened to other people, like winning a competition or going abroad.

'Would you like a coffee?' The man had just filled up the machine, so her mother wouldn't get the runt of the litter like last time.

'Not me. I read a report. I've given it up, switched to tea.'

'Tea, then?'

'Not if I'm going to walk home with this little one.' She leaned forward, a bearer of secrets, 'You know what my bladder's like.'

No drink, no news, no two-way conversation. Had her mother walked all this way purely to criticise her again? When she *did* have Esmond, why did she bring him to Jeanette's workplace? Couldn't she take him to the Early Learning Centre or the park? The launderette wasn't an ideal playroom for a three-year-old. If it had been, she'd have brought him with her to work.

Wanda was going to take him to the museum, to see the train engines. She'd also promised to take him back to the zoo. He'd been there before with David. He'd seemingly laughed out loud as the Prairie Dogs scooped out their tunnel home.

As soon as something suitable came on, Wanda was also going to take Esmond to the cinema. He'd never been before, though he watched cartoons on TV. David didn't like crowds, or he and she would have taken him. David wouldn't go anywhere which involved sitting close to lots of people he didn't know.

She remembered their one visit to the theatre in the short period they'd dated. The Kings Theatre, it had been: he'd insisted they take a box. It had cost more than the stalls: she'd thought he was trying to impress her. Mother said that men with one thing on their minds went all out to impress.

But he'd had that thing – must still be interested in pleasing her. She had appreciated that he was trying so hard. Even now, she could remember wanting to cuddle him. Instead they had collected their tickets then climbed the stairs to their little four-seater box. Sitting sideways to the stage, she'd leaned over the little wall to see better. She'd felt embarrassed whenever anyone in the seats below looked up.

David had been happy, however, avoiding the common herd, what he called 'the proletariat.' He said their muttering disturbed his concentration. He said he felt nauseous when they slobbered over their sweets.

'I'll need to get on, Mum.' There was a crate of individual soap powder packets in the back needed unpacking. And they were low on pound coins, she'd have to get some more. When Susan who covered at lunchtimes came in, Jeanette would leave pronto. She'd just reach the bank before it closed for lunch. She'd got her mother to go once, but was trying to rely less and less on her. As David said, you had to make your own way in life.

'Don't let me stop you.' Mrs Landrew looked round the shop with half-lidded eyes She looked like a camel whenever she did that. Esmond had climbed onto one of the chairs and was facing its back.

'Giddy up,' he murmured uncertainly.

'David still working in that health food store?' She made it sound like a brothel, something Underground.

'Yes, Mum. You could go there to buy decaffeinated coffee.' She tried hard, couldn't quite meet her mothers gaze.

'*He* should be doing this. You should be at home with the kiddie.'

'He can't work such hours, Mum. He has to write his songs.'

'Has to, does he?' A camel-like snort to rival the eye movements, 'Which means you have to do this.'

How to explain the safety she found in the routine? 'I don't mind. It's straightforward, quite well paid.'

'But if *he* wasn't so lazy, you could get something part time that was interesting.' *Or sit in the flat with you, Mum, you mean…*

Jeanette took a deep breath, looked up at her mother. 'David isn't lazy. He looks after Esmond as well as writing songs.'

'Ach, that child almost looks after itself.'

'Just as well, for all the attention you're giving him.' The last few words came rushing out, as she realised what Esmond was up to. She saw the beginning of her mother's flush before she rushed past. 'Don't touch that, Esmond,' she said, lifting him back from the abandoned whirring machine. 'You could hurt your hands.'

'Touch. Hands,' said Esmond, his small face serious.

Jeanette walked him back to his suddenly quiet gran. An awkward silence. 'Did I mention I'm about to join an Assertiveness Training class?'

'Doesn't sound like you need it,' Mrs Landrew said. She took Esmond's hand, not looking at him. 'We'll be back at five-thirty, then.'

'Yes, thanks, Mum.' She looked beyond the stiff back to wave to Esmond. 'Bye, Esmond. See you tonight.'

Tonight she was going to talk to David about her annual holiday. Two whole weeks of freedom scheduled for next month. OK, so they couldn't afford a vacation, but they could manage an afternoon at the nearby village of Crammond. It had a river and swans, little boats. Maybe she and David would take Esmond to the zoo and invite Wanda. She, Jeanette had only been once, with the school. Or if they ran out of cash they could drive to Blackford Pond and feed the ducks, then climb up to the Observatory.

Her thoughts raced. If they left Esmond at Wanda's as usual on the Wednesday, she and David could even climb Arthur's Seat together. Drat, no – he worked then. Maybe Mrs Melloway would give him the day off?

Wanda had been lending Jeanette magazines, the type that cost a lot and came out monthly. Some neighbour passed them on to Wanda when they'd become well-thumbed. Jeanette had read several articles about communication. They said that you should ask calmly for what you wanted from everyone.

She wanted to spend more time with David – *talking* time. Some of the articles had shown how *together* good relationships could be. They gave you a little case study in which the couple weren't communicating. Then they began to talk and iron their problems out.

Not that she and David had problems, exactly – they were just a bit too busy. She worked full time, he held down two different jobs. They had a young child, she had household chores and shopping. Until now, she'd never had a friend.

Not that she'd let Wanda know that. You had to maintain a distance about some things, like Mum said. In the end she'd done what David did, mentioned strangers as though they were friends. 'I was just saying to this friend the other night…'

The first time David had done that, she'd felt embarrassed. The 'friend' had been a cold-canvasser from some newborn religious group. David had invited him in for a drink, flicked through his pamphlets. Led him to believe he was interested, then torn his beliefs to shreds. Now he was letting Mrs Melloway think that the man was a regular visitor when in truth, they would never see him again. Or the Market Researcher who'd wanted his opinion about male perfume. Or the double glazing firm whose painstaking estimates he'd spurned. Friends, suddenly. 'I was talking to this friend about home improvements…' Friends only referred to as such when they were far away.

Not that she could blame David, not really. It was hard to strike up meaningful relationships when you worked in a shop. It was all talk about the weather, about prices. You couldn't suddenly invite a customer to the pub.

The keep fit class, now that was different. Maybe David could ask around, and find one that took men? Mind you, he was happy being a loner. Creative people were often like that – self contained.

But not self contained enough that they didn't need wives and fun and holidays. Jeanette smiled inside as she led customers to vacant washing machines. Tonight, when Esmond was in bed, she'd talk to David. He'd probably be glad she had opened up.

'… So if we could plan my holiday.' She'd got all three of them settled with trays of quiche and salad in front of the TV.

'I'm going out after this,' said David, putting his parsley garnish carefully to one side. 'I've got other plans.'

Jeanette felt a strange ache – hurt? disappointment? – in her stomach. She didn't ask for anything, as a rule. 'When do you have to leave?' She kept it friendly.

He kept his gaze on the TV as he spoke, kept eating. 'As soon as I've finished this.'

'Well, could you even spare me half an hour?' She must have sounded different, for he glanced at her.

'It's a difficult time. I've to go to the Music Library before it shuts.'

After a day at the store, the poor man was still working. She felt the familiar feelings of inadequacy and guilt. 'Sorry, I didn't realise. I thought now that you ordered from these music mags all the time.' They'd had words about those, once, and she'd hated that. Hated him lying in the lower bunkbed refusing to say goodnight. It was one of the few arguments they'd had since getting married. Well, not an argument really – no harsh words. She'd commented on the amount he was spending on CDs. He'd seen it as interference and his mood had turned dark.

'I'm not buying at the moment. Got to pay for the car, remember.'
Of course – the service. it had cost more than they'd thought.

The Scottish news headlines came on and he reached over to switch channels. He must want something lighter for a change. One day, Jeanette promised herself, they'd have a remote control handset. One day they'd have a 26 inch screen.

Was the discussion about holidays over? She watched David cut carefully into his quiche. *Don't give up. Keep talking.* Women had to ask for what they wanted, and be firm.

She tried again: 'Maybe after the library…?'

'Not possible. I want to go on to Salisbury Crags.'

To help, no doubt, with his song writing. If it hadn't been for Esmond, she could have come too. When the men in the magazines couldn't do what their partners wanted they said, 'Sorry, dear'. Sometimes they made up for things by buying chocolates and flowers.

'We could talk about this at the weekend' said David, raising his voice a little to compete with a film preview, 'I'd forgotten you had these two weeks due.'

'You'll not be going to another weekend conference?'

Another sharp look: 'No, no. At least, not for a while.'

'I mean, I don't want to do anything exotic. Just plan a couple of day trips, you know.'

She realised they could go to the university town of St. Andrews. A strange place, with its crumbling castles and imposing cliffs. Best not to mention it till Saturday though, best to let David unwind in his own good time. Jeanette looked proudly over at his dark hair and well-dressed body. She must never smother him the way her mother had done to her. David was a free spirit, needed room to develop. She must always give him licence to be himself.

CHAPTER THIRTEEN

Hurrying up the old washing green, he hoped Pauline would be pleased to see him. It had been difficult, getting away from home. Goodness knows why Jeanette had suddenly come over all talkative. Suddenly wanted to enter the tourist trap.

Usually she came home and just smiled and said, 'Not long till tea time,' went into the kitchen and began to cook the meal. Sometimes she'd say something negative about her mother. He'd encourage her to get it out of her system, add some comments of his own. More often, he'd keep listening through his headphones till the food was ready. Then they'd take up their usual stances and watch TV.

Even Esmond didn't say anything when the set was switched on. It was a way of life, a known yet unspoken rule. But tonight she'd queried the hours he intended to spend on song-writing research. She'd kept looking at him expectantly, refusing to let the matter drop.

Bad, that. David brushed away a diagonally-growing weed as he reached the foot of the challengingly steep embankment. He hoped she wasn't turning into a shrew. They'd done all right so far – a casual, flatmates-like relationship that gave him freedom. Yet he could still appear mature to strangers by mentioning his wife and child.

A man with a family, a man with a future. A future which didn't involve lots of questions and time-wasting trips. God, he wanted to be here, at The Secret House, throughout the mild weather. Wanted to lie in the sun with his mistress and talk about life. Any minute now, he'd be doing more than talking. The slight uncertainty about getting away from Jeanette tonight had lent excitement to his prick.

Most men, David decided, wanted sex without commitment. They just didn't know how to achieve their goal. Women tried to hold out on them, to mould them into armchair companions. It took a strong, determined man to put them right.

Take Pauline. Christ, he'd done so. The first two nights he'd tried it, she hadn't liked giving head. She'd spat and gagged, even when he'd only pushed the tip in. His erection had subsided and he'd fallen out.

Cue the chocolate freeway. He'd flipped her over, reared backwards. A man had to be flexible, and he was the innovative type. She hadn't liked that either: had grunted like a piglet. Writhed exquisitely against his cock, though, so he'd persevered.

Again the body lotion had come in handy. White lotion tainted with the spreading stain of pink. If only she hadn't fought so much, it might have been easier. There were supposed to be erogenous zones in there.

Pauline didn't seem to have erogenous zones anywhere. No whimpers of pleasure when he touched her hard, cold nipples, the silken contours of her tits. Sometimes she squealed, more often she just breathed raggedly. Spoke when she was spoken to – rather like Jeanette.

And watched, eyes following him everywhere. Jeanette at least didn't put him through this. Did Pauline find him too thin, find him wanting? He tried to hold back his shoulders and puff out his stomach as he walked around the room. He fed her and washed her, supervised her two minute crawl outdoors as she disposed of her waste matter. He did everything for her and got nothing in return.

Well, not nothing – she gave a reasonable blow job nowadays. Anything, he suspected, to keep him from taking her in the arse. Now when he walked in she flinched, started rocking. Seemed to remember what she was here for, and stared hungrily at his zip. God, but she took it in deep when she was running on empty. Sucked overwhelming sensation from his balls.

Reaching the top of the embankment, David began walking towards The Secret House. He'd planned on having a woman that gave more than sex. The silly girl had never tried to talk to him. When he spoke to her she trembled, gave halting replies.

'Don't be frightened,' he'd said often at the beginning. But now she'd been here for almost two weeks and he was bored with repeating himself. How long could you reassure someone before your patience deserted you? How long before you settled for being what they took you for, a hard-driving boss?

Maybe tonight they'd ascertain the answers. Maybe tonight she'd open up, begin to trust. He was writing a song about urban existentialism. She'd been alienated in her bedsit, ought to understand.

He unlocked the door and realised she understood nothing. She was lying where he had left her, half propped up against the window wall, on the floor. The room smelt slightly sweet, and he unhooked the shutters. Opened the windows an inch from the bottom, to let in the warm evening air.

When he walked over to her commode, he realised he'd have to open the door for a moment. Let her disinfect things, let the odour escape. Trying to pretend she hadn't moved since his exit. was she? At some stage since last nights visit, she'd obviously struggled over here to defecate.

And made it over to the shutters. There were brand new wood shavings beneath the locks. She must have been trying to make a run for it. He'd have to make her blood run colder now.

Pity, that. It would have been nice if she'd been sitting in one of the chairs, reading. She could have looked up, looked pleased to see him, smiled then asked about his day. Even with the handcuffs on, she could have finger-combed her hair a little. Could have pinched her face to bring some colour to her cheeks. He went into his inside pocket for the henna shampoo he'd stolen earlier. Cold water or not, he was going to have to wash her head.

But first he'd have to take her dress off so that it didn't end up getting soaked. He told her what he was going to do, and she stared. Rocked again – the damn girl was always rocking. Back and forward on the floor like a rocking chair.

When he reached for the material she didn't try to fight him. Didn't help either – just let her upper limbs go limp. He got the dress off, noticed it was dusty. Yellow stains beneath the arms and above the hem smelt strongly of urine and sweat.

So did her blanket, and the old quilt he'd brought her. As soon as he could come here for the day he'd wash them out. It would take several hours in the sun to dry them. Well, he couldn't exactly hand them in at the launderette.

Grimacing at the irony, he uncorked one of the gallon containers of water. When his wife went to her keep fit class he'd bring hot water here. He tested the cold with his finger: found it was bearable. Walked over to Pauline and tipped some of it over her hair.

Her head jerked back, her mouth opened wide, but she wasn't screaming. He rubbed in some shampoo: it lathered hardly at all. Added more water, more liquid. Spread and rubbed then rinsed and rinsed and rinsed. Scented water ran down her breasts and belly, making her smell better. He found the facecloth, knelt, and scrubbed her hard.

And grew hard in doing so, hard and eager. Her eyes were at crotch level, she must have noticed the change. He looked at her face, and she looked up at him, and she was shaking. Got her tongue out, and ran it enticingly over her lips. Looked at his bulge, and back at him, and repeated the gesture. Reached, with her handcuffed hands, for his groin.

He watched, feeling happier, hopeful. The cuffs made it hard for her to cope with the zip. She struggled for a while, the metal clanking. When she'd succeeded, she could go no further and put her hands in her lap. He stepped back, undid his top button, adjusted himself. Felt the heavy tension in his scrotal sac.

Naked, she rose to her knees, still staring, staring. He wished that her hair could have been blow-dried in compelling waves. He stepped back slightly, so that she went forward onto all fours to reach him. Just as her mouth opened, he moved smartly to the side.

Gotcha. He hurried back to stand behind her. Pushed her down on her belly and lowered himself till he lay upon her back. Sorry, baby, my move again. And whatever game they were playing, it wasn't chess. Pauline cried out as his cock teased the entrance to her anus. Wriggled and bucked – but she wasn't going anywhere.

He was, though – to Nirvana. To wherever you went when your balls shot their angry load. OK, so it wasn't what she'd planned, but she wasn't the planner. When *he* hadn't been in charge, his life had been a veritable hell.

Never again, never, ever. He was controlling things now, control-ling the way his prick shoved hard. David began to thrust more deeply and more strongly. Genius deserved obedience and respect.

CHAPTER FOURTEEN

The following Sunday, she was especially respectful. It had done her good, then, spending a night, a day, and another night alone. He hadn't planned it that way – it had just happened. He'd meant to pop in on the Saturday morning for a couple of hours.

Then Jeanette had dragged him to the Tourist Information Office, saying the excursions they'd find out about would be good for Esmond. He wanted his child to enjoy life, couldn't quibble with that. They'd gotten leaflets and a catalogue on Edinburgh's finest. Gone on to a horribly crowded McDonald's for outsized cokes. He'd wanted to find somewhere quiet, but there wasn't anywhere. They'd sat beside the window with their leaflets, and Jeanette had insisted on reading every detail out loud.

Would he like to go to the castle, she'd asked him. She'd been with her mum once, but they'd done it up since then. Or there was The Camera Obscura or The Ghost Tour. He'd noticed an advert about a Torture Museum, decided to go there on his own. Ah, they'd had the right idea in the olden days. Got rid of the human vermin with an entrail-eating rat.

Talking of vermin – he'd left the car at home to outwit the traffic wardens. You had to park so far away from Princes Street it was quicker to walk from home. Then Jeanette had said she wanted to walk back again, as part of her keep fit campaign. He hadn't relished the idea – had another hard night's thrusting into Pauline ahead. But Jeanette had said they should get their circulation going properly, could use the bus fares for something else.

So they'd walked, with Esmond running ahead of them. Had decided where they would go during her holidays the following month. It would be October, he'd said, it might be cool, it might be raining. Two day trips a week, on Mondays and Fridays, was the most he had to give. Other spanners in the works had included the cost, time out for his songs, Esmond's proneness to all sorts of ailments. But she'd been adamant. It would be the first holiday, of sorts, that they'd ever had. At night they'd been tired: she'd made them baked potatoes. He'd chopped onion for the filling, got out sweet pickle, grated the cheese. He'd left the onion out of Esmond's – he didn't like it. Felt pleased that he was catering for his little child. Cue TV for the braindead – a typical Saturday. He'd added a library book to his dinner tray and started to read. A good place, the Central Library. Meant he could save his money for DIY…

Soon Esmond and Jeanette had fallen asleep, and he'd switched off the flickering television set. Picked his son up and taken him to his little alcove bed. Tonight he'd have to sleep in his day clothes until Jeanette put on his pyjamas. He hated to see young children undressed. Christ, such hellish vulnerability. Poor little bastard, with his puny white torso and thin arms and legs.

Efficiently, he laid Esmond on the mattress in his dusty shorts and T-shirt. Covered him with his duvet, and let him sleep.

He'd meant to slip out, then, but the book was absorbing. Looked at the Church's attitudes to sexuality from ancient times. Looked – and dared to tell the truth about the damage. And so he'd read, vaguely aware of Jeanette sleeping on.

Easy to sneak out – but he wasn't motivated. Didn't feel like cleaning up after Pauline, or having sex. No, the last few weeks had been tiring, and he had to recharge himself. He'd left a jug of juice with a straw sticking out of it – she'd survive.

What else had he left? Ah, yes, dried fruit and a cream cheese sandwich. He'd put them on the sink unit, reminded her that they were there. He'd had to unwrap them – handcuffs got in the way of bags and clingfilm. She'd gotten semi-hysterical when she couldn't get a banana free of its skin.

He didn't want to leave more than she would eat at one sitting. Rats might scent any leftovers – that could be bad news, rats finding a girl handcuffed and with her ankles tied. No, he'd left just enough to keep her going till Saturday morning. Now that he wouldn't see her till Sunday she'd have to go without.

Her own fault, really, for not being enticing enough, for not connecting with him. He'd done his best to make her comfortable, make her feel at home. But she was void, somehow, lacked that vital creative spark. Perhaps, then, he'd have to settle for just keeping her as a sex slave. Take a second Mistress who'd appreciate his work.

Someone like Wanda, beyond mere sex, a superior being. He'd seen her once, briefly, since the first time that they'd met. He'd been picking up Jeanette and Wanda had just been leaving. He'd given her and her alterations a lift back home.

Of course, he heard about her from Jeanette at regular intervals. 'Wanda said,' had become a regular opening comment in their two minute talks. 'Wanda and I,' came a pretty close second, after the keep fit classes. Now they were both attending some kind of woman's group as well.

Yes, they'd all three of them have to arrange a cultural evening. He'd buy in wine for the women, Jeanette could show off some of her fancier knits. She'd done up some fantastic patterned jumpers for Esmond. Had already knitted things which would fit him for at least the next two years. Wanda would ask about the songs, and he'd offer to show her some. It would be the start of many evenings of intelligent talk.

Talk to me today, he thought silently as he drove to The Secret House on the Sunday. Maybe hunger and loneliness had made Pauline voracious for wholemeal bread and words.

Carbohydrate – that was the best thing to give people after a mini-fast. It was palatable, digestible, took the headachey feeling away. He'd pretended to make himself some toast last night, had put four slices in his pocket. This morning he'd added two individually wrapped portions of processed cheese. Cue brunch. As he parked near The House he felt rejuvenated. She'd definitely have missed him this time – her stomach would.

Time for the risky bit. He got slowly out of his seat and locked the drivers door. Looked casually up and down, then crossed the road diagonally and walked smartly to the close. If anyone ever saw him at this stage and followed him they'd find the handcuffed girl and he'd find himself in prison. Thrown in with the very class of people he'd fought to escape…

A miracle, really, that the old man had never even been up on an assault charge. The neighbours and an auntie at the very least had seen him lunge at David, when he was but two years old. And once he'd kicked a boy at work for fooling about in the lifts of the factory. Sixteen, the boy had been, and he'd been crying when the other factory hands had led him away. 'I showed that little bastard,' his father had said as they sat round the tea trolley. 'Some of the lads said he might report me, but he's not that daft.'

His father had been a fool – but an uncaught fool. So, he, David, with his superior intellect should also be able to avoid being caught. Should be able to hide, as so-called families hid, behind honeyed words to strangers and firmly closed doors. Few people questioned their relatives too closely. Few people wanted to get involved and complicate their own small lives.

It wasn't as if he was keeping an enormous talent from the world in holding Pauline. No, she was at the bottom of the most missed league. He'd scanned the papers, but hadn't seen a column inch about her. She was just one of the many voluntary disappeared. The disappeared who took lovers, got pregnant, went elsewhere. The housing agencies probably took their possessions in lieu of back rent. At worst, there'd be a paragraph in the papers, a few weeks of the police being quoted as 'concerned'.

He unlocked The Secret House and was immediately concerned himself. Christ, no. Surely she hadn't gone and died on him? Just lying there but not making eye contact. Not flinching, not whimpering, not even as much as a blink.

Leaving the door open for once, he knelt beside her. 'Speak to me. Say something.' He shook her arm roughly and she moaned. Opened her eyes, moved her head, took a while to focus.

'I was busy,' he said awkwardly, 'couldn't get away.'

He reached for the cheese sandwich and held it to her mouth. She tried to nibble the edge, but began to hack and cough. Was she coming down with something? Surely the place was free of germs when she only saw him. No breathing in others colds on stuffy buses, no getting caught out when the heavy heat turned to sudden, clammy fog.

Her eyes swivelled to the side, then focused. He followed her gaze, saw the water jar nearby. Either she'd knocked it over or he'd underestimated how much she'd be drinking. The gaudy straw traced down to sparkling dry glass.

Hurrying to the cupboard, he got out another gallon container of orange juice. Put a little in the jar, and placed the straw between her lips. In the few seconds it had taken to do so, her access to the open door had been total. Either she was too weak, or too clever, to run away. He watched as she sipped slowly, finishing the liquid. Gave her back the sandwich, and this time she wolfed it down. Did wolves really eat so quickly, or was that one of mans' unthought-out expressions? There was so much shallow thinking in the world.

This world, however, could be the exception. In this little world it should be possible to make things right. This time, before he left, he'd fix the jar to the surface with adhesive. No more spillage, though she'd have to stand up and hop over for a drink. The store had started selling foil packs of juice which appealed to schoolchildren. Surely one or two wouldn't be missed?

Crouching down beside her, he began to talk of the foods he could bring in the next few days. Did she have any preferences? Curled up like that, she looked like an appealing child. 'Want some of those things at the store?' he said generously. 'You know, the ones in the fridges and the freezers that you couldn't afford.' He could cook them on Mondays and Fridays while Jeanette was at work, rush them over. Maybe she'd be more communicative with a hot meal inside. 'What would you like?' he prompted, when no answer came.

'Anything.' An affected whisper.

'You're not making this easy for me,' he said evenly. She began to tremble again. What did you have to do for some women to win their approval? Food, liquid, toiletries, body-cleansing, talk. He'd brought her a book on day one but she still hadn't opened it. He'd left her with two years worth of his songs. Copies of course – at home he still had the originals. She might tear them up or defecate on them out of spite.

No, she really didn't like him – he had to face it. She was boring, thoughtless, hopelessly immature. She deserved all she got with her silly posturing. All this whispering and trembling – it was only a matter of time before she developed a lisp. And a cut on her hand with wood splinters that would become infected. Serve her right for scratching the shutters all the time. Here she was, sucking his cock and playing up to him and saying 'anything', when really she wanted to run off into the night. He knew the ways of women – had watched mummy. Take that awful time when his father had gone to the doctor for a line wearing his one tight suit. He'd used the opportunity to hide the bastard's belt. Dad had come in as usual and sat down at the wooden trolley.

'What kind of a day did you have?' His dad said that to his mum every teatime.

'Oh, so so. I put the washing out.'

'The doctor was saying we should try to get away somewhere.'

He could feel his mother grow more tense: 'Oh aye?'

'Of course, I said on one wage it wasn't easy. I said to him, it's not even as if the wife's willing to get a job.'

'You'd miss it if you didn't come home to find the trolley set and all your meals cooked.'

'There's plenty of women manage both.'

'And a clean bed once a fortnight?'

'Better to spend a week in a bed 'n' breakfast somewhere else.'

Don't, Mum, don't, Mum, don't.

'I found your belt, by the way.'

'Did ye?'

'M'laddo here had hidden it behind the cooker. Needed a coathanger to fish it out.'

Afterwards, when it had all been over, she'd come to his room to tuck him in. He'd been lying wet-faced on his stomach, kept his head turned away. She'd smoothed the covers out all round, not saying anything. How had she felt, telling on him, causing such pain? She'd promised, promised – and he'd believed her. She'd made him trust her and then she'd lied.

Now it was her turn – she deserved it. As he unbuckled his belt and walked forward, Pauline began to shriek.

CHAPTER FIFTEEN

'I'd like him home a little more often,' Jeanette said quietly, looking at Marie for assurance. She risked a quick glance at Wanda, who glanced back and smiled. Everyone else was leaning forward, frowning. *Don't stare, don't stare.* She transferred her gaze to her denims, 'I… no, I don't have anything else to say.' She raised her eyes, lowered them again. 'That's about it.'

'And have you told him what you want from him?' This was Marie's favourite question.

'Yes… well, sort of. I got him to go into town with me on Saturday.'

'And that wasn't difficult?'

'No.' Again the watchers seemed to expect more of her. 'We had a very nice day.'

Marie nodded encouragingly. 'So what makes you think there could be conflict?'

'Well…' Talking about what David did was always difficult. 'He writes songs, you know… He hates to spend time away from thinking about that.' A pause. That made her sound as if he lived in some fancy creative world. *Make them like you.* 'He's good about looking after Esmond for me. I mean, there's lots of men just don't have a clue.'

'And what do *you* do for *him*?' Jeanette felt a blush start and quickly overwhelm her. She dipped her head again. Surely Marie wasn't asking about sex? 'I mean, do you split the household chores, or…?'

'No, I do most of the cooking and cleaning, things like that.'

'Do you see it as quite an equitable arrangement?'

Equitable? Presumably that meant equal. Marie must have sussed this, as she rephrased the question: 'I mean, do you think the way you divide up your leisure time is fair?'

'I used to… Now I just want us to do more things together. You know?' *Like the families in the magazines do.*

She didn't know any real families – her dad's early death ensured that she'd never been a part of one. She'd never had to chance to learn, observe.

'Then keep making your wishes clear to him. You're not asking for anything unreasonable, after all.'

'It is difficult, though, isn't it?' said Wanda, looking at Marie, leaning forward. 'You know, changing things that have been the same for years?' Jeanette smiled at Wanda gratefully. Wanda smiled back.

'Yes, it's often best to start small, get the other person used to the idea. Can anyone suggest how Jeanette might proceed?'

Odd to have strangers talking about her. Odd to tell them long-concealed truths about her married life. But everyone was doing it, talking openly. Talking of debt-ridden or adulterous husbands, rude sons. She herself was beginning to feel quite privileged. She had a relatively straightforward life.

'You could ask him to stay in and watch a film with you,' one woman said. Jeanette half-nodded, trying to picture the domestic scene – she and David liked such different films.

'Or tell him you want to go out somewhere,' another classmate suggested. Difficult again, when money was scarce. Maybe their largely separate lifestyle was right for them, then? Maybe she was expecting too much?

Marie leaned towards her. 'Are those suggestions not helpful, Jeanette?'

'Well, David likes documentaries… I prefer nature programmes.'

'What *would* you like to do together?'

'Just sit around and talk.'

'You feel you're lacking the opportunity to tell him things?'

'I suppose so.' God, she felt such a bitch. She could feel waves of empathy coming over the room towards her from Wanda. Pity they hadn't managed to get seats together tonight. The others had arrived early – must be keen, or desperate. Still, now that she had started talking, it wasn't too bad.

'All right. Let's get involved in some goal-setting,' Marie said, returning to her strange assertiveness talk, 'Do you both get up in the morning at the same time?'

'Sort of… three days a week, that is. The days when he works at the store.'

'OK, well let's be realistic about this. Probably neither of you are at your best first thing.' Low level laughter. Jeanette looked down at her lap and smiled 'but try talking a little more over breakfast. You know, discuss the mail, any plans you have for the day.' Marie reached for a slim sheaf of forms beside her, started to hand them round. 'Don't fill these out now, but we'll discuss the kind of things you might like to write on them. Take them home. Give the issues some thought.' The form contained sections for minor and medium goals, major changes. There were printed examples on an accompanying page.

'A medium change might be if Jeanette asked her husband to come out for a walk with her one evening,' Marie said. She went on to outline other goals which were manageable. On David's songwriting days, maybe they could cook the evening meal together? They could chat and catch up with the days news at the same time. By then he'd have had more than eight hours of writing songs, of doing what he wanted to do. 'It's too easy to start relating to each other simply as parents,' said Marie.

But we don't do that either, Jeanette thought, confused.

Perhaps they could finally reach a situation where they had certain evenings together, the facilitator continued. They could agree to spend others in solitary pursuits. It would help Jeanette to have more stability, and David might feel that he was being needed, was more part of her life.

Needed. She'd never thought about it like that. Maybe he thought she was tired of him and his writing, didn't care what he did? She'd thought she was doing well, giving him his freedom. What if she'd gotten it all wrong?

'Try the breakfast talks for a week or two and see how it goes,' Marie said smiling. 'You can bring the subject up here at any time.'

'Thanks.' Big wet circles were expanding under her armpits. She hoped against hope that no one could see.

'Moving on – does anyone else want to change the behaviour of family members?' Ah, blessed words – moving on.

'My fifteen year old son has these girlie magazines,' the woman next to her said. Jeanette felt herself blush from her neckline to her forehead. She kept her head down, swallowed hard. David had such mags, but David was an adult. Surely an adult could have whatever he liked? Well, yes he could – within reason. She had the right to ask him to keep them private, Marie said.

'He keeps them under his bed. I have to lift them out of the way to vacuum,' the woman continued.

'Ask him to move whatever is there to his cabinet, then.'

The woman grimaced. 'But I hate the idea of mentioning them.'

'Be matter of fact: tell him you want his floorspace free so you can clean his room. Tell him to put everything lying around out of the vacuum cleaners way.'

Jeanette twisted her wedding ring. David's magazines were in his cabinet, but that worried her. Esmond wandered round the house, and the cabinet didn't have a lock. What if he looked inside and saw the pictures? Would he be traumatised? Would he understand?

She hadn't thought about this before – she'd been too tired. Funny how keep fit increased the energy you had. She felt more alert these days, more vital. It was good to have places to go other than work.

Sex mags. Keep focused. What to do with the sex mags? Harmless for a man, surely, but not for an innocent child. There was a drawer between the two bunkbeds which could hold them: Esmond didn't like using the ladder, couldn't reach. Should she just take them out of the cabinet and put them in the drawer and then mention it? Sound casual: 'I was tidying the house.'

Once he'd shown her one – it wasn't as if they were a secret. It had been before they were married, before the third time they'd made love. 'A friend gave me this,' he'd said, taking it from behind the settee cushion, ultra casual. What friend?

She suspected now he'd bought the thing himself. 'Oh,' she'd said – or something equally gormless. She'd seen one before, brought in by one of the older girls at school.

Girls with big breasts, girls with perfect buttocks. Girls like you saw going in to those expensive gyms. Mind you, Jeanette, was now firming up a bit. Her waist felt smaller, improved the line that led to her hips.

One day, she thought, feeling hopeful. If we talk more and take walks then maybe we'll start to touch each other again. Kiss and hold and ever so slowly unbutton. Touch much less clumsily than they had in the months before Esmond's birth. You couldn't just come home from work and have sex with someone. There had to be a build up, something before.

Perhaps they'd even look at these publications together in the shadows of the lower bunkbed. One of Wanda's magazines had said that erotica increased couples' arousal tenfold. Another had said it should be subsidised by the government rather than reviled and threatened with being banned.

Banned from Esmond, though, until he was a teenager. He'd been exploring the house more since he's started going to Wanda's and to the creche. No, when she got home she was going to move David's soft porn publications to a childfree setting. He wanted what was best for Esmond, so he'd understand.

CHAPTER SIXTEEN

It was hell, now – Jeanette was in the house all the time, was on holiday. Even when she went out to the shops he didn't feel safe. She could come home at any time, find him missing. He'd have to explain where he'd been. Worse, he felt obliged to look as though he was writing. She'd even asked if he wanted to talk about his songs.

What songs? These past few days he'd been constantly interrupted. She'd asked him to help choose the wool for a jumper Wanda was paying her to knit. Not *for* Wanda, either, but *from* Wanda to her mother. A Christmas present, no less.

She wanted him to help with the tea, now, came into the lounge for him on her way to the kitchen. Before she'd just smiled in passing, said hi. It wouldn't have been so bad it he could afford to experiment. Make Duck a la Orange, Tandoori Prawns. Instead, it was omelettes and salads, wholemeal spaghetti, vegetable chilli with rice. When they had meat it was usually a quarter of something from the supermarket. Not blood red pleasure, but something pressed, cooked, sliced.

Slicing into his time, his privacy with her new found questions. Could they go to the zoo? Or to that park with the chute he'd told her about the other day? He'd invented the park to explain one of his absences. She wanted him to return to places he'd never seen.

Lies, damned lies – he might have known they'd catch up with him. He'd said he'd been everywhere from The Botanic Gardens to the Music Library in recent weeks. Now she wanted to visit these places with him and the staff there wouldn't know who he was or anything about the research for his songs. If she suspected him of having an affair, he'd be in trouble. She might leave or get the flat changed over into her name.

She could, he knew that – easily. She had the cash, and now she had a friend. Maybe her seeing Wanda wasn't such a good idea. The camaraderie seemed to have gone to her head.

Now he wanted to head off to see Pauline. He stretched, laid his pen down, put the lyrics he'd been struggling with away. Jeanette was around so much now that he couldn't use the sex lines. The pressure was building up, up, up in his cock and weighing him down.

'Think I'll walk over to The Commonwealth Pool.' A safe bet, this – she couldn't swim and didn't like the water.

'Would you like me to sit in the cafe and spectate? Wanda took Esmond, remember? I told you earlier, I'm free.'

Had she told him? He'd paid lip service to her some of her recent monologues. Part of his psyche was still reeling at the change. 'No – you just relax with your magazine.' He stood up and began to move towards the door.

'I don't mind.'

He forced himself to laugh. 'I'm a bit rusty – you know how long it's been. A spectator will make me feel worse.'

He wondered what she was up to when she stood up and walked towards him. 'See you later, then.' Rising onto her toes, she placed a quick closed-mouth kiss upon his cheek. He fancied she blushed slightly: she was certainly beginning to look different. Same clothes and hair, but the body and face seemed prettier, more assured.

She was beginning to look ugly, shrinking. Her facial skin was dry, her eyes lacked shine. He didn't want to take her into the light nowadays. She seemed a thing to be hidden, of the dark.

But for now it was light, a cool October Friday. He stepped through the door, and she began to moan. Maybe she hadn't stopped moaning since his last visit. It was hard to imagine her existing when he wasn't there. But exist she did – the waste in the commode proved it. He'd lined the thing with a bin bag, and now disposed of it outside. He'd dug a special hole, just like cats did. It was quicker than getting her to do it herself.

Re-entering the House, he gave her a container of water, a phial of perfume, one of liquid soap. She sponged herself slowly, like a clockwork soldier in its final moments. He wondered if she was play-ing for time.

It was time she finished her ablutions, he'd decided. He took the things away, and she breathed hard and fast. He touched the cloth at her shoulders and her dress slid off, revealing smaller breasts than those he'd remembered. Disappointedly he weighed their reduced-ness in his palms.

'Please me,' he ordered. Her shaking intensified. 'Imagine that I'm a private patient and you're my personal nurse.' He hadn't had the money, or the courage, to buy her a nursing uniform. She'd just have to do the verbal – and the physical – work. He handed her the pre-mixed oil he'd stolen from the Health Store. 'Here – give me a full massage.' He lay back and watched as she spilt oil over his stomach. She was equally inept at rubbing it in.

'No, down a bit. More circular.' It spoiled the fantasy if he had to give her instructions. She was supposed to want him more than anything. 'Softer.' Christ, her nails had almost scratched his balls there. He must remember to cut them, and those on her feet. Maybe he'd trim her hair a bit, shampoo it. As usual, he was having to do all the work.

And how. 'Left a bit... right a bit... to the centre.' Just like that awful programme, The Golden Shot. His mum had watched it the same time each week, at teatime. 'Come on. Come on,' she'd cheered. Rooting for complete strangers who were trying to hit a target in some silly game. Urging them to win whilst he sat and stared at food he didn't like...

He had his hands round her throat before he realised what he was doing. He was on top of her: she was on the ground. He felt his thumbs touch each other and tighten, making a human choker across her neck.

Neck-ties. Tie-baby. Baby blues. The blood was rushing like some freak weather storm through his arteries. Soon she stopped gurgling. Then her torso stopped jerking. It had briefly been like riding a wild mare. And subdueing one. He put the finishing touches to his handiwork. Well and truly broken – fit only for dog food, now. Staring down at new death, he felt spaced out, tremulous. Maybe he hadn't eaten enough today? He'd brought her some salted nuts from the grocers near his flat before getting into The Escort. Lucky he'd been insightful, thinking ahead.

Backing away, he went into the sink cupboard for a foil carton of orange. Sat facing her, and had his energy-giving snack. Once her leg twitched, and his heart did an encore of pounding. If she recovered, he couldn't look her in the eye.

Or anywhere. He didn't know if he'd come, but he no longer felt like doing so. Maybe when she'd been bucking like that against him, he'd lost control. He stared down at her body and felt disgusted at its ugliness. Nude, white, stringy, soiled, splayed.

Despite her initial promise she'd had nothing to give him. Was Jeanette the only woman who wasn't on the take? He felt a momentary affection for his wife – they had a connection. She was improving herself, and her future – *their* future – now.

Funny how ambivalent he always felt about Jeanette. He'd hated her lack of education when she spoke to the more upmarket customers at the store. At home, though, it sort of suited him. He liked when she asked his advice about Esmond, about the launderette, about her mum. Now she didn't do that so much, but she loved him. She'd kissed him on the cheek before he left.

There was much left to do here before he could go home again. Picking up the spade and key, he went outside. Locked the door, in case anyone appeared unexpectedly. You could explain a hole in the ground more easily than you could a ten-minute-old corpse.

Push down, tilt: the wood mould gave way like soft scoop icecream. He dug and dug till his back and shoulders ached. She'd soon be a corpse without a coffin, without a gravestone. Buried only in a dirty lemon dress. He stopped the thought – it was a stupid one. If he redressed her it would make it easier for her to be identified.

No, he'd leave the clothes in the Secret House for many months to come – but not the body. He checked his watch, resumed digging. This had to be the biggest swim in the history of competitive sports. He'd have to tell Jeanette he'd bumped into someone – say from that so called Song Writing Conference. He'd say the guy bought him some chips at the Commonwealth Pool's restaurant.

Wood chips were all he was going to be seeing for the rest of the afternoon. Wood chips and sawdust and wood mould. Wood lice like grey, oval crabs. He waited till one of the slow-moving bugs was free of his spade blade. Continued to carve out a rough oblong, five foot six by three.

God, it was unbearably close for early Autumn. He threw down his jacket, continued to work. Stopped for a rest, and added his wet shirt. He stank of fatigue and uncertainty and sweat. Digging, digging – he had to get this finished soon. Digging for his safety, his sanity, for a better day than this.

It was deep enough – it was ready, but he wasn't. He wished he had a triple alcoholic drink. Going back in there, touching her... What if she came back to life, wasn't really dead? He'd taken off the handcuffs – she could do anything. Might have gone to the cupboard, picked up her high heeled shoes.

You could hurt a person a lot with a heel if you lashed down in a temper. It left strange, scary dents which smarted and changed texture for days. Mum had said you could get cancer if someone else nipped you. Imagine, then, the damage she could have done with her shoe.

But the damage done by a decomposing corpse in an outhouse could be greater reaching. Animals would come, attracted by the smell. Maybe someone would follow their cat or dog, join the sniffing. They'd either break in or call someone official who would.

Even if she wasn't found, it would mean he couldn't return to The Secret House. And he couldn't bear to give up his refuge now. Not now, when Jeanette was taking more and more of him daily. Not now, when he didn't know what he had left to give.

He had to give up this brooding, had to go for it. Squaring his shoulders, he walked to the building and unlocked the door. She was lying where he'd left her – but that meant nothing. You couldn't trust a situation that looked safe and calm. No, a moment's relaxation, and anything could happen. Beatings, beratings – any living nightmare at all.

Now he had to pick her corpse up – had to. He was a man of action, a man destined to succeed. He put a hand behind her back, put another under the strangely flaccid buttocks. Gagged slightly, and a little of the orange juice came back up.

Keep going, going. He staggered, her head was lolling. He got through the entrance, and dropped her in the hole. Au revoir. He doubted if she'd known any languages. She'd been ignorant, backward: it was a pleasure to see her go.

His need for oxygen returned, and he gasped in lungfuls of air, faster and faster. A cover up – he coaxed back mounds of mould. Pushing them over her with his spade, with his feet, seeing less and less body. No eyes, then no hair, then... completely, irrevocably gone.

Gone to graveyards, everyone. He shovelled in the final few spadefuls, flattened down the wood mould by stamping over it again and again. It was over. He'd repossessed the place. His House was his alone and would be welcoming once he'd made it clean. Exhausted as he was, he couldn't leave it like this. Couldn't return days later to shit and sweat and blood.

Disinfectant. He went back in and used a bottle of it. Poured bleach in the commode, and left it there. Put perfume over where she'd been lying to remove the mustiness of the area, her strong stale scent. Pouring on the lavender water, he blinked, whimpered – for a second he'd seen her shrivelled outline in the dust.

At last he was ready to leave his sanctuary. He'd washed himself as best he could with the water and toiletries that remained. Now he'd go to The Commonwealth Pool and have a bath or shower. He could both check the place out and get really clean. He couldn't afford to come home with another woman's scent on him. Not now that Jeanette was around, and doling kisses out.

As he was locking up he noticed a movement by the graveside. He cried out, whirled round, saw a cat hurrying past. It had been pawing at something with a vengeance. Dear God, was it digging her up?

He approached slowly, ready to turn and flee down the embankment. Saw the large woodlouse lying by the side of the grave on its back. Its off-white legs were a marked contrast to the dark grey carapace. It wriggled quickly but unstructuredly, just as he remembered from his childhood days.

Easy, easy. Finding a little stick, he gently righted it. Its hair-thin feelers flickered as it searched for a crevice-like space. He'd spent hours on the embankment as a little boy with the hordes of woodlice. They'd tickled gently as they ran from palm to palm.

Jesus! This one was a saviour – it had reminded him of something. In his exhaustion he'd forgotten to camouflage the grave. Fine thing for children to stumble on this body sized rectangle of freshly dug wood mould. 'Dad, dad, we found a dead woman today.'

Bushes, leaves, pieces of wood, an ancient bicycle wheel. He gathered debris from all over the embankment and scattered it over the topsoil in disarray. He had to start thinking ahead, be extra careful. His Secret House now had a Secret Burial Ground. He must keep it safe.

CHAPTER SEVENTEEN

Drat. She'd forgotten to remove David's magazines. At Assertiveness Training the following week, Jeanette remembered her earlier promise. She'd have to tell him not to put them in one of the usual bin bags if he decided to throw them out. They'd started buying the thinner refuse bags as they were cheaper. She didn't want to see his copies of big breasted beauties grinning through the see-through sacks.

Talking of saving money, the bills were still high, and her wage had stayed medium. She wished she could find a way to ask David to work Saturdays at the store. She knew he'd been offered them on first going part time. In those days, though, they'd agreed that three days a week was enough. David had said that prioritising was vital. They'd agreed that he should put his songs first.

But he wasn't putting the songs first, he wasn't. In the days she'd been on holiday he'd just listened to music or made hesitant notes on his pad. Was he failing, scared, did he want to move on to something different? He could tell *her* – she'd never, ever laugh. Even if the songwriting didn't work out, she'd still admire him. After all, he had tried, had followed his dream.

Maybe he wasn't disillusioned – maybe he was just going through a low patch and felt trapped by circumstances. There had been some talk about the music charts being rigged. Maybe his path to fame was blocked, or he had writers block. Either way, those past few days she'd seen that he was anxious, restless, bored. Some extra time at the store might give him a diversion. They could use the extra money to eat better: he'd said he'd like to cook more exotic meals.

'How's David's song writing going?'

Jeanette cringed and hoped the class would start promptly.

'Oh, same as usual, Wanda, OK.'

'Has he found another partner?'

'*What?*' The pain went through her like scalding water, and she blushed.

'A music partner – he said he was looking for a replacement.' Wanda was nodding and smiling to the other women as they came in.

A music partner. He'd never really had one of those. Oh, he'd contacted a couple of guys through the small ads in the music press, but it hadn't lasted long. He'd dismissed one local guitar player as 'naive and puerile'; another, a Glaswegian, 'had a parochial view.'

'I think he's happiest solo at the moment.' She wished, for a second, that she could tell Wanda the truth, that he didn't seem to be making progress. But that wasn't fair to David – she was prejudging him.

'How's my mum's jumper coming on?' Wanda asked lightly.

'It's fine, nice. I'm on the second sleeve.' She felt at her calmest when she was knitting – it seemed so magical, somehow, making soft shapely garments from a simple ball of wool. 'I think Esmond wants one. He'll be the only boy at the creche dressed in rose pink.' She thought he liked it because Karen at the creche wore a similar colour. It was good that he wanted to be like the other children there.

Maybe she'd knit one for herself next, dare to be different. Wanda had suggested that last week. It wouldn't be ready in time for this term, but she could wear it to other evening classes. According to Wanda, she could even do Advanced Assertiveness Training elsewhere.

Jeanette smiled to herself, thinking of the possibilities. She wasn't sure about attending Advanced classes – it was hard enough speaking up here. But if she and David started going out together she could wear something brighter. He himself liked to dress in cream, pale blue and white. Of course, it was different for him – he met interesting customers. You felt silly getting dressed up to work in a launderette.

She wouldn't feel silly today because she wasn't going to say anything. Would listen to the others stories and pick up clues. If she did admit to their lack of cash, Marie would tell her to ask David outright to work longer. He was a free agent, Marie would say, he could always refuse.

But he'd be hurt, withdraw – he'd think she didn't believe in the songs anymore. She did, it was just… well, they couldn't live on dreams. Maybe she could give him the impression *she* was the one who wasn't coping? She could say that she'd overspent on food. Then a few hints about rising prices, a comment that if only she had the energy to take on a Saturday job.

Strategy, subtlety. These evening classes were teaching her about talking. You never laid blame at the other person's door. Instead you asked them for help, explained the situation gently. In the videos they showed, the couples never got upset.

Well, she and David never had arguments either. She knew she was lucky – some men shouted at or punched and kicked their wives. David had hardly raised his voice at her, and never, ever at Esmond. A man so gentle with children was a wonderful sight. Yes, he'd understand about her moving his sexy magazines when she explained that it was for Esmond's sake. She hoped he wouldn't consider her a prude. Sex was… well, the women's mags said that it was vital to a healthy marriage. Maybe if Wanda took Esmond for the night?

Two in a bunkbed – better make it his, the lower one. Even if they could just cuddle a little, kiss. She'd been feeling a few twinges since starting the keep fit classes. All those scissored thighs and thrusting hips. Jeanette winced, remembering. She'd been such a shy teenager that when David had undressed her she'd just froze. Had stayed frozen as he pushed in and out of her tight opening, just running her hands tentatively up and down his back. Then she'd started to get morning sickness – and he'd stopped touching her. They'd rented the flat with the built-in bunkbeds, and so slept separately from the start of their marriage every night. After the birth they'd both been exhausted and he hadn't even kissed or cuddled her. But maybe now…

A feature that she'd read last week had said that some men preferred women to make the advances. Maybe David kept waiting for her to make the next move? Perhaps she could get aroused by reading sexy stories? Some women did – one of Wanda's mum's

Sunday supplements had told her that. There was a world of information in the material the student passed on to her. Totally different publications to the genteel weekly titles Jeanette's mother read.

If only she'd discovered them years ago, her life would have been so different. How to cope with your parents, the latest type of contraception – they told you everything you could want to know, and often more.

The level of conversation in the room dropped as Marie entered. She handed out new information sheets and the two hour session began.

'Has anyone made any progress?'

They had, and wanted to talk about it. Jeanette drew pictures on her notepad and shifted in her seat. David was looking after Esmond at home for the evening. She'd left them both a salad in the fridge. Esmond had a book of farmyard animals to look at, and David had said he'd work on one of his songs.

When she came home she'd put Esmond to bed, then sneak into their own bedroom. Have a flick through David's magazines, see if they had any effect. She could decide at that stage whether or not to mention them directly, or just say 'I moved some things while cleaning,' like Marie had told that other woman to say.

Really, Esmond should be in bed long before she got home, but she knew he wouldn't be. For some reason, David refused to undress his sleepy son. Either she did it herself of the poor little mite sweated away in his day clothes. David seemed to both love and fear the night...

'You were miles away,' said Wanda, as they stopped for a teabreak.

'Sorry.' She accepted a plastic teacup from the smiling student. 'I'm just not in the mood for this tonight.'

'We could sneak off early, say we've got a train to meet.'

'Better not.' She didn't want to draw attention to herself.

At last the class was over, and she and Wanda walked most of the way to Jeanette's together. Then she waited with Wanda at the bus stop, till her only friend got on her bus. While they waited, Wanda talked about what it was like moving into third year. Each year seemed to have pressures all of its own. As Jeanette walked the remaining few yards to the flat, she reflected again on how lucky she was. You knew what to expect when you worked in a launderette.

Knew what to expect at home, too. She walked in to find David in the lounge, wearing his headphones. Esmond had fallen asleep on the settee clutching his book. 'Have you both eaten?' She always felt obliged to ask that.

David took off his headphones: 'Sorry? What?'

'Tea all right?' As usual he'd cleared away and washed any dirty dishes.

'Mmm. Fine thanks. Esmond had a couple of biscuits as well.'

She knew he'd rather Esmond didn't eat biscuits – but her mum had given them to the little boy the other day. And David would never, ever interfere with what his son wanted to eat.

'I'm... em, just going to change the beds in a moment. Do you want a drink or anything? I'll make us a cup of coffee first.'

When he said he was all right, she felt her heart begin to race faster. She was amazed she hadn't peeked at his erotica years ago. Something different, in a life which was famed for its sameness. Something grown up, a little bit forbidden. Mummy wouldn't approve, but that was standard. Would Wanda? She had a Sex Report by Shere Hite at her flat.

Feeling strangely guilty, Jeanette shut the bedroom door and walked towards the cupboard. She put her hand on the cabinet door and it opened easily at her touch. The latch had been awkwardly stiff when they bought it. Maybe he looked at these all the time when she was at work?

His 'The Church's Attitude To Sex' book was lying on the top of the pile. Beneath it, she found some song books he'd bought second hand at a Conference. Then the first magazine – a colourful, top shelf read. Breathing faster, she studied the cover and then opened it, stared at women's bare buttocks and bellies and breasts.

Such smooth, tanned skin, such glorious curves and contours. She could understand why any man would want to stare at these. The women looked at you as if to say: 'I want it.' They wouldn't have to pluck up courage to give their husbands a kiss on the cheek. Or a kiss anywhere, to look at some of them. The kind of girls she'd been forbidden to talk to at school. Still, there had to be a happy medium, a kind of sexual meeting ground. She began to read the articles looking for clues.

One woman said she and her husband had spiced up their love life by using a vibrator. Another swore by sessions on a sunny beach. Jeanette felt her face prickle and grow warm as she read them. Breakfast chats were one thing, but imagine saying 'My mail order vibrator has arrived!'

Maybe the next one would be more helpful. She pushed the copy she was reading from the pile. And stopped, feeling as if someone had just plunged her into icy water. Surely that cover picture must be a very lifelike doll? It couldn't be human, it couldn't. The skin was blue, the pupils glazed and fixed. Half-hoping for explanations, she turned to the inside pages but the writing was all in a language she didn't know. Cut out blanks showed where six other small photographs had been. The rest of the publication was foreign text.

Maybe he'd been given it by somebody? He could have had it for years, forgotten it was in there. But it had been second on the pile. Jeanette watched the goosebumps prickle her upper arms into ugliness then she pushed down her sleeves.

More, more. Shaken, but compelled to continue, she looked at another one. A hand was holding a penis, a yellow stream of fluid spurting from it into a woman's open mouth. Even if it was fake urine, the idea was disgusting. Could a man really masturbate to that?

Not *any* man – her David. David who often took two baths a day, and who was always putting his white slacks and shirts in the wash. There was something very pure about David's appearance. Those dark brown eyes, that gorgeous, gloss-black hair…

Eyes that stared at this, that grew large, excited? A hairline that sweated as he imagined a woman's urine-filled mouth? No they must be to do with his songs, some kind of research. He'd always liked to upset the status quo, be his own man. Maybe he was writing something about hard porn, wanted graphic images. The explanations felt hollow even to herself.

What now? She wished she'd never looked, she felt disgusted – the kind of emotion her mother expressed all the time. David was always on about other people's small mindedness. But she'd *wanted* to like his magazines, become aroused…

Putting the pages of song words and his book on top she stood up slowly. Esmond must never ever see such photographs, such loss of life. She'd just put them in David's bunkbed drawer, not say anything. Hopefully he'd be shamed into throwing them out.

As she turned towards the bunkbeds, he barged into the room.

'Esmond wants you…' He stopped, saw what she was doing. Said, more slowly, 'He's just woken up, confused.'

'I… thought it was time I tidied. You know, put in new drawer liners, made the cupboards fresh.'

He nodded, staring. She looked at the book and songs, thankful that they covered the mock-death photograph. He was standing in place as if rooted to the carpet.

'I'll put those in this drawer here,' she said.

'Mummy?'

She put the magazines in their new home, was just closing the drawer when she felt the small pressure on her knees and upper legs.

'Did you just wake up, did you? I think it's time you went for a proper sleep. Have you finished your animal book, then?' Her voice sounded hectic, 'It's late, you know. Let's get you into bed.'

David stepped aside as she walked towards the door, but she could feel his eyes on her. Though she strained her ears, he didn't appear to leave the bedroom for a long, long time.

CHAPTER EIGHTEEN

They'd be here any minute. Wanda looked at her tiny flat, and saw it through the eyes of relative strangers. Saw it through David's eyes – David who looked as if he'd appreciate quality and good taste. She was willing to bet that one day he'd be able to afford interior decorators. Well, he'd have to. Left to her own devices Jeanette would paint the walls a guarded beige.

Disloyalty again. Why was she so disloyal? She *liked* Jeanette, was pleased that she had gone to all nine Assertiveness Training classes, was continuing to go to the keep fit. OK, so they'd never be soulmates, but it was great to see someone exploring how much life had to give. Her friend was reading more, talking more, thinking. Sharing her thoughts with the intriguing David Frate...

That one time he'd driven Wanda home from the launderette, Jeanette had settled down in the back seat with Esmond. The child had been reluctantly handed back by his gran, who'd then stood on the pavement, ostensibly to wave them off. My God, but Mrs Landrew could stare for Scotland. If looks could kill, the woman would've committed murder there and then.

At last she'd waved, a kind of grudging flapping of the upper hand. They'd all waved back, feeling silly, as the car edged away. Except David, that was, who'd glared into the driving mirror, then smiled.

'I almost didn't get here. Brought this book I was reading into work, and forgot all about the time.'

That had led on to her asking about his working conditions at the health store. Didn't his boss mind him bringing in a book? 'No, I more or less run the place – she has other interests. Providing every-thing's in order, I can do what I like.' Madness, though, to think of that eager brain reduced to stocking items on display shelves. Madness to think of the hours spent reading fairy tales to a toddler and making bite-sized meals. Didn't he want to spend all of his time penning modern classics? Didn't he yearn to be free of such restraints?

She smiled to herself as she sat on the floor of her lounge, remem-bering, and Esmond smiled back. What had she read somewhere? Genius shouldn't be exempt from doing the dishes. Maybe it was a good thing, then, that David had family ties? She supposed it injected a serum of normality – of structure – into a creatively-charged, uncer-tain life.

Designing clothes was a lottery enough – but you could survive by diversifying into related areas. Buy in material and make clothes to sell to neighbours and friends. You could do alterations, hire yourself out as a machinist. Make soft toys to sell from a car boot sale.

But what could David do, in the periods when the music compa-nies weren't buying? What could David do, but wait and hope and write? She admired his certainty, his perseverance. His songs might not be bringing in much now, but Jeanette had made it clear that he believed completely in himself.

She reached out and stopped Esmond tipping over his juice. This time it was real orange, not cordial or diluted syrup. She could just about afford it with the money she was getting for this extra babysit-ting work. The Wednesday childminding was now established but this was the first time the Frates had asked her to look after Esmond on a Monday night.

Strange that Jeanette hadn't been more enthusiastic about seeing a film on this otherwise dull November evening. It had been David's idea – he'd phoned and booked the seats. 'He hates crowds, but the cinema has a section with bigger seats for a pound or so more a ticket. Tracey at the shop and her husband went.'

'All right for some.' Wanda had said enthusiastically, half-hoping to be invited.

'So if you could look after Esmond…' Jeanette had said looking pale and strained. So here she was, half looking forward to, half dreading the Frates visit. Someone seeing your house when you hadn't seen theirs put you at a disadvantage, made defenses run high. But what could she do, short of inviting herself to Chez Frate? Jeanette had never asked her to call round.

'Will I put the kettle on for your mummy and daddy?'

Esmond nodded, smiled, ran the yellow truck she'd bought him along the carpet. She noticed he rarely used the words mum or dad. Still, when Jeanette talked to him she rarely referred to herself as Mummy. Maybe David was modern, and believed children should call their parents by their christian names?

'Gran,' said Esmond quietly as Wanda walked past him.

She stopped, ruffled his silky head, 'Silly, I'm not your gran.'

The bell pealed out, breaking the prolonged quiet of a subdued, uncertain autumn.

'That's your mummy and daddy,' Wanda said.

Esmond climbed onto the armchair and sat down, his little legs sticking out in front of him. Didn't children usually run to greet their parents, play hide and seek?

'Coming!' She hurried down the hall, and pulled the outer door open. 'He's been fine,' she said, standing back to usher them in. Jeanette followed David into the confines of the lounge, smiling wanly. She was wearing an oatmeal-coloured jerkin, her light blue blouse and cobalt blue jeans. She held her body awkwardly as they walked down the hall in tandem. She looked pale, the flesh over her facial bones stretched and thin.

'I used to have a flat like this.' David sounded relaxed, almost jovial. He looked well groomed and comfortable in his brushed fawn jacket and light summer slacks.

'When you were a student?' Again she felt a connection.

'Yes. I never did see my furniture deposit again.'

'In that case I'll take the carpet with me when I leave.' She led them into her main room, and gesticulated towards the two seater settee.

'Have you been good, Esmond?' Jeanette asked, ignoring the seating offer. She scooped him from the armchair then sat down on it with him seated on her knee.

'Good film?' Wanda queried.

'It was very illuminating,' David said.

'Hang on – I'll make tea, then you can tell me all about it.'

'I'll help,' said Jeanette, gently depositing her child onto the rug. Wanda left the room, aware of David's gaze following her. She wondered if he approved of what he saw.

By the time she had everyone settled with mugs and biscuits, it was clear that Jeanette wasn't going to be at her most forthcoming. Was she pre-menstrual? Had they had a row? David had been sitting on the settee when they'd returned, but instead of joining him, Jeanette had again opted for the armchair. Would it look odd if she, Wanda, sat next to him? Suddenly shy, the student took a seat on the floor.

'You were the only female in our row who didn't look ready to cry when the boy killed himself,' David said to his wife, leaning towards her.

'Was I?' asked Jeanette. Her voice sounded unusually flat.

'So, give me the plot in fifty words,' Wanda joked to David.

'I can do it in ten.' She listened to his account. He was quick, incisive, entertaining. He'd sought out a rerun of a film that had been a hit many months before.

'I knew it had a statement to make, was quality. Not some big budget adventure epic without a plot.'

'You should try film reviewing,' she said, meaning it.

'For TV you mean? You need the right contacts. It's a closed shop.'

So much for being helpful. She tried to meet his unsettlingly steady gaze. 'What about reviewing for the broadsheets, then?'

'You have to know the right people there too,' he said, stretching out his long, cream-trouser-clad legs.

'Yeah, you're probably right.' She sipped her tea, waited for Jeanette to contribute something. She fancied she could hear her alarm clock ticking away in the adjoining room. 'What about journalism?' she asked curiously, 'Getting taken on by a newspaper with in-house training? My former neighbour taught a course…'

'It takes at least three years to complete.'

But didn't songwriting? It seemed hostile to ask. Of course, maybe he wouldn't be able to train as a journalist and still earn money working part time at the health food store.

'So what have you been selling recently?' she asked.

'Oh, various pieces.' He tilted his head proudly. 'There's a band in Fife wants to use my material for a charity gig.'

'Great!' Exciting, one day, to say she'd known him before he was famous. Had known him when he was a struggling artiste with a shop job, a rented flat and a young child. 'Maybe I could sell tickets for you at my College? We have a noticeboard. I could get a poster put up.'

She noticed Jeanette gave him a swift look of what seemed to be disapproval. Did she want to keep her husband's talents hidden away in an Edinburgh flat? You got men and women like that, people who wanted to keep their partners dependent. Did Jeanette fear losing David to fortune and fame?

'It's all taken care of. Now I'm writing a song about American carnivorous plants. Britain imports them. Most die within a couple of years.'

'You should sell it to Sting!' Wanda looked to share the joke with Jeanette, but Jeanette was murmuring to Esmond whom she'd seated on her knee again. Maybe she should try talking to them as a *couple, talk* about more domestic things? 'If you ever get tired of him I'll take him off your hands, you know.'

Jeanette looked up, seemed startled. 'Who?'

'Esmond, of course.' She waved at the child, 'He's a great little guy. He and I have been getting on really well.' She kept smiling at them both, digging her fingers into her knees to help rid herself of her bodily tension, until Jeanette managed what could best be described as a wan grin. She looked back at her child again. The conversation crashed to a halt.

'I'd like to read some of your songs,' Wanda said, back to David.

'Come round anytime,' he said. Though he tried to sound casual she noticed that he sat up even straighter and squared out his shoulders. It was obvious that he was pleased. Twenty minutes later he hung back as all four of them reached the door. 'We'll arrange something soon – a music night.'

'I'd like that.'

'Great. Jeanette can give you the details at the launderette.' He smiled, showing white teeth that looked like they'd never needed a dentist, and she smiled back at him.

She was still smiling two minutes after he'd left.

CHAPTER NINETEEN

Bastards. The rage drove simultaneously through his head and lower belly. He squinted at the signature. Was it a woman or a man? A cunt, either way, a complete dickhead. Some wealthy bastard who'd completely missed the point.

Most people have a collection of personal scribbles under the bed. Yours should stay there.

Words from a jealous non-starter, designed to destroy. He crumpled the letter up, put his rejected songs in his folder. Got the letter out of the bin again, and smoothed it out so he could study the address.

Many companies sent standard rejection slips, but this was personal. Standard slips said the company already had too much work to consider, that they'd prefer a cassette tape rather than a printed page. This letter was different, pure targeted antagonism. Patronising bastards... they'd get theirs.

But not immediately – he had to go to the Health Food Store. Had to get through eight hours of Christmas cake, gingered figs and equally overspiced mulled wine. Order boring menus for bored and boring women. Only then could he could write back and tell this musical jerk what he thought of him or her.

Shock and hurt were scalding through him like a steam burn. A psychic burn changing texture and hue and shape. Writers and artists like himself had always suffered. Van Gogh had lived off his brother all his life. Thomas de Quincey and Coleridge had been drug addicts. Many other scribes had quietly killed themselves.

Because of idiots like this, no doubt, who held the purse strings. Fools who wanted saccharine lyrics, not surreal sounds. He drove to the store faster than the build up of traffic deemed advisable. Hooted back at length at the staid slow cars which hooted at him.

There was dust on the tins, and Mrs M gave him a duster to polish them. Bitch, bitch. He gave the tops some half hearted flicks.

All day composing, composing.

Dear Sir/Madam, In answer to your reply...

What a coward they were, just putting a first initial rather than a christian name. He'd show them – with some well-chosen words, some real life politics.

Sugar free sweets that glistened with sugary honey. Supposedly healthy fruit cakes that were heavy with vegetable fat. As he stocked the display fridge his calves itched with anxiety. He hoped Jeanette didn't want him to make the meal tonight. He needed to be waited on, deferred to. He needed to feel that someone still gave him respect.

By the time he got home his eyes hurt from behind, as if someone was pushing on them. The divide between his buttocks felt sticky: all day he'd wanted a bath. Taking the car to work had been a mistake – the tailbacks made his teeth hurt. Half the traffic lights in Edinburgh seemed to be out.

Home, and she was in the bath, god damn her. He rattled the door.

Her voice sounded breathlessly high. 'I'll be a few minutes. It was so close today – this weather.'

Esmond brought over a drawing he'd done at his gran's. What was it? What was he meant to say? He knew you shouldn't shout at children or be dictatorial, but what *did* you do to make them happy? How did you bring comfort to their frightening lives? Most books said to cuddle them, but he shrank from the alienness of that.

Christ, but he felt ill tempered. Said, 'That's nice, isn't it?' and Esmond nodded and took the much-thumbed piece of paper away. Going into the kitchen, David checked that the bath water immersion was still on then fetched himself a tumbler. He hated having his mind controlled by toxic substances, but today it was begging for a drink.

Vodka, they always had vodka. Just in case, Jeanette said, someone came to first foot them at the New Year. You couldn't offer people just one drink, so he'd brought home various quarter bottles in the time they'd been married. Gave himself two bottles of organic wine from The Health Store, too.

Now he poured clear spirit into his glass, added a centimetre of lemonade. Downed it, grimaced, waited for the heat to subside. Freshened his glass again, aware of Esmond watching. Sat down at his desk and began to work on his reply.

Dear Sir/Madam, *Pity you didn't have the decency to reveal yourself...*

'Did you want in?' asked Jeanette, appearing with her head swathed in a towel. God, but she looked plain like that, insipid.

'I'll have to wait till the water's warmed up.' Calm, calm, he didn't want her to know about any of this. It was vital that she always believe in his work.

'Mail any good today? The postie must have arrived later cause I missed it.'

God, it was almost as if she knew. 'Nothing important,' he said, in case she was testing. The pain behind his eyes had extended to the veins that criss-crossed his cheeks. Maybe he was coming down with something, like sinus trouble? At least if he was ill he'd escape from that cow at work for a day.

But this cow here looked destined to get her hooves into him. Did he want to help her with the tea preparation? Had he taken the car today? She'd almost phoned him to say it was stolen when she'd first looked out the window and seen the empty parking space. All friendly now that he couldn't be bothered with her. Yet she'd been distant enough those past few days. Distant because she'd seen his adult magazines. He'd rather that she'd said something: he could have explained it. How some were born to lead and others to serve.

Anyway, those nude stills models liked doing that; it was easy money. Easier than being treated like a piece of shit in a wholefoods store. You should try it, Jeanette, he thought: you'd look better painted with a blue tinge. A nice mouthful of urine would stop you going on about cooking the bloody tea.

'Hard day?' she asked, looking closely at the vodka bottle. She'd never had a creative thought in her life.

'I've just about had enough of that place,' he said disgustedly.

A pause, she hesitated: 'We could go to the Jobcentre, help you look for something else.'

'Like what?'

She looked at the floor: 'Anything.'

'Part time, of course.'

'Whatever you think would suit you best.'

What was she suggesting? He forced himself to sip his drink slowly, pushed his pen and paper away.

'Working already?' she asked.

Was she needling him? 'Just a letter. I'll do it after my bath.'

Fed, bathed, brushed, bottle of booze by his left hand.

Dear Sir or Madam…

Hatred bubbled into the envelope but gallons of vitriol remained.

'Want to go feed the ducks tonight?'

Why had he married someone with such a limited imagination?

'No, I want to do some thinking. I thought I'd go out for a drive.'

Give you a chance to look through my dirty magazines. Give you a chance to find out what gets you aroused.

If anything. Jesus, what a bummer. He with a prick like the Eiffel Tower, married to a frigid little prole. There were women out there who were crying out for a good session. Women who wanted it thick and fast and hard…

'You're going out, then?' She had followed him into the hall like a Milk Monitor.

'Mmm… I'm restless tonight. Need to think.' Maybe she'd think he was considering leaving, and it would put the frighteners on her. She'd find it hard to get another man as bright as him. Not to mention as creative – he was quality. He'd come from one of the worst homes and would end up, in time, in the best. If she'd just *be there* for him, she could share in that opulence. If she could be there and not ask questions, not hold him back, not nag…

'Drive carefully,' she said, and his hands tensed into fists inside his jacket pockets.

'I might go for a drink or two. Don't worry if I'm late.' A few months ago, he would never have dreamt of saying that. A few months ago he'd have known she wouldn't query his whereabouts the next day.

Now, nothing was certain – and no one. Everyone in his life so far had at one stage let him down. His relatives, his song writing partners, his mistresses… Yes, they especially: what a mistake that

Pauline had been. He'd left out blusher and lipstick, but the lazy bitch had never once experimented. Next tart he put in there – she wouldn't be given the choice.

Tart or tarts. He parked the car two streets away from a well-known disco and walked to an adjacent bar. It was 10pm: well past the Happy Hour, with more than a few of the women already looking glum. Nothing to say to each other when there wasn't a man around. Or tired of buying their own drinks, the greedy cows.

They were desperate now, because it was getting close to Christmas. Desperate for someone to make the buying of a turkey worthwhile. Small minds, lapping up the ancient carols and modern jingles. Small tongues, lapping at his cock. Soon they'd move on to the disco across the street, and he'd stay here, waiting. Eventually they'd trail heavily out, with hunger and hopelessness in their eyes.

Finding a place at the bar beside a group of laughing thirty-somethings, he tried to merge in as part of the crowd, become invisible. Hated the cheap jokes, jarring elbows, beery breath. But a loner always looked suspicious, attracted attention. People feared the lone man, who thought and lived for himself. Thought differently to the way they did, maybe. Thought – no, *knew* – that he didn't have to be one of the flock.

They'd flock to him later, those girls would. Already they were unshy of cleavage, showing more and more stockinged leg. He looked sideways, checking out which of them was scanning the room for likely boyfriend material. If they fancied you, they started talking more and more loudly to their friends.

He put down his empty glass: he could only afford two more drinks. Normally he'd ask Jeanette for a fiver, for petrol money. But he couldn't demean himself that much when he felt this mad.

Now he wouldn't be able to enter the disco, which made things more difficult. Not impossible, though, if you had a quick mind and a smile. He practiced the smile, and the barmaid, who was nearest, smiled back at him. 'Same again?' she asked. At least she didn't call him that trashy 'love'.

She'd noticed him, so he'd better move on to stranger territory.

'No, the wife's expecting me,' he said. Went next door and ordered a small fresh orange. You had to keep a clear head when you were going to do something like this. You wanted to know exactly what you were doing, as you were doing it. You wanted to enjoy every sexual act.

✛

He didn't have to act well to get her into the vehicle. She was pissed, pissed off, came clumping out of the noisy club at half past twelve. Early enough for no one to notice her in particular. Late enough for people to be concentrating on their own pick up lines.

He was standing against the outside wall when she stumbled onto the pavement.

'Did you see a girl with red hair in there?' he touched her arm.

'What? No. I wasn't paying much attention.' Her face was hectic with the purply effects of the drink.

'Could you do me a favour, maybe look for her? I've lost my ticket. These gorillas on the door won't let me back in.' He waited, holding his breath. If she wanted rid of him she only had to offer him *her* ticket.

'Lost mine as well,' she said with a shrug.

'One of those nights, eh?' He sent out smile waves of empathy. 'I know how you feel. My girlfriend and I just had a row.'

'The redhead?'

Full marks for observation. 'Yep. I think she's found someone else and is hiding in there.'

'Her loss.' she said, giving him the once over. He had already appraised her own short black skirt and sparkling silver top. Her clothes were was saying, 'Rescue me, admire me.' In a few hours she'd probably change her mind. But in a few hours she wouldn't have the option. Silly girl. He could afford to toy with her now.

'Sorry to have bothered you,' he said, taking a measured step away from her. Saw her mouth slacken – she'd been waiting for his pick-up line.

'Maybe you could walk me along the road?' she said. 'The girl I came with has gone off with some guy from work, so...' She was shivering, under dressed, must have planned to share a taxi home.

'I can do better than that. I can even give you a lift.'

She hesitated then, and he took another step away from her. Turned as if assuming she would follow, began to walk along the street.

'I live in Comiston.' She fell into line with him.

'No problem. I'll have you home in five minutes.'

'Dad worries if I get back late,' she added, a bit too emphatically. The evening air had taken the excess of colour from her cheeks.

'Here we are.' He unlocked the passenger door, sounding jovial. She got in and he walked round and unlocked the driver's door. 'Comiston here we come. What street did you say?' She named one. 'If I hadn't brought the car, we could have walked.'

She said nothing, looked down at her shoes, and grimaced. Why on earth did girls wear such impossible spiky heels? 'My girlfriend and I often used to walk home from here,' he said wistfully. And when she turned to look at him sadly, he grabbed her wrists.

She tore at his shirt once before he got the handcuffs on. She had time to scream once also, but he'd chosen his moment well. No one on the street, but noise aplenty: car doors slamming, women mock-shrieking drunkenly in the surrounding roads. With her hands restrained, he quickly pushed her head down and reached under his carseat. He'd put the scarf there earlier tonight.

Mrs Landrew had bought it for Jeanette, to prevent her getting colds and throat infections. David had explained that colds were caused by a virus, not by being scantily dressed. Jeanette had never worn the item, which had remained in the chest of drawers with other unwanted presents. He wanted it. He'd taken it tonight.

He put the material in the girl's mouth, threaded its ends round to the back of her head, and secured them. At last he was putting Mrs Landrew's thoughtfulness to good use.

'Keep your head down or I'll hit it.' It took him a second until he realised she was gagged, and couldn't reply. 'I just want to have a bit of fun... a bit of excitement. Just do exactly as you're told.'

Or else. He started the engine, and drove as quickly as he dared to The Secret House. Kept one hand ready to strike her, but she stayed hunched, invisible from the road. Invisible to her girlfriend who'd deserted her. Even if daddy phoned the police in the next few hours they couldn't connect him with her.

Welcome to my world he thought as he pulled her up the close, the backgreen, the embankment. The House was sweetly perfumed, the surfaces recently cleaned. He pushed her in, locked the door, switched on the flashlights. She stood there, trembling, eyes bigger than Bambi's on speed.

No foreplay now. He brought the trunk over right away, tugged it into the centre. She deserved this, the whinging, teasing little bitch. Everywhere, people doing the dirty on him – or wanting to. Everywhere, cheap little nothings like this. Nothings who got places in life, and had fun, and had drinks bought for them. Were admired for showing a flash of leg, a curve of tit. And he, David, slaving away day and night was appreciated by no one. Was told to dust tins and hide his magazines and make the tea.

Slut. He got her tied over the trunk within minutes. He was getting good at this: had a lot of built up strength. And how. He took off his belt and threw it over his shoulder and brought it down with reasonable force. Harder than he'd thought? He could hear her shrieks through the gag. No matter – he liked a bit of variety. He stopped and took the gag off and the subdued sounds turned to echoing, endless screams.

All the ills of the world centred in one pair of buttocks. All the ills of the world to be beaten out by a higher, fairer hand. What a noise she was making for someone who deserved to be punished. What a noise to come from so obviously wicked a girl.

But not for long. She obviously realised it wasn't worth the effort. Settled for just jerking her buttocks in an impudent way. He'd teach her. He put down the belt, flexed his arm, undid his trouser zip. Spat copiously at her rectum then invaded in one single driving thrust. Was amazed to find she was lubricated till he licked one of his wettened fingers. Christ, she was a bleeder – his hands were smeared with blood.

Paused, continued – in for a penny… Well, a freebie, actually, he hadn't as much as bought her a drink. Cheap slut, making herself so available. Offering her arse over a wooden trunk to a strange man.

But what an arse. He came, came out, got his breath back. Unbound her – God knows, he wasn't finished with her yet. The rage had kept him hard, kept him rampant. He wanted her to suck her blood from his cock.

'Turn over.' When she didn't move, he did it for her. Mouth open, eyes open but already beginning to film. He felt for her pulse, found it missing. The spineless little tramp had gone and died.

It was early morning before he finished digging a new grave. Every centimetre of muscle felt cruelly racked. He'd have to sneak in and have a bath before Jeanette woke up, fabricate some story. A trio in the pub could've asked him back to their flat for a game of cards. As he drove home through the deserted streets, David at last began to feel tranquil, almost sedated. He'd put his affairs in order once again.

CHAPTER TWENTY

David had ripped his shirt – David, who was always so careful. The material to one side of the fourth button had a long, thin tear. Frowning, Jeanette took the rest of her newly cleaned laundry from the machine and transferred it to the tumble dryer. How on earth had he managed to do that?

She hoped he hadn't got into a fight – that wasn't like him. She didn't know when he'd come home last night, or in what kind of a state. Not that she hadn't stayed up for a while, waiting. He'd insinuated he was unhappy at the store, so she'd wanted to talk.

The information sheets Marie had given out at the final class had said that couples should set time aside to discuss important issues. She'd mourned each solo Friday night since the sessions came to an end. She could have told them about David going out again, if they'd continued. About waiting up, not knowing what to say. 11pm, midnight, rehearsing casual opening lines. Finally, at 1am, she'd gone to bed. And lain awake, worrying about their future. Where David worked was important to them all. She wanted him to be happy, wanted them to have more money, more outings. When Esmond went to school they'd need cash for uniforms and books.

She'd been planning to ask him to do a Saturday shift, but now that wasn't appropriate. She'd wanted to say something about the death-style magazine, but he was distant, tense. Could he have met another woman last night, and... *been* with her? Some women tore at their partner's backs or clothes as they came...

There'd been an article about it in one of Wanda's magazines. '*Are Your Passion Quotients Similar?*' Seemed some men wanted to come several times daily. Which was strange, because the female orgasm was more powerful than the male.

She didn't know much about those things, but she did know she wanted David. Wanted him as husband, father, joint provider for the rest of her life. Not for her the endless round of lovers, and stepfathers for Esmond. Just a simple life of coupledom with a little more fun.

And if David's fun came through looking at strange, posed pictures, so be it. Just as long as he didn't contact such a woman in real life.

'Just the one bag, is it?' she said as a confused-looking woman wandered up to the counter. Thank goodness no one could read her thoughts.

Her own laundry finished, she put it on the little screen in the back to dry. David wouldn't want her to try to mend the tear herself. It would remind him of his childhood poverty. Of eating leftovers, wearing hand-me-down jumpers and second hand shoes.

She'd give the shirt to Wanda, the professional. Invisible mending was her forte, after all. David liked forging ties with other creative people. He would appreciate a good job well done.

'No. I don't want her touching it.'

She stared at David and clutched his shirt more tightly to her chest. 'Why not? It's too good a shirt to throw out.'

'She'll... she'll think we're cheapskates, not getting a new one.' She could see he was calming down. Already he must feel silly about reacting like this. In a moment she would ask him what was wrong...

Silence. He was looking down at his desk again, as if the matter were finished. Jeanette walked over to him. Hesitated. Patted his back. 'No, she won't. She knows we don't have much money. She doesn't either, David. She's got a tiny grant and this big student loan to pay back.'

'I have been to university. I do know about the grants system.' She felt the muscles tightening in her belly again. She hadn't been getting at him – she hadn't. He was being childlike. He wasn't the only one who'd had a tiring day.

'What do you want to do about it, then?' That's what Marie would have said. She had always urged them to sound reasonable in the face of unreason, to try a different approach. 'I mean, you only have seven shirts.' she added, 'one for every day.'

'I'll replace it.'

This was madness. 'But David, it doesn't *need* replaced.' He insisted on buying good shirts from established tailors. This one had cost forty pounds, maybe more. Wanda would mend it for four pounds, and be glad of the money.

'It's *my* shirt' he said, insistently.

'Then pay for it yourself.'

'Oh, don't worry – I intend to.'

She hated this cold, calm rage, hostility. She wanted the offhand, introspective David back. She hunted about for neutral ground. 'I thought I'd make omelettes for tea.'

'I'll get myself something later on.'

Miserably she backed away, went into the kitchen. Made herself and Esmond a sandwich and glass of juice. She couldn't back down on this, with Esmond needing shoes and Christmas presents. Someone had to be practical, think ahead.

She couldn't ask where he'd been last night now, she just couldn't. He might lie and say he'd slept with a woman just to hurt her even more. His life was going wrong, and he was blaming everyone. Best, for a few hours, if she just kept out of his way.

For the first time she wished Wanda was on the telephone. Wished she could talk to someone who, unlike her mother, wouldn't just tell her to leave the man. Seated at what passed for a breakfast bar, she stared out of the window. Was she really going to have to stay here till David went to bed?

Odd, to be shut out of your lounge by your husband's tantrums. She only ever went into the bedroom to clean up or go to sleep. It was so cramped, barely had space for a cabinet and the bunkbeds. There was no way in which you could relax in there.

''Lo.'

She looked down to see Esmond walking past. 'Hello, Esmond.'

Flopping onto his stomach, he began pushing his beloved fire engine in front of the fridge.

Blasts of rock music crashed through the walls from the lounge and kept going. Spilling out onto the street, where strangers could complain. This was unknown for David, alien. Was he opening the vodka bottle? Opening old wounds?

She looked round the kitchen, in search of relaxation. Her knitting was in the other room, alongside the TV and compact disc player. It was going to be a long and tedious night.

Then she saw the freesheet lying on the stool beside her. Normally she didn't have time to read much, but her mother seemed almost to memorise it so she got a second hand account.

Evening classes, sports clubs, a competition. Items wanted, goods for sale, film reviews. And a headline query:

Missing Pauline: Can You Help The Police?

She couldn't, but she read on anyway. Pauline Clark, an eighteen year old unemployed girl, had disappeared. The date she'd gone missing was uncertain. She'd definitely been seen by neighbours in early August and had signed on then. Thereafter confusion, mystery. She hadn't paid her rent for her bedsit. Hadn't paid her bills, though she'd been putting aside the money for them up until she disappeared. For her to just take off would be quite out of character, said the girl who lived in the adjoining bedsit: she was a quiet girl who kept herself to herself. She didn't go out at nights, didn't have a boyfriend. She was from Glasgow, and didn't know Edinburgh very well.

'Brown haired Pauline may have become depressed through being unemployed,' the article continued. 'Her parents, in Milngavie, say that they are very concerned.' The remainder of the description could have matched thousands of girls throughout Britain. A caption admitted: 'The photograph shown here was taken when Pauline was fourteen years old.'

Probably run away, Jeanette thought, staring at her. The eyes staring back from the printed page looked as though they were seeking something more than what they had. You could start your life again if you had the courage. If you didn't have ties you could just leave everything and go. Go to a fresh start, make things the way you wanted them to be. Go to excitement, to a man who loved you, to outings and fun. Wherever Pauline was now, Jeanette hoped it was working out for her. She looked as if she was long overdue a break.

That film she'd just seen on TV had had a great motto. She'd written it on her shopping list: *seize the day*. Jeanette wasn't sure if she was ready to seize it yet but she could at least touch it in passing. Could start to connect with the world a little more. A slight new excitement prickling through her veins, she began to look through the entertainments section for cinema films that she and Esmond might enjoy together. As Wanda said, you only lived once.

CHAPTER TWENTY ONE

'*H*ello. *I'm glad you called. I want to tell you my little secret...*'
David gripped the receiver more tightly as the recorded message began.

'*You see, I'm only eighteen and still live at home. But when mummy and daddy leave for work, my boyfriend Geoff calls round. He's really special. He likes us to play dirty games.*'

No wonder with a sexy voice like that, thought David, unzipping himself. He lay back in his chair and peeled away his trousers, then slid his hand into his boxer shorts. The girl spoke in a whisper, which hinted at possible discovery round every corner. He could imagine her learning about biology firsthand whilst daddy thought she was being taught religious studies at school.

Sucker. He wondered if she would suck, or at least try a nibble. Some girls didn't – maybe it was the taste. This one hadn't said what her games entailed, her sexy secret. But he'd soon hear what she liked to do between the sheets.

'*He likes to put his shaft between my tits, and move it up and down. He liked to come over my pouting pink nipples, rub it in.*'

Some boys have all the luck. He'd had nothing, woman-wise, for three and a half weeks now; nothing since the night he'd fucked that disco brat. And she'd been literally dead boring. There was a limit to the fun you could have with a not-so-strong silent type.

For a while, after marriage, he'd been happy with his hand. Even then, he'd rarely had the energy. Esmond's crying had been exhausting, the Health Food Store's new homoeopathic section had been queued out. Plus he'd been finding out about the music industry. Had been overworked and under strain.

Whereas now... well, he knew all there was to know about writing songs, and as the novelty of alternative remedies had tapered off the shop had grown quieter. And, illness aside, Esmond more or less took care of himself. Which meant David now had regular erections, a constant need.

Usually he phoned the sex lines, but he hadn't felt like it recently. Probably because Jeanette had been hanging around in the lead up to Christmas, with all the hypocrisy that festive planning seemed to entail.

And for what? They'd had three days of acid indigestion. a stupid plastic whistle from a cracker, a glass of blackcurrant cordial and 24 hour canned laughter from the TV. Plus – ah, glorious contrast. – Mrs Doom-Bringing Landrew prophesying tomorrow's disasters and listing the world's current ills. Clock-watching, tendon-tightening hours trapped in the same surroundings. Even Esmond had yawned a lot.

This little phone flirt sounded lively, though. He wondered what secret she was about to reveal. The line had just been called 'Find Out What I've Been Up To.' The drawing beside it had been of a woman in school uniform who'd long outgrown her low cut and waist-tied white blouse.

'Anyway, the other day, Geoff came round at ten o'clock, as usual. I'd put my see-through nightie on. Mummy and Daddy don't know about it. It's made of this really flimsy white stuff which clings like a wet T-shirt to my bottom and my breasts. Geoff calls it my come on clothing. He almost tears it off me every time.'

A little girl giggle. This one could win an Oscar if she put her mind to it. Well, maybe not her mind... He stroked himself, feeling the familiar tightening. Another few moments till he christened the tissues again.

'So far, we haven't... you know... done it. I'm an old fashioned girl really, wanted to wait. But Geoff bought me this ring the other week, which changes things. It means we're practically engaged. So...' So? Sliding, squeezing. Tell me, tell me. *'We decided it was time to go all the way. I put on the CD-player – put on his favourite classic. It's really sexy. Just listening to it is enough to make him hard...'*

The strains of 'Je T'aime' began to float down the receiver. C'mon, thought David, angrily. He already had this record in the house.

Music, breathing, promises in a breathless French voice. The lyrics went on and on. Bitch. He realised she was going to play the full three minutes. He rubbed his erection, watching it begin to soften and shrink. Demi-hard, at the irritating stage. Hard to come, hard to think, hard to piss.

Damn her, damn her. This was supposed to be his first real pleasure in weeks. Christmas Day, just past, had been Hades revisited, a living death for intellectuals, with Mrs Landrew talking of game shows, freesheets, family films.

And so it went on.

And on. By early evening, when she'd been with them for eight hours, he'd felt almost ill with irritation. It was like being attacked by midges during a marathon climb. He'd promised Jeanette he'd sit this one out, wouldn't go off on his own, go driving. He envied Esmond, who had escaped into sleep in his chair.

'That child should be in bed.'

'He's fine, Mum.' Good for you, Jeanette. One of the few times she'd put her foot down that day. The rest of the time, those same feet had been treading lightly. Shall we watch this? Let's give Esmond his crackers. All that shit.

Shit, but he hated hanging on the telephone like a lovesick teenager. It would cost more, though, to hang up and listen to the drawn out introduction of yet another bitch. He listened to the breathing on the CD, the music gradually fading into oblivion. Christ knows how much that little musical interlude had cost.

'Yes, Geoff loves that record. He can almost come just listening to it. But what he wanted most was to come inside me. He's been wanting that for months and months and months. Anyway, mummy and daddy went off to work, as usual, and I lay on the bed in my nightie, waiting for Geoff to come up the stairs. He's got his own key, you know. Means he can sneak in to see me at any time.'

Jesus. How long had he been on the line now? Too long. And she still hadn't done anything with anyone, and he was still semi-erect; Monday morning blue balls bringing on the Monday morning blues.

Esmond was, unusually, with granny. Granny had taken him to the sales to spend the Christmas money she'd given him two days before. At least, for once, she'd been unconventional: 'Madness buying things beforehand, when they go cut price immediately afterwards. Anyway, he's too young to understand.'

Whatever the stupid cow's faults, she was helping him to have a family-free wank in his lounge today. Jeanette had left for work two hours before. She'd be home again before he'd shot his load, the way this was going. He moved his fingers gently down to his scrotum and held it within the sanctuary of his palm.

'*Before long, I heard the door opening. I flipped over onto my stomach, and edged my nightie up. "Just do it," I said, burying my face in the pillow. I was a little bit scared and very shy.*'

David was rooting for Geoff by now – go on, fuck her. He could imagine the wonderful round globes of her arse, the tanned young thighs.

'*I felt him get down on the bed beside me, slide his palms round till they brushed my nipples. He circled his thumbs against them and kissed my neck for a long, long time.*'

Neck kissing – this was boring. Get the bitch sexed up, stick it in her hole.

'*I got all wet and squirmy – he could tell I wanted him. I felt him rear back, then he slid all the way in.*'

And? And?

'*It was really great, my tummy felt all trembly. I started to clutch the top of the duvet and push my hips back. Geoff was moving faster inside me, really slamming forward. I was whimpering and writhing, ready to come…*'

That makes two of us, baby. He was beginning to pulsate again, elongating. Soon fluid would make its first tentative appearance from his tip. Followed by bingo, Nirvana, pay day. The hours of contentment that led on from explosive release. '*Geoff reached for my tits, and pushed forward and I started to shriek, and moan. It was wonderful. He gave this odd sounding grunt, and collapsed over me. And…*' And? '*… this is the amazing thing. It wasn't Geoff. It was Owen, who I've fancied since I was in second grade.*'

So much for love, honour and obey. He slammed down the

phone. His cock was going flaccid. Who could he ring now? He'd promised himself he'd relax this week, no matter what. He picked up his directory of sex lines, and thumbed through its pages. 'Call Me Any Time. 24 Hour Satisfaction' This one must sleep with the phone by her bed. 'Tell Me Everything.' No way. A brunette with long hair seemed to stare at him invitingly from her celluloid setting. The caption read: 'I'll Do Exactly What You Want.'

Prove it, baby. He reached for the phone.

The bell, arrowing through the house, made him jump physically and mentally. Christ, no. He fixed his underwear, pushed his now flaccid flesh back in. Zipped his trousers up, and gulped air, trying to get his breathing back to normal. Who? Who? Anger replaced by new hope. This could be the arrival of some exciting package – maybe a music competition win – via parcel post. Special deliveries could come at any time.

Walking to the door, he practiced looking casual, authoritative. He'd brought his pen with him in case he had to sign a form. He opened the door, saw them, saw *her*, nodded. Granny and grandson in smiling tandem: 'Here we are.'

'Here you are, indeed.' Though he kept his voice neutral, he stared at her with unconcealed hatred. She was holding Esmond's hand, and he wanted to break the connection, sever her's at the wrist.

'Didn't take us long to get what we wanted. We've brought back some mince and onions. I thought I'd cook us all a proper meal for lunch.' *Her* cooking for *him* – this was unbelievable. She hated being alone with him. God knows, though, he hated it even more. 'We phoned Mummy at work, didn't we, little man? And she's going to come home for lunch today and see what we bought. As I told her, Christmas is a tiring time for young mothers. If she's going to do all this keep fit, she's got to start eating right.'

Right. There *was* no right any more. Day by day, everything was increasingly, horribly wrong. 'I've got to get back to my writing,' he said, excusing himself. To keep the natives happy, he left a notepad on his desk at all times. In reality, he didn't always have the urge to write meaningful lyrics. At moments like this, though, he had to pretend. Sitting at his desk, he picked up his pen and put it against the whiteness.

'Mince all right for you?'

Immediately she waltzed into the lounge. Was she checking up on him, reporting back to her daughter? She'd taken her bright green woollen coat off, but was still wearing her hat. God knows why women wore hats these days. It was archaic, ugly, sad.

Where was Esmond? He hoped she wasn't giving him junk to eat. 'No mince for me, thanks. I'll get myself something later on.' Polite, always polite, but as cold as a butcher's freezer. Why didn't she get the message and fuck off and die? She had come to stand to one side of him and he hated people standing close who weren't being sexual. Like those affected actressy women, who kissed everyone on the cheek.

'Got an idea, have you?'

'Hundreds.' *Like stringing you up, you old cow.*

'Sold anything lately?' she asked, looking into his eyes, with a gaze that said 'Liar'.

'I've a couple of leads.'

'I'll let you get on with it, then. Check on Esmond.'

If looks could kill…

Confronted by the page, he tried to think up images, concepts, word games. What would reach out to the nation? How could he best communicate with fellow free thinkers today? Placing the nib against the paper, he urged himself to go for it. Cue automatic writing. Cue psyche. Cue Muse.

For an hour he sat there frantically moving the pen, whilst the cloying smell of mince filled the apartment. But all that came out were blackening whorls of fear and resentment and hate.

CHAPTER TWENTY TWO

January sales didn't extend to health food stores. Other than a rush for mineral water and fruit juices at around 11am, things had been agonisingly quiet. At least when the place was busy the time passed more quickly. At least he didn't have to pre-bag so many portions of dried prunes.

His few customers today had had headaches caused by tension, tequila, tremendously unrealistic expectations. Everyone seemed colourless and low. The third of January had brought a return to work, fat rain clouds, slim wallets. New Year resolutions, like bonhomie, soon faded away.

Jeanette had been up last night with period pains, a common problem. He'd heard her moaning and going to the tiny kitchen to refill her hot water bottle again and again. He'd stayed in his bunk bed, shutting his eyes against the light which filtered under the door and cast long, hideous shadows. Woman's trouble – nothing a man could do.

Or would want to. Awful, really, knowing you could bleed at any time, and spasm in agony. Like childhood, nothing under your control. Terrifying that life could inflict such uncertainty. Terrifying, that absolutely anyone could spawn a child. Wanda was keeping *his* child for the day – reliable Wanda. With Jeanette feeling ill, he had to pick Esmond up from her college tonight. Fancy, his son at an educational establishment so early. One day he'd graduate from such a place. If he wanted to. Wanda was good at finding out what he wanted to do. Jeanette had heard her ask Esmond if he'd like to see where she worked. 'I'd like to pop in for five minutes, collect some materials,' she'd told Jeanette, 'but if Esmond doesn't want to, or you object…?'

Esmond had said 'want to' in typical parrot fashion, and Jeanette had said that that would be fine.

Then Wanda had offered Jeanette the chance to see round the place; and so it had been arranged that his wife would have a guided tour round the College at 6pm tonight. When he'd taken Esmond to Wanda's house this morning he'd had to tell her that Jeanette was off sick, that there was a change of plan.

'Nothing serious, I hope,' she'd said, and he'd felt a small hollow of disappointment. That was the kind of standard remark Mrs Landrew would make.

'Hormonal problems.' He tried very hard to make his voice sound casual. She was a woman of the world: he could talk to her adult to adult about such things. Euphemism was for the proles and genteel non-thinkers. He hated that kind of shit.

'Oh, well… maybe I'd better not take Esmond to the college.' She'd looked suddenly sad. He knew how hellish it was when creativity was undermined.

'No, keep the plan – *I'll* collect him.' He'd appreciate the chance to look round.

Now, as the day trickled on like an almost-blocked egg timer, he welcomed the prospect of her company even more. Great to just sit over a coffee or a drink and talk to someone. Nice to see embryonic talent at work. Maybe she could come back with him to the flat, see some of his earlier material? The freshness he'd brought to his first few songs had definitely given him an edge.

'Quiet, isn't it?' Mrs Melloway sneaking up on him again, probably checking on the number of pistachio nuts he'd eaten. It would be blissfully quiet if she wasn't here, was gone for good. At least he could read a book then, make a phone call. On second thoughts, he'd had enough of sex lines for now.

And he'd had enough of mother-in-laws, of boring bosses.

'Maybe you could price these tins of soya protein, and put them on the shelf?'

That 'maybe' was so inaccurate, completely dishonest. She paid his wages, so he didn't have any choice. Replies buzzed through his head like killer bumble bees: maybe you'd like to suck my cock, lick my arse? One day he'd be so famous he'd be able to say these things. One day they'd smile and nod as he said exactly what he liked.

Did what he liked as well. Like now, he wanted to be with Wanda. Wanted to have a meaningful interchange whilst he still felt alert and at his best. The store fed off him like a daylight-loving vampire. Took his energy, his status, his potential, his very soul. If he had a soul – he couldn't be sure about that. Mum had been a church-going believer, yet still destroyed all that he had had.

'I'd like to get away at five thirty,' he said to Mrs Melloway. She looked defeated. She hated it when the shop wasn't bulging with customers trying to find, maintain or improve their state of health. Funny how little attention she herself paid to her lifestyle. Only pounds and pence gave her that get up and go.

'Yes, of course. I can always stay on for a bit myself, see if things pick up a little.' Mean bitch that she was, she sometimes didn't notice what the time was when it came to dismissing him for the night.

Handy, though, Jeanette having worked for the woman. Meant she knew of her foibles, her tendency to keep staff late. It bought him lots of excuses as to where he'd been when he went to the DIY store to buy something for The Secret House. She'd be suspicious if she knew how often he prowled around the town.

'Going somewhere special?' Christ, the woman was so predictable. Her finger was on the pulse – but only of the lentil variety. So much for Britain's entrepreneurs.

'I have to collect Esmond from his babysitter.' A pause. Eat your heart out, Mrs Shopkeeper. 'She's a student. I'm collecting him from her college at six.'

And where did you get your education, oh demanding one? He loved to humiliate the uneducated, if only in his thoughts. They were almost back to back now as she scanned the tins behind his counter. Scooping more nuts onto the scales, he tried to pretend he was a scientist doing research work.

'If she's got references, I'm sure she'll be all right,' she mused.

His top teeth bit down hard on his lower ones. Trust someone like her to take the conventional line. References said that you were polite, biddable. They said nothing about having the courage to be yourself. References. He was glad she couldn't see him. Sometimes it was a battle to hide the way he felt.

'So how *is* Esmond?'

'Deep in thought.' He refused to say, 'Oh, he's stretching up – getting big.' God knows, people treated children as if they were fish on a line, sea trout to be weighed and measured. The difference being that none of the poor bastards ever got away.

Unless they died, of course: he'd read somewhere that more and more children and teenagers were taking their own lives. The fear that the Hell his mother spoke of might be worse than the one he was living had kept him from doing that.

'He's a lovely little boy,' Mrs Melloway added warmly; 'you must ask Jeanette to bring him in some day soon.'

Conceived after your night out, he thought sourly. He wondered if the pair of them had set him up. He'd never wanted to father a child, had never intended to. The sheep could do that: those mindless hordes of people who had offspring because it didn't occur to them to do anything else. He'd intended to be a batchelor, not so much gay as rampant, leaving behind a network of tunnels of lust.

'Off you go, then.' He didn't realise he'd been day dreaming till she hauled him out of it. Patronising as ever, sending him off like a little boy. Come, heel, good dog… good *bitch*. He could train her. God, he'd love to have that woman chained up in his House.

No sex, please, we have aesthetics. Just the kind of thrashing her backside would never forget. And some slow strangulation, to take her mind off her money. Seemingly if you increased then released the pressure, you could keep the person alive for hour after hour.

'I'll just cover up this mushroom pate – it hasn't been selling.' He would never ever leave exactly when she said. You had to exert your will, maintain some power. Otherwise, you became a puppet, a tool.

His tool was unsatisfied, unspent. His balls felt heavy: he'd have to take a new magazine into the bathroom with him tonight. It had been a while – it should be easy. Just a new centrefold and some moderate touching would be enough.

He'd had enough of this place: 'See you later.'

He walked out jauntily, with a backward wave of his hand. Even when you were feeling low, you had to keep up appearances. At least you did where people like Mrs M were concerned. They did fuck all of any importance with their lives, but were always ready to have a go at anyone who dared to be different. The fool had looked as if she was humouring him on the few occasions he'd briefly mentioned his songs.

Walking to the car, he increased his pace a little. The temperature had plummeted these past few days, and he wasn't really wearing sufficiently warm clothes. But he felt right in the light grey jacket, and even lighter grey trousers. His Winter coat, a mid-brown trenchcoat, made him look too thin.

Jeanette had bought it for him. God knows, she meant well. He'd been recovering from flu at the time. 'I know the shade's too dark' she'd said, all pale and hopeful, 'But if was the last one the supermarket had in the sale.'

No, you couldn't wear supermarket clothes to a fee-paying college. Couldn't risk embarrassing a girl who would want you as a mentor, special friend. She'd be surrounded by fashion statements, forward looking individuals. Thankfully his creativity would help him compete.

Let the competition begin. Reaching the Escort, he checked his hair in the mirror, examined his teeth for residual debris. A fig seed or an orange cell caught between two molars, could detract from everything you said. His father had been a slovenly eater, disgusting to sit with. Like a mental defective: egg yolk running down his chin.

Those years were over, over. He had to be forward looking, forward thinking, take a forward stance. Life was different now, encouraging – one day it would come exactly right. He was going to see an intelligent new friend, collect his child who had never once been terrorised or bullied. He, David, would see the fashion 'n' fabric students paintings. He'd have to think up suitable things to say. He smiled to himself, thinking up original questions. Lucky poor Jeanette hadn't been put in the position of having to do that.

Nice, though, that she trusted him. Lots of women would try to stop their husbands meeting an attractive female friend. Women treated men like children, if they could get away with it. Some women treated children like shit.

The blast of several horns made him jerk, and the car veered slightly towards the wrong side of the road. Christ. Had he jumped a light or something? For a moment, he'd been miles – no, years – away. Back to the present. driving to meet Wanda. Shared knowledge and warming tea.

Parking the car in the college's car park, he made his way to the main entrance. She'd said she and Esmond would meet him in the cafe. He walked corridors with big clear sign posts, following the instructions she'd initially written down for Jeanette. Finding the place, he stopped for a moment and patted his hair, smoothed down his jacket. Checked himself in the glass of the cafe's door.

Then walked in strongly – it was important to make an entrance. He looked around, almost casually, with a slight, superior smile. Waiting for the moment when their eyes would meet and she would smile back at him. Waiting to walk over and make his opening speech.

For a second he saw no one – the huge hall was empty. Then he looked again, saw movement, two nodding heads. No, three – Esmond was sitting back sipping from a carton. His features were hardly visible above the table, he was so small. Wanda was facing the door but she was concentrating on the girl opposite her. David could only see the back of the girl's head.

Brown hair, with fading brick red streaks in it sprayed on out of a tin, the kind of thing bought for fancy dress parties. Her head didn't move as much as Wanda's: it looked defeated, de-energised. He began to walk towards them, trying to smile.

Wanda looked up, waved, continued her conversation. She said something to Esmond, who waved as well. Then his little fair head dipped down to concentrate on what he was doing. Reaching the table, David saw he was moving lines of spilt ash about with his straw.

'Tanith – this is David, Esmond's dad.' Was that how she thought of him? He wished she'd said a fellow artist, or a friend.

'Hi.' The girl's voice was soft, almost husky. She looked as if she lacked the energy to speak. A bit like Jeanette had been until recently. Did Wanda collect and transform such retentive types? He hoped she wasn't on some Christian mission to save lame souls or something. She had struck him as brighter, more her own person, than that.

'Hi.' He sat down in the only vacant seat, beside Tanith. She smelt of smoke and of perfume that had been applied several hours before. He breathed in again: it was more like aftershave. Maybe she'd been with some man earlier in the day?

Something must have tired her out – she looked exhausted. Her face looked slightly puffy, alarmingly white. The streaked hair was spikily short; looked dry up close, overheated. She was wearing a white T-shirt, had goose-pimpled arms.

'Tanith models for us,' Wanda said, as he pushed his chair away slightly.

'Really?' He looked back at her pale, expressionless face. Obviously the artists concentrated on the body. It looked reasonable: maybe a little overpadded around the stomach and the hips. Which meant the thighs would be jodspur-like, bulging. One of Jeanette's magazines had said that most overweight women carried some of their surplus poundage on the thighs. 'So, do you do classes or…?'

'Mm. But only part time.' The words came out almost as a sigh. He saw Wanda looking sympathetic. He and she would talk about this girl after she'd gone.

'And what do you do the rest of the time?'

'Em… I'm looking.' She pulled out a cigarette, lit up, looked away.

'She occasionally does private sittings for me,' Wanda said quickly. Both girls drained their paper cups and set them down again. 'I promised David I'd show him round,' Wanda said, leaning towards Tanith. Tanith shrugged.

When Wanda stood up. Tanith remained seated. David stood up also, went over to Esmond and lifted him down from his seat. He saw the women exchange smiles: they liked that. Liked a maternal man. Was there genuinely any such thing?

He took Esmond's hand, keeping up the pantomime. He didn't often do this: it didn't feel right. Still, he didn't want the child running off to be abused by some lecturer. He mightn't be able to feel the sort of love Wanda thought he did for the little boy, but he didn't ever want him to suffer in any way.

Parting is such sweet sorrow. He began to edge away from the table, towards the cafeteria door.

'D'you want to come with us?' Wanda was saying to Tanith. The older girl – she must be at least thirty – was looking at David with her dead brown eyes.

'No, it's been the same for ages. There won't be anything I haven't seen before.'

Wanna bet? She didn't like him. He felt his stomach muscles tightening Now she was spoiling their exit. Esmond said 'Ouch,' and tried to pull his hand away. Something about that voice tugged at his consciousness. Did she sound like one of his school teachers? Like a neighbour he used to know?

No, teachers sounded brisk, even bossy. This girl was Marilyn Monroe incarnate, if only in voice. All little girl lost, almost whispery. He found her about as sexual as one of Mrs Melloway's figs.

'All right, so we'll see you later.' Wanda seemed unflatteringly reluctant to go. 'Listen, you can read this magazine,' she added, bringing a heavy glossy publication from her shoulder bag, 'You can give me it back next Thursday after the class.'

'Cheers.' Tanith was a girl of few words and fewer gestures. When she looked at the contents page of the magazine, Wanda seemed to see it as a cue to walk away.

Cue the guided tour. He felt proud to be with her, held the cafe door open. Smiling, jaunty: 'Are all your models as animated as that?'

'Tanith? Oh, she'd had CFS – you know, chronic fatigue syndrome? Or says she has. She keeps going for jobs she'd not qualified for. Poor girl gets so depressed.'

'That explains it.' They began to walk in a trio up a broad flight of stairs. Wanda obviously liked Tanith, so he tried the sympathy line. 'Are you her only support system? Maybe she's got brothers or sisters who might help.'

Wanda frowned. 'I think her family have largely disowned her. Tanith for an hour or so is more than enough.'

'I can imagine.' This was great, great – they were chatting. Usually he found small talk quite hard. 'So what made the college take her on as a model?'

'Well, it's not a job everyone wants to do.'

Obviously nude work, then, as he'd suspected. The aftershave on her body might indicate a liaison with some artist who got carried away. The students didn't have classes today, but Wanda had indicated the girl did private work. God knows how she earned enough to survive... The answer hit him, and he almost stood on Wanda's heel as she stopped abruptly.

'The Life Sciences students did this collage.' She began to point to the various materials used as they sidled slowly along a much-decorated corridor. Her voice was drowned out by his rush of thoughts.

Of course – Tanith sounded like that phoneline bitch who'd ripped him off the other day, appealing to rock hard manhood. Until you *saw* that the promises weren't genuine, you'd been conned out of your dwindling cash. Christ, but he'd like to show her what he was made of. He'd have fun demonstrating just what she'd missed.

'This next room we're coming to holds examples of Photography and Audio Visual Studies,' Wanda said. Posters on Information Technology, Health and Recreation. An article about a girl doing Business Studies who had been interviewed for a careers-related book. Dutifully he nodded, lifted Esmond up to see the brighter photographs. But his mind was already elsewhere.

With Tanith. At The Secret House. If he could get back to the cafe, arrange to meet her... He smiled at his son. 'I think this little one's thirsty. You'd like some juice, wouldn't you, Esmond?'

'Juice,' said Esmond.

Wanda looked surprised. 'Oh, well, he's already had...'

'With him getting so many colds, we worry that he'll get dehydrated if he doesn't keep his liquid intake high.'

That did it. She nodded, frowning: 'Have you got some ten pences for the machine?'

Thinking fast, he dug into his pocket, came out with some. 'No problem. Do you mind keeping Esmond here? It'll be quicker if I dash along by myself.'

'Sure.' She pointed to a door with a poster on it, 'We'll be in there, it's got mobiles he might like.'

The cafe contained something daddy might like... well, like *punishing*. He hurried back the way they'd come, heart beating fast. And reached the place, and sauntered in And it was empty. Damn. She'd ruined his plan, run out on him, escaped.

Mind racing, now in contrast to his feet, he walked leisurely back to Wanda. If he left now, they could drive around and maybe find her. But no – he had Esmond with him, couldn't let him see The Secret House. He'd wanted to get her alone to make a date.

'Didn't they have any?'

Strolling through the door, he stared at Wanda.

'Any juice?'

Christ, he'd forgotten his reason for going. 'Um… the machine was stuck. I kicked it twice.' He tried to grin, the epitome of the unviolent, put upon male.

'I could get the janitor…'

'No, it's all right. We'd better be going. Thanks for looking after him again today.'

'I enjoyed it.'

He felt surprised, could tell she meant it. 'I'd be happy to give you a lift home,' he said, and they both smiled.

He'd drop Wanda off, then Esmond, then go on to the DIY store. He wanted to buy a rail or hook to put above the fireplace. Men were getting taken for a ride every day by cheap-talking women. He hadn't been nearly innovative enough yet.

CHAPTER TWENTY THREE

Was he seeing someone else? He was more preoccupied than ever. She'd thought that things would get back to normal after Christmas and New Year. Instead, they were getting worse.

Perspiring heavily, Jeanette shifted her position, and put a cushion over the hot water bottle she was cradling against her stomach. Hopefully it would help keep the fading heat in for a bit. She'd been about to ask David to refill it for her when he'd rushed out again.

He'd rushed in just minutes earlier: 'Hi, we're back from college.' Esmond had hurried over to show her six coloured pencils someone had given him there.

'Was the exhibition good?' she'd asked curiously, eager for conversation. Once the worst of the cramps had passed, she'd felt lonely in the house on her own.

'The usual – a mixture of talent and pretension.' David always said things like that: he never just *described*.

'Have you eaten anything?' She wished for the hundredth time that he wasn't so difficult to talk to. He cut off every opening and returned, with indecent haste, to his thoughts. She wondered if he'd taken Wanda to one of the wine bars he'd once worked in. He'd like a chance to show off his new artistic friend to the bartenders there.

She studied him as he took money and a pad of paper from his desk drawer.

'No.'

'Where are you going?' she asked, and was suddenly convinced he was about to lie in answer. In a strange way, menstrual cramps gave you a kind of strength. After a few hours, you didn't care about anything except the dragging pain in your belly. When the cramps subsided you were so tired you were beyond emotional pain.

'To the Central Library – I'll just make it.'

Ah, the blessed library. As he turned, she looked at him: 'Don't forget your books.'

'I'll probably go on to the pub for a quick one.' He moved towards the door again, 'What with the college after work, it's been a tiring day.'

'Did *you* like the college, wee man?' She looked down at Esmond who had sunk down at her knee and was resting his head in her cushioned lap. Already his eyelashes were flickering: he'd probably been denied his usual afternoon sleep.

'Thanks for bringing him back,' she started to say, then stopped herself. My God, Esmond was his *son*. 'Thanks for asking how I'm feeling,' she changed it to, drily.

He stopped, stared: 'If you like, I'll buy you a fish supper on the way home.'

Ah, so he intended to be back before midnight. That was encouraging: she hated those evenings when she'd no idea what time he'd return. 'With a pickled onion,' she said quietly, grimacing as her stomach rumbled and the heavy feeling intensified between her thighs.

'Whatever,' he mumbled. The doors slammed seconds later, indicating he'd gone.

Esmond had gone as well, to all intent and purposes. Out for the count, little blond head emitting equally junior snores. Stretching out further in her chair, Jeanette joined him. She'd feel better after a sleep.

She did – eventually. Woke with foul, furred mouth, feeling shaky, stomach mercifully still. Laid Esmond on top of his bed, stumbled to the kitchen. Made tea, drank it, ate a banana then had three of the chocolate biscuits she'd bought during her premenstrual days. Eyes opening up, rubbing the crusts away. Mouth enlivening, full of caramel energy and breath-sweetening crumbs. Returning to the lounge, she switched on the television, couldn't find the enthusiasm to change channels. Esmond whimpered in the recess, reminding her he was still on top of the quilt.

Mummy's here. She tucked him in, impressed by the depth of his slumber. Sat down again and picked up a monthly magazine – nowadays she sometimes bought the better ones herself. An article on being a second wife, one on masturbation. Another on the empty nest syndrome. Uh-oh. Time to phone Mum.

She had to phone the woman every Wednesday evening, let her know 'how Esmond got on with that Wanda girl'.

A difficult call. What to say? How to say it? Mum, Mum, I wish you wouldn't criticise, that we could talk.

Instead, a duty call – British Telecom must survive on them. People bound together for sixty years or so by an accident of birth.

'Mum, it's me. How's it going?'

'I was watching something good on the telly. It's been on for half an hour.'

Damn. A typical comment: instant rejection. 'Oh. well, I can phone back, or you can phone me when it's finished.'

The reply, as usual, came suspiciously quickly. 'No, no, I'll get a chance to see it some other time.' A sigh. 'There's that many repeats nowadays. It's only the licence fee that doesn't stay the same.'

A pause. 'So what did you do today, Mum?' Make it happy.

'Me? Oh, nothing much. I still miss my wee man.' The usual dig at her, for employing Wanda.

'It's good for him to have variety, Mum. The psychology books say–'

'I brought you up fine without the help of psychology books. Half these so called experts don't know if they're coming or going nowadays.'

So there. Conversations like this had upset her before she'd done Assertiveness Training. Now she refused to take the blame. David had helped lighten the situation, pointing out a comedian in drag who sounded just like Mrs Landrew. Platitudes ruled OK.

'He's fast asleep, Mum, you should see him. Wanda took him to her college and David collected him there at night.'

'In his element, was he, amongst all the hippies?'

Jeanette wasn't sure whether her mother was referring to her husband or her child. 'They both liked it. Well, it made a change.'

A pointed silence: 'And how come you weren't there?'

'I wasn't too well. You know…'

The voice sharpening: 'Not pregnant, are you?'

'No, Mum, quite the reverse.'

Silence. Talking about periods wasn't quite nice, wasn't proper. She could still remember her mother's face when she'd brought home the little booklet from school. It had featured a nurse, who said you should ask your mother if you didn't understand anything. Mrs Landrew had kept saying: 'Not now,' and: 'What on earth are you going to ask me next?' Finally she'd said: 'There's a package on your dressing table. Keep them hidden.'

She'd been keeping things hidden ever since.

'You'll take it easy for the rest of the week, then.' Periods, to Mrs Landrew, were synonymous with a cruel and wasting illness.

'I'll be back at work tomorrow, Mum, if you can pick Esmond up?'

'Just remember to eat liver for the iron.'

Another pause. 'Right, well, I'd better go – freshen my hot water bottle.'

'Wait; while you're here I'll tell you about what that besom next door's been up to.' Her mother launched into a tale of 'she did, I said' that could easily have kept. Jeanette drew little faces on the telephone pad as the minutes crept reluctantly by.

Poor woman. At least Jeanette had David coming in eventually, and Esmond, who trusted her one hundred percent. She looked over at his sleeping figure, the little hands curled at either side of his face like a defensive boxer. She loved him, yet sometimes felt she couldn't quite *connect*…

You saw it sometimes in other mothers, the way they looked at their children. As if what they had was special, as if they would always be linked. Esmond didn't look at her like that, though he came to her if he fell over. Sometimes she felt they were more like casual friends.

'What do you make of that, then?'

Jeanette flinched at the question. She hadn't been listening: usually an answer wasn't required. 'It's… Mum, I have to go. There's someone at the door.'

'Well keep the chain on, and ask to see their ID before you let them in.'

Escape. Tranquillity. One white lie equalling freedom. She broke the connection, cut herself a generous wedge of cake. She was eating more these days, trying out some of the recipes in the magazines. Doing the keep fit class weekly was probably stopping her from putting on weight.

Now what? It was 10:30pm. Normally she'd be tired by this time and ready for her bunkbed, but she'd slept away part of the evening after lying about all day. If she stayed up, she could have that fish supper David had promised. Meanwhile she might as well write cheques for the most recent bills.

Electricity, telephone. She looked at the latter envelope, and was tempted not to pay it. Imagine her mother's face if she heard that the Wednesday phone calls were over, that they'd been cut off. But the phone was vital for checking on who was looking after Esmond, for phoning in sick to work.

She opened the manilla envelope, read the amount due, winced and exhaled noisily. She hadn't put away enough in the bank to pay for this. Moving on to the enclosed sheet, she studied the listings. So he hadn't cut down on his song lines dialling, despite what she'd said to him when the last phone bill came through.

It wasn't fair – she paid more of the bills than he did. She'd told him he must only phone the music lines at the cheap rate: nights and weekends. It seemed a small sacrifice to make, but he hadn't made it. He had no idea she'd requested an itemised bill.

She read on. Strange that he hadn't made any over Christmas. She'd suggested he do so on several occasions when he'd been at a loose end. 'I'll be in the kitchen for half an hour, or so, David. You can do some listening in peace.' He said it gave him access to the Indie charts, to offbeat singles. But the times listed showed he always phoned when he was on his own. Or when Esmond took his nap, or when she, Jeanette, was at her keep fit class. Why the ongoing secrecy?

Only one way to find out. Jeanette poured herself a gin and tonic, gulped down half of it. Dialled the first number... Heard the '*I'm glad you called...*', sounding slightly distorted. She had obviously gotten through to an answering machine. Or a sex machine? As the woman said something about her tits needing sucking, Jeanette slammed down the phone. Felt colour scald her face in a molten rush.

This was like going through your husband's pockets whilst he was sleeping. This was like getting her pregnancy test result all over again.

Shock. Horror. Amazement. Replaced, after a few minutes, by curiosity, a desire to see things through. She looked over at Esmond, but he was still sleeping. Looked out of the window – there was no sign of the car.

She keyed in another number.

'I'm Suki. I hope you're seated comfortably. We're going to go on a long journey together on the biggest motorbike in town. You can't imagine the affect that bike has on me. It throbs between my legs for hour after hour.'

Cut. She'd heard enough, got the picture. Was this why he never felt the need to touch her in any way? These girls sounded dirty, wild, exciting. And David had always championed the out of bounds, the little known. Suddenly anxious to avoid him, she put the bills away in her handbag, went round switching off the lights, hurried to their room. Quickly she undressed in the dark, trying not to think about her bloated stomach: she wouldn't risk encountering him by going to the kitchen to refill her hot water bottle tonight.

Almost safe, almost. She climbed the little ladder to her bunkbed, got carefully under the duvet. Lay staring at the ceiling, straining her hearing for noises, trying to decide what she had discovered tonight. David phoned recorded sex lines, and presumably masturbated to them. The magazines said masturbation was OK. He'd lied about what he was doing, but that was understandable. He probably felt inadequate, even ashamed.

So where did that leave her? The same as usual. With a man who played at being a husband, rather than a genuine mate. There was more to most married people's lifes – she knew that now, was learning. But she didn't have the desire or enthusiasm for too sweeping a change.

They got by as they were, coped without crisis. It wasn't a conventional partnership but it wasn't all bad. Later, when childcare became less tiring, they would have time to make love. Maybe they could go to marital counselling after Esmond went to school.

He was a man, so he had needs, requirements. Now she knew how he dealt with them, which helped. She'd always realised, deep down, he must use *something*. As she slid into sleep Jeanette decided that the situation could have been a whole lot worse.

CHAPTER TWENTY FOUR

'Sacked?' He stared at Mrs Melloway disbelievingly, 'My God, you think I've taken a few biscuits and you...'

'Don't *think* – I *know*, David. I've been watching you for some time.'

Weakly he steadied himself against the table in the back shop. This couldn't be happening. Not at 6pm on an otherwise normal Thursday night.

The day had passed much as any other: he hadn't seen much of her. He'd looked forward to being let loose for his usual long week-end. He'd popped into the back just before closing time, found his earlier cup of tea, his music mag in the little alcove there. Usually she put his wage packet on the table next to them. It was noticeable by its absence tonight.

Rotten bitch – playing games again. He'd gone back into the shop and served a couple of stragglers, covered up the open bowls of salad in the display cabinet, given the counters a wipe. She'd come out then, and locked the shop door, flipped on the 'Closed' sign. He'd followed her into the backshop, keeping it light.

'You mean I'm to keep this ship afloat without a fee, now?'

Then she'd taken the packet from her overall pocket, and said it.

'This will be your last wage packet here.'

His brain must have garbled the words: there was some misunderstanding. He looked down at the packet, but the figures on the front weren't the same. They were higher than usual, the packed was bulkier. Surely it couldn't be severance pay?

'You're letting me go?' He waited for her explanation, apologies.

Maybe she'd gone bankrupt, had invested elsewhere? She was standing further away from him than was normal during a conversation. His skin felt like taut canvas across his cheeks.

She couldn't have decided to close down so quickly, she couldn't.

'David, I don't like having to do this, but you're fired.' Her features were composed, if slightly blotchy. How long had this been on the cards?

His mind was racing, rejecting possibilities. Had she sensed his hostility, seen him pull a face? 'I don't understand.'

'I know about the stealing.'

Jesus. 'What? What stealing?' His voice sounded as if it was coming from above his head.

Like it had done when he was accused of things as a youngster. Things he hadn't done, things that in the outside world weren't crimes. The accidental knocking over of a milk carton. Not being able to tie your shoelaces. Crimes like getting up to use the toilet in the middle of the night.

'Those biscuits in your inner pocket, for starters.'

That's when he'd said it: '…You think I've taken a few biscuits?' And she'd gone on to list all the times she'd suspected him before. The face creams, shampoos, even the organic wine and mineral water. She hadn't been able to prove it at the onset, had kept watch.

'I wanted to be wrong, David. It's not easy to find mature staff these days. For a while, it seemed to stop…'

Stopped because he didn't have anyone to feed and clean at The Secret House. Only at stressful times, like the New Year, did he steal stuff for home.

Christ, if she'd only give him another chance, he'd never repeat his actions. He said as much: 'I've been under pressure… it won't happen again.'

'I'm sorry.' She walked ahead of him to the door, and he stared at her neck with loathing. Two hands, clasping hard, or a sharp blow with a can of soya chunks to the back of the head… She undid the lock and turned to him, eyes flickering.

'I can say you're a reliable worker, but obviously I'll have to mention this if anyone asks for a reference at a future date.'

✛

Doomed. He was doomed. An unknown area, an unknown pub, an unknown warrior. A warrior who was tired of fighting everyone all the time. Mums, dads, mothers-in-law, bosses: all out to get him, all out to see him ground into the earth. One fuck, thirty-odd years ago had created him – he hoped he wouldn't be able to *give* a fuck by the end.

But for now he did care, as per usual. Cared that he wasn't achieving the things he had set out to do. How could he write, now, with no income? How could he face Jeanette and explain that he had been sacked from such a low level job?

Jeanette did well in the launderette, was highly thought of. The company had said that if they opened a bigger branch in town she'd have first option as manageress. He couldn't admit to being fired: couldn't think of a reason. She'd be suspicious, might even check up on him. He didn't want her to regard him as a common thief.

Which he wasn't, really. That Health Store bitch paid him so poorly that he'd merely been taking his due. He bet she didn't put all her profits through her tax accounts, but her type always got away with it. The law made allowances for white collar crime. But let the trampled on worker steal a bite, and he's thrown onto the street within minutes. Left to drive round these same streets, to drink and reflect alone. Around him, the unwind-after-work crowd were similarly drowning their sorrows. At least they weren't having to use their severance pay.

'Same again.' He was on gin – it seemed appropriate. Mother's ruin: that was him, the poor little sod. Mother had fucked up his life, and escaped into oblivion, leaving him to face each year as best he could.

Women everywhere, with growing bellies. Bellies which took in seeds last summer, when spirits were high. Thoughtless bellies, belonging to thoughtless bitches. Who came and conceived and contracted and pushed out new flesh. Pushed offspring out, into a hostile universe. Cruel, to push down, push away, and never make things right.

Slice that belly. Cut it. Kick it. Make sure it never performs its deadly little pantomime again. He looked round the pub at the various hags with their unsubtle, lipsticked come ons. Looked at the barmaids with their smoke weary eyes and rough, dried hands.

He didn't want anyone from here – not a good area. He'd kill one of those cretins the moment he got her outside. No, he needed a slightly less drink-fuddled woman. Someone who knew what was happening to her, and why. He needed agirl who was clean: these hags looked grubby. He wanted white flesh on which you could see trickles of blood.

'Same again.' Three gins in thirty minutes – this was a record. Screw your organic wine, Mrs M.

Bloody music. Everyone was penning singles nowadays – well, almost everyone. Even some of those vacant teeny stars were having a go. He raised his glass angrily and gulped from it. Give a bimbo a short skirt and a breast implant and some fucker gives her a Rock and Pop Award.

Sex songs, hurt songs, love songs. As the words of pain flowed over him, he remembered about the phone sex line playing 'Je T'aime'. Remembered Tanith, who at this very minute was probably displaying all she had for the benefit of over twenty student guys and girls.

What had Wanda told her? 'You can give me back my magazine on Thursday, after the class.'

That had been a week ago, but it was logical to assume Tanith worked there *every* Thursday. And Wanda had said she did a class at night.

He stared at the remaining half inch of clear liquid in his glass, and willed himself not to drink it. He'd already had too much for what he intended to do. If he was stopped, breathalysed, before or even during... But, Christ, the way things were going, he had very little to lose. No reputation to maintain: already branded a criminal. At least, he would be when he went for another job. She'd said she wouldn't tell the police, but you couldn't trust her sort. They loved to gossip, had tiny, vicious minds.

Rage making each limb rigid, he set down his glass and walked from the pub, elbowing the punters. Breathed deeply of the cold,

January air. He had to locate his brain, his car, his street map. Found them all, drove around until he reached familiar roads. Now he could work out how to get all the way to the college. Now he could determine how to deal with that ball-baiting strip-teasing miss. He'd teach her not to play music down the line to a man that needed proper sexual stimulus. He'd teach her not to take off her clothes in front of supposedly artistic men. Luckily he'd fastened that towel rail above the fireplace the other week. It had been intended for someone else. Someone anonymous. Choosing a girl that a witness had seen him with was not his usual style at all, was slightly risky. If she disappeared, and Wanda was questioned by the police... But, no, he and Tanith had hardly exchanged a sentence while she was in the student cafe.

Anyway, the girl was a high suicide risk, with her ill health and depression. And no one had linked him to Pauline whom he'd spoken to time and again.

Go for it. He was going to go for it. God knows, he felt reckless. Wanted to push down the accelerator, aim for maximum speed ahead. Mow down bodies and bicycles. Cut through walls, smash through buildings, bring down trees. He'd like to kill the whole bastarding community of laughing, loving cretins. He'd love to leaving mangled limbs and mania in his wake.

Wake up. He had to wake up to the master plan. Stamp the anger down into his stomach, wait for a safe place to let it run its course. Find the slight smile – he'd never been a grinner. Locate a light voice, tap into his store of jokey asides. He had to get this one right, had to be careful. Half an hour from now he could be having the time of his life. The time of her death. Well, a dress rehearsal. Teach her not to steal his money or cheat on 'Geoff'. Some people missed the subtlety of verbal reprimands. You had to administer a short, sharp shock. Or a lengthy warning. Let's face it, he was going to have lots of time on his hands. Lots of flesh *in* them, and various implements. A challenge, taming fire with fire.

Not that Tanith was fiery – more waterlogged – but she'd pretended on these cheating tapes to smoulder into life. What had she said? *'Let me tell you my little secret...'*

He had secrets of his own, though – a Secret House.

Secret rituals, secret needs, secret punishments. Already he was getting his life back under control. Women were always hurting him; it was time for retaliation. They had to learn he wouldn't be treated like this.

Landmarks, familiarity, security. People hurrying home to defeat the January cold. Any minute now, he'd be at that Hall of Learning. He drove round the vicinity looking for a safe place to park. Seeing but unseen – that was his motto. Waiting till she walked along the road. From here, he could see everyone who left by the front gates of the college. Could also, by straining back, follow the progress of those who left by the smaller door at the side.

The clock on the dashboard showed that it was 8pm. Night classes were usually from seven to eight, or to eight-thirty, so he shouldn't have very long to wait. Watching, he practiced his opening line: 'Hi, you look in need of a lift.'

A lift home in a warm car, light hearted talk to lift her flagging spirits. He wasn't her type, if she had a type, but he was willing to bet she was literally sick of being alone.

He'd got her sussed. It hadn't taken long. Like a slogan on a faded T-shirt, some women's faces showed their lives. Nondescript at school: he bet she'd left early. Worked in a supermarket, flirted fruitlessly with the boss. Then got a bit smarter – or thought she had. Found a job on a sex line, paid to make titillating talk. Which was all fine and well if you gave out what you promised. But when you lied and cheated, and led men on, and effectively stole...

Not stealing like he did – that was *legitimate* stealing. Tanith took from those who were already desperately in need. Took from those hungry for release, for sensation. Took their hope, took their manhood, relaxation once again denied.

No longer. He wouldn't put up with it any longer. He leaned back against the driving seat and took long, deep breaths. There were lots of cars parked around here, with waiting occupants. The Escort was so ordinary, he didn't stand out.

Exodus. Suddenly there was a flurry of bodies leaving the building. Most in twos and threes, the occasional grey haired male going it alone. Funny how women always managed to strike up a conversation with someone. His mother had been like that.

Tanith wasn't a talker – at least, not in company. Probably worn out making all these promissory tapes. When it came to conversation, he liked a switched on woman. One who knew a lot, but who knew that he knew more. Like Wanda. He watched as she traipsed delicately down the front stairs, carrying a folder. Shit. Tanith was at her other side. He was too far away to tell if they were talking, but the older woman's head was turned towards the younger girls.

What would Tanith be – around thirty? A round thirty. He smiled grimly at his little joke. If she was to reach 31, she'd have to play her cards right. She'd already set things in motion for Russian Roulette.

They were walking along the road – he followed them in his adrenalin-charged imagination. Started up the car when he figured they'd have reached the intersection of all the main roads. That way he could see which route they were taking, if they were going to Wanda's. If so, he could park near her flat, wait outside.

Slowly, slowly. He edged out into the traffic, let a car overtake him, steeling himself not to forge ahead. This was no time for an accident. He had to be totally in command.

There they were, heading up the street, not watching the traffic. He drove on, took the lane that ran parallel with the street they were on. Parked and waited till they came out the top and turned right. Did the same, drove on quickly, keeping his head down as he passed.

Stop. Park. Wait. Watching. Hoping. He had drawn into the kerb half way down an avenue: in a few minutes they cut across the top. And faltered. His heart leapt – had they seen him? Then Wanda walked smartly out of sight, and Tanith strolled towards the car.

He dipped his head, began to rummage in the glove compartment. Any second now she'd tap on the window and he'd say... He found a tape, slotted it in, straightened. She had disappeared. Christ, no. Which way had she gone?

Maybe she lived in one of the blocks of flats and he could locate her? His plan faltered. He didn't know what her fucking surname was. He started the car, drove down the road, thoughts volcanic. She could have turned smartly to the right.

Driving more quickly now, he overtook her. Forgot his opening lines, went round the block, came back. Easier, now, that he could see her from behind and fully assess her. Stocky calves in black leggings, an ugly green cagoule over her top. Walking dumpily, as if her feet were flat or hurting. She seemed to be wearing some kind of training shoes. Appropriate, really, as he intended to train her. He'd been lax with the others, letting them do their own thing. He pulled into the kerb, just ahead of her. Quickly scanned the other parked cars: there was no one in sight.

She was parallel with the vehicle when he wound down the window. He leaned out, smiling: looking confident, looking good.

'Hi, aren't you Wanda's friend?' Voice tinged with surprise and pleasure.

'What? Yeah.' A look that said *who are you?* He saw recognition in her eyes as she moved closer. 'I left her just a minute ago,' she said.

Uh-oh. Was she going to ask him to pick Wanda up?

'Her and that bus pass,' he said. A pause, 'Every time I see her she's just stepped off a bus or is getting onto one. I think she likes to get her money's worth.'

Was he overdoing it? She wasn't saying anything: was just standing there. He breathed lightly, shook his head: 'My wife hasn't learned to drive, yet – she's just as bad.'

Gotcha. He saw her relax a little, then she shivered. 'Freezing, isn't it? Can I give you a lift someplace?'

Such lacklustre eyes: no intelligence, curiosity. 'If you like. It's not far from here.'

She clambered noisily into the Escort, and tugged and pushed at her seatbelt. He got the impression she wasn't used to cars. Or to small talk; or to handsome semi-strangers. She seemed to lie back and tune out.

Which suited him, as it was too early to use the scarf to gag her. Too many people about, too much light. The handcuffs were still at The House: he hadn't foreseen this. Hadn't known he'd get sacked, then drunk, on an ordinary Thursday night.

'Busy day?' he asked. She jerked – her eyes had been closing. Shit – what an idiot. He'd virtually woken her up.

'What? Oh, sorry. Yeah, modelling's tiring. You have to concentrate so hard on sitting still.'

Not for much longer, baby. He wanted plenty of movement. They were coming to the derelict area – almost there.

'Have you known Wanda long?' she asked, looking at him, yawning.

'A few months. She's a friend of Jeanette's.'

'Jeanette's your wife?' Her voice was low again, fading. He sensed the tremendous effort she was making to find her voice. She reached into her windcheater for her cigarettes, lit up without asking if he minded.

'Yes, she and Wanda go to night classes together, and work out.'

That sounded impressive, though he hoped she wouldn't ask him for too many details. Where did Wanda and Jeanette go nowadays? Was that women's group still on, or had she dropped out of it? The main thing was to keep the talk upbeat, positive. He didn't want to admit his wife worked in a launderette.

'Is your wife a student? I might know her.' The car filled with her irritating smoke.

'She's mainly a mother.' *Mind your own business.* He felt the tightness return to his throat.

'And what do *you* do?' Her eyes were heavy lidded as she questioned him.

Pulling in to the entrance which led to The Secret House, he said, 'This.'

CHAPTER TWENTY FIVE

'I'll be turning into a muscle woman at this rate.' Jeanette handed the self defence leaflet back to Wanda, and smiled.

'Only I thought that now the Assertiveness Training was finished...'

'You're sure we wouldn't be better doing Assertiveness at Advanced?' Jeanette stepped to the left to avoid a sniffing terrier, and continued walking. Having just finished an hour of keep fit it was hard to imagine doing another weekly class.

'The Advanced AT's being held on a Wednesday night, but there's no creche for it this time. That's why I thought something with childcare would have more appeal.'

'I didn't realise.' Jeanette made an inward face at the thought of no creche facilities. That would mean Mrs Landrew taking Esmond again. David could look after him if he came straight home from work, but that wasn't a good idea at the moment. Her husband was so preoccupied. 'How about macrame, something we can do sitting down?'

'Jeanette, you already sit down a lot at the launderette,' Wanda said, stopping to tie one lace of her neat little black ankle boots, 'And you can knit so well, macrame's not much of a challenge. She smiled as she straightened up again.

It was true. She was a coward just to keep doing safe things. Wanda was prepared to look silly, take risks. 'A trial period?' she said, pressing the button for the traffic lights, 'just in case...?'

Wanda put her hands on Esmond's shoulders. 'Watch for the little green man – he'll tell us when it's safe to cross.'

She looked at Wanda, and Wanda laughed, and said they could indeed go to one class and see how they liked it. Esmond walked over and held on to Jeanette's coat tails.

'And it's definitely women only?'

'Yep. Though the article in the freesheet said they'd give us a real man to practice on.'

'Not karate, or anything?'

'Karate,' said Esmond, and they both laughed.

'Maybe we can ask some of the other women at the keep fit to join up for it? It'd be nice for Esmond to play with the same kids.'

'Nice for us, too, to be able to take care of ourselves.'

Jeanette looked over at Wanda, reckoning the student did OK.

'Surely at the college you're safe enough?'

She knew Wanda had bolts and a chain on the door of her flat and also had window locks.

'Well, I thought I was, until yesterday when a policeman and policewoman came round. This girl I know, she disappeared sometime before Friday evening.'

Jeanette's scalp prickled. 'Did she live on her own?'

'Yes. Her cousin just came through from London to stay with her for a week, didn't get a reply.

'There seems to be a lot of that in Edinburgh.' They crossed the road which led to Wanda's bus stop. 'Do the police think something's happened to her, then?'

Wanda pursed her lips together. 'They didn't say.'

She gave an odd little grimace, 'It's silly, Jeanette, but I feel almost guilty. I was with her the night before she... disappeared. She might not even have made it home after I left her. She walked me almost to the bus stop. Then when her cousin came round the next day...'

'And she didn't seem any different?'

'Well, yes – happier than usual, if a bit tired. She's been ill for a year now, thinks she's got CFS – you know, chronic fatigue? She mentioned this cousin was coming to stay, said she might bring her to the college and show her around.'

A bus arrived, and they squinted through the dark. It wasn't Wanda's.

'A female cousin?' Jeanette murmured.

'Yes – just a teenager. First holiday away from home.' A pause. 'I doubt if the poor kid knows anything about it. She just wanted to see a bit of the world.' Wanda looked sad. 'It wasn't as if Tanith went home and packed a suitcase. It's not looking good.'

It wasn't. Strangeness in familiar streets. Jeanette felt suddenly colder, wrapped her arms across her chest. Esmond's head with its little bobble cap was resting against her leg, warm reassurance. Stooping a little, she played with the pom-pom on it till he smiled.

'Um... do you mind walking the rest of the way to the flat with me? David should be in by now – he'll give you a lift home.'

Wanda looked concerned. 'Fine. Oh, I'm sorry. I'm scaring you. It's just... Tanith's disappearance has been preying on my mind.'

'Tanith,' Jeanette said, as they set off again. 'That's unusual.'

'Mmm. Doubt if it's her real name – more likely acquired. She wasn't content with her life, wanted to change it.'

Jeanette raised her eyebrows, a look that said 'How?'

'Oh, you know – she wanted to be someone exotic, someone special. She had some artistic talent, but not enough to get into art school or anything like that. Then she applied to do design work at various greeting cards companies, but all of them turned her down.'

'But I thought she was still a student?' She kept forgetting that Wanda knew lots of people who had other jobs.

'No – she did some modelling at the college part time.'

'Oh, I see.' She wondered if it had been life modelling, didn't like to ask. Some weirdo who couldn't handle female nudity might have followed her home or somewhere. She looked round for a change of subject, focused on her son. 'Are you warm enough, wee man?'

A soft shy, 'Yes.' Under his little duffle coat he had on the pink jumper she'd recently knitted him. David had complemented him on it, and her mother had virtually had a fit.

Fit to drop. She'd be glad to get home, put her feet up. Have a bath, wash away the business of the day. They tended to overheat the centre in winter, forgetting their particular group were exercising. You came away feeling dehydrated, limp.

As they neared her close, she hoped David would be in to take Wanda safely home. He should be, wasn't often late on a Tuesday night. His first day of the week at the Health Food Store seemed to tire him most, despite the impression he gave that song-writing demanded that much more.

She had a horrible thought as she turned her key, and shouted his name loudly: 'David, it's us. I brought Wanda back.'

Took time hanging up her anorak in the hall, slipping her shoes off. If he'd been phoning one of those sex line girls he'd had time by now to get off the line.

They walked in, to find him sitting on the floor with his head-phones on. He looked beautiful – she felt a sudden rush of love. He smiled when he saw them, freed himself, put off the music system.

'Hi. Does this hungry trio require supper? I'm willing to give of my best.'

'No, we had chips as usual,' said Wanda, patting her non-existent stomach bulge.

'And a pickle,' said Esmond importantly.

'I told Wanda you'd give her a lift – there's been some trouble at her college.' She'd give him the details later: it would give her some-thing to tell him when they were alone.

'Do you want to go now, or…?' He looked so thoughtful, he was being so reasonable.

'I think I'd better,' said Wanda, 'We've aerobicised ourselves into the ground.'

Aerobicised ourselves into the ground. Why couldn't she, Jeanette, think of things like that? She'd just have said, 'The keep fit tired us out'. David was looking at Wanda with obvious admiration. Why put temptation in his path?

'We'll all come,' she said lightly, 'After what you've been telling me, I don't feel safe alone in the house.'

Chatting easily about the class, they drove through little popu-lated streets to Wanda's. Watched as she got out and let herself into her flat. She looked vulnerable standing there, clutching her Yale key. Was she still thinking of her missing modeling friend?

As David drove herself and Esmond home again, Jeanette looked at his profile with renewed thankfulness. She was very glad he was here. There had been too many single girls disappearing recently in Edinburgh. It was safer being married to a strong young man.

CHAPTER TWENTY SIX

'You've been here six days – I really don't think you're trying.'

The stupid little cow had looked up at him wordlessly as he came in the door. She whimpered and ducked her head as he began pacing,

'It's not as if I'm asking you to do anything hard.'

Hard. He seldom was, nowadays, and no wonder. Looking at her was enough to make anyone soft. Only when he took her to task could he get interested. And that had limited appeal as she kept passing out.

It was a problem that shouldn't be insurmountable. Some dictators used doctors who specialised in reviving their unconscious victims. You could cut down on time-wasting, then, discipline them some more. His time at The Secret House would be much more rewarding if he could just find a book on such medical techniques.

He sighed, studying her now, wondering how long it would be before she slid back into oblivion. Previously he'd tried throwing cold water at her, but she'd stayed out. Then he'd slapped her face, shook her insistently. He'd even risked giving her some fresh air outside. Like a dog, which was what she was to him. A dog that's just been whipped and is suitably cowed. Dog. Cowed. Ah, the complexities of language. He felt a new surge of bitterness: once, he'd written songs…

… And worked in a Health Food Store. Tomorrow would mark his first week of unemployment, though it was unofficial so far as he hadn't signed on. He wanted to go straight to another job then tell

Jeanette, to avoid her disapproval. He could speak of new opportunities, more pay.

He shivered in the January chill, and resolved to buy himself a blanket from one of the charity shops. Keeping a fire alight in this place had proved to be such hard work. He sighed, planning a mental list of things to buy for warmth and sustenance. He would also buy the Friday editions of the papers which contained the jobs.

Till then, Tanith was his work, his raw material. He'd fixed her up with a makeshift collar and double rope lead. No muzzle required: she definitely wasn't dangerous. He'd seen more life in an overweight Pekinese.

Not that she was so heavy now: in the six days since acquiring her he'd noticed a difference. Now that he no longer had access to the Health Food Store, it was more difficult to keep her in food. Which didn't seem to matter, as she just picked at the fruit and sandwiches he bought her. He hoped she wasn't working up to a hunger strike or some similar rebellious plan.

He snorted his irritation, and her semi-clad body stiffened as she stayed on all fours before him. He'd let her keep her cagoule and underlying jumper and blouse for warmth but had taken away her leggings and flower-dotted pants.

It was cool in here now – he couldn't deny that. And he only wanted her to suffer when she let him down. The rest of the time she could exercise her mind, build her body. He'd shown her the books that Pauline had left unread.

Difficult to tell where Tanith was at, if she was anywhere. When she'd arrived, he'd wasted no time in teaching her to obey. In a round about way she'd lost him his job: her, and women like her. They used their sexual power to sweet talk him out of his cash, ensured he had to steal to feed his child.

He stared ahead. One of the latest women in his life had sacked him, refused him references. The first woman, his creator, had programmed him to fail. Tanith had failed the first command by not staying conscious. Thrashing unresponsive buttocks didn't set his anger free. Rather it brought newly fuelled rage that she'd cheated him. Escaped to her own little world to leave him contemplating his own.

That very first night he'd brought her here, she'd soon become oblivious to him. One moderate beating, and she simply fainted away. The gin had been wearing off by then, pulsing its farewell message. His eyes had hurt, his arm felt stiff from bearing down.

So that was how she wanted to play it. He'd unfastened her from the chest, let her flop down like a carcass on the floor. Had spent ages lighting the fire, planning to heat her up a bit. Throbbing his own heat as he imagined how it would be. Only… His mind went on, on, to the days which had followed. Friday to Monday, he'd hardly seen her, had been doing things domestic with Esmond and Jeanette. Not that he'd wanted to visit The Secret House especially: he'd have lots of time for that on his supposed health store days.

On the Friday afternoon he'd walked to The Job Centre with his son, head full of hopefulness, only to find that suitable employment was thin on the ground. Thin on the cards, too – there hadn't been many suitable ones. Cards with details of engineering, clerical and temporary posts.

Nothing ventured… 'I'd like further details on that part time job in an off licence.'

'Qualifications?' A forty-something matron, looking him up and down. Esmond had picked up the little calendar displayed on her desk and she'd glared at him.

'I went to university…'

'We're not really here for graduates. Try University Careers.'

Cow. He'd had to admit then had he hadn't actually graduated, had admitted he'd just finished working in a shop.

She'd got out a file about a post in a wine and spirits shop:

'You'd be working alone until late sometimes. They'd need two written references – at least one of them from your most recent job.'

'That shouldn't be at all problematic,' he'd lied. Keeping his back rigid, he'd said he'd go and get them, but had gone home.

Home to think about his latest prisoner, to plan out her future. Home to an absence of mail about his songs. Tanith had had twenty pounds on her, which would keep him going for a day or two. That disco girl had had about the same. With Pauline, he'd fared some- what better. She'd carried fifty quid, presumably as a contingency in case she had to pay part of the meal. Kim, poor little sod, had had two pound odds in assorted silver. That totalled over ninety, more than his three day wage. Usually he gave Jeanette sixty, and she paid part of the bills with it. The rest was for his personal use, for stationary, CDs, snacks. If he hadn't found a job by next week he could eat into his personal savings. He still had money from his salesman days.

Not that the bucks ended there: the disco queen had been flashing a heavy gold locket. Pauline had had on a bracelet with lots of little charms. He could pawn them at some stage, when the heat had died down: had it even started? He wouldn't take chances until money got tight.

If money got tight – he had to think positive. He'd had some bad luck, but was still in control. No more tugging forelocks, no more Mr Nice Guy. Only coercion – take what you want and when.

He sighed, and Tanith trembled slightly. He'd tried being nice, from that first infantile smile. Nice to mummy, nice to daddy, nice to his teachers. And what had it brought him?

'Face stuck in a book… bad at games… clumsy sod…'

Tanith wouldn't call him names, wouldn't stare at him. When he'd trained her right, she'd remember not to look.

Look what she'd missed because she wasn't tall enough. She didn't know how lucky she was, how close she'd come… That night when she'd passed out, he'd got the fire burning. He'd fastened a towel rail above it on his most recent trip.

Time to trip the light fantastic. Hot to trot? The flames spread their glow around the Secret House. He'd stripped her naked, dragged her over towards the heat, Held her up over his shoulder, got one of her limp hands handcuffed to the firm rail. He'd had to hold her there and tie the other wrist in place. Tomorrow he'd send for a second set of handcuffs, would do this properly. He was learning all the time.

Meanwhile he'd got her unconscious body fastened. Then he'd let her go, waiting to see her revive. And dance a little jig against the fiery backdrop. And scream and plead and promise all manner of things. Instead, she'd hung for a second, still immobile. There'd been a tearing sound, then the towel rail had torn free of the wall.

All fall down – he had put the rail too high to hold a body. He'd imagined a taller girl, held taut, whose toes would touch the ground. The rail, then, wasn't strong enough for the purpose. Meant for a cotton towel, not the drag of a woman's weight. Fat cow. His rage had been such that he'd kicked her in the belly, If she'd been pregnant, she wouldn't be any more.

Yes, she'd gotten off lightly, though she didn't know it. When he'd next come here he'd been calmer, burning her had seemed too severe. He hadn't been thinking straight when he'd attempted it. Now all he wanted was subservience and respect.

'Tell me what you've been instructed to do again,' he said to her calmly. They went through this each time he arrived. If he could prove she was being difficult he'd thrash it out of her immediately. But she might just have a memory that was blank.

Her head was hanging towards the ground, so the words were muffled. 'Don't look at you, sir. Don't speak unless spoken to. Stay on my hands and knees.'

'Except when I'm out of the room. I'm not a monster.' There were men who did much worse things than he was doing to her. She kept looking down. He said: 'Say "No, sir".'

'No, sir.' Her body was shuddering with the effort of holding up her weight. Taking a few steps back, he squatted down with his back to the door, took his belt off. He wondered how long she'd be able to stay like that before her arms gave.

CHAPTER TWENTY SEVEN

'The thing is–' he put some more vodka into his glass, tipped in a small amount of orange juice– 'I've no connections in the industry. It's who you know…'

Tanith's head was down again: hadn't he just given her permission to look at him? Two days ago he'd had to beat her for not staying on all fours.

'All those bastards busy networking. No aptitude, yet the talented unknowns have got no chance.'

He leaned forward from his seat on the floor and stared at her profile. The short hair was beginning to look matted, the spikes now flat. He'd have to show her the shampoos, remind her to keep herself clean and scented. Not that he wanted to touch her, but he still wanted things to be right. Dad hadn't been big on washing, on changing his underclothes. Excepting family weddings, there'd always been the faint whiff of ammonia, three day sweat. A big greasy mark on the backrest of the armchair where his head rested. A sickly sweet smell, all too human, around the seat. Gross memories, where other children had carefreeness and candyfloss. Lucky children, with lives like the sitcoms on TV.

Real life, for people like him, contained no luck, no silver spoon promises. He was the afterbirth – something unwanted, thrown away. Thrown by people who liked the idea of cute little babies. People who couldn't cope with children who cost money, and cried and got sick.

He sipped from his glass, feeling depression weigh down on him like a dream about suffocation. Being an afterbirth was about unbelonging, standing apart from the crowd. Apart from the individual, too – at least, individuals like this one. He wished she would say something, *do* something, somehow switch on and connect.

Words in his head, turned inwards, unheard and unwanted. Others laughing, joking: himself always outside. He brought someone here, and she wouldn't even communicate. Slid into silence after he'd risked his freedom for her, his civilian life.

A prisoner. He didn't think he could bear to be a prisoner. Life measured out in tobacco tins: a sentence carved out of petty rules. At least here he could leave when the day became oppressive. Or teach her to sit up and beg, come to heel.

'This is the first time I've been unemployed in years,' he said, gazing at her wearily. No answer. He tried a different tack, 'You can sit down now.' Ah, so she *was* listening after all. Her head came up, and after a slight hesitation, she sank back on her heels, moved her legs out in front of her. Said something through swollen lips. He assumed it was a far from genuine: 'Thank you, sir.'

Lies, lies: he hated others lying. As a small boy he'd always told the truth. Later he'd lied out of fear, lied to protect himself. Now he lied to gain short term respect.

'Tell me about your modelling, then.' He needed company, conversation.

She shivered and said, staccato-like: 'What do you want to know?'

'You do it nude?'

Her pupils moved from side to side as if seeking enlightenment. 'Some models do both.'

'What do *you* do?' He moved closer, so that the soles of their feet were almost touching.

'Night classes, for the general public. Not nu... fully clothed.'

That was it, then. She wasn't even defying dull convention. Nothing exotic here – no colour, no verve. He sat back against the door, and wished that he was a smoker. It would give him something other than drinking to do with his hands.

Something to do at all, at a time like this, damn it. He didn't really know what to do with her next. With the loss of his job, he hadn't been feeling much like anything. And, as lovers went, she didn't exactly try too hard.

Here's to tranquillity. Grimacing, he picked up the vodka bottle again and filled his glass up. Not like him to indulge like this, especially not during the day. But what could you do when there were hailstones outside and you weren't supposed to be at your own house? Where else could you go to effectively hide away?

Hideaway. Where he'd once kept his hide away from further punishment. If only she wasn't here, if only he could have peace. He'd been wrong to take her – he'd known that from the onset. A flash of anger, a solitary lapse.

But now she *was* here, making the place untidy. Was here until… well, until she died. He flexed his hands, his shoulders: realised he didn't have the stomach for it. The others had been foolish, had somehow brought about their own premature deaths. He looked at her legs, sticking out from the cagoule like mutant lollipop sticks. Spreading white calves with goosebumps on a grey concrete floor.

Better buried. The idea came to him, and rocketed through his consciousness. Prime burial ground outside, awaiting a grave. She would die eventually – of her illness, of natural causes. Fitting that she should dig her own resting place whilst he remained at rest.

Issuing instructions would help quell his boredom, give her purpose. She blinked when he said they were going outside.

'Put on your leggings,' he ordered, fetching them and her pants from the cupboard. He undid the handcuffs, watched her get awkwardly to her feet. Come on, come on. She tugged on the garments and shoes with teeth grinding slowness. He noticed she had to steady herself against the wall.

No such support outside – and he was glad of it. Just a windless chill, glistening shrubs and weeds. He held a cautious hand and foot out – the hailstones had stopped, the ground was squelchy. Easier to dig, he supposed. She'd soon find out.

CHAPTER TWENTY EIGHT

Now his pocket was torn. Jeanette felt a shock of discovery sprint through her. First his shirt ripped, and now this. Health food stores simply weren't dangerous places. What on earth was he doing in his spare time?

The day had started out with such potential. The launderette had recently added dry cleaning to its services list. Not that they did the work on the premises – it was contracted out to a larger agent. But it made getting David's jackets cleaned much less work.

No more Saturday morning trips to a dry cleaning outlet some distance away. She could bring them here with her. Then he could ferry them, and her, home in the car. They'd save money as well as time, for the new place was cheaper. She'd gone to work that Friday leaving David and Esmond still in their respective beds.

And found this, as she went to bag his second favourite jacket. This one cost most, was the one he wore when he was feeling down. A heavyweight pale grey, with a darker grey edging round the pockets. Sleek, well made – too well made to suddenly give at a seam.

The January sunlight filtering in through the shop's postered windows suddenly appeared more diluted. She pushed the jacket onto the table which dominated the launderette's backshop and something fell from one pocket – a key.

Not the key to their house door, their car, his workplace. A different key: one she'd never seen before. The key to another woman's house or to a rented third house? The magazine articles said to look for clues like that. She'd have to keep an eye on the situation, watch for other signs that he might be straying, somehow stop him going out every other night.

Jeanette forced her thoughts to go down this least welcome of paths. Who might he want to…? He could have met a female song-writer that time in Glasgow. But the car hadn't clocked up much mileage recently: it must be someone nearby. Not a pub person: for all his little jaunts David didn't like them or their occupants. Which left someone he'd met over the health store counter. Or someone who worked on the same side?

Like Tracey. Oh, she was married, but that didn't mean anything. The magazines said lots of bored housewives had affairs. And Tracey only did a morning shift – was bound to have spare time. Easy to spend it with an attractive married man.

Trembling slightly, Jeanette held the key and gazed round the backshop. Let him ring the woman's doorbell in future – he wasn't getting this back. The table drawer, the cupboard… she mentally discarded places to hide it. Finally she pushed it down into the soil of the wandering sailor plant. Was he wandering in the direction of Tracey's duvet? Inhaling deeply, she picked up the phone.

She must be mad to even consider this. As she hurried along familiar streets towards her former health store employer. Jeanette dreaded the conversation that lay ahead. Mrs Melloway had been so nice on the telephone, so gentle. If she'd been surprised to hear from Jeanette she'd hidden it well.

'Yes, of course I can see you at lunchtime. If I'm in the backshop, Tracey'll show you through.'

So here she was, at ten to one, approaching the health store. Prepared to see Tracey's look of embarrassment or surprise. Would her presence be enough to make the other woman reveal herself? Would she flinch, blush, somehow give the game away? If not, she'd have to try saying something slightly threatening and ambivalent. Like: 'I'm here to talk to your boss in private, Tracey.' That should make her quake.

Almost there, almost. Breathing a little faster now, damp patches under her arms despite the cold. She was going to lie to Mrs Melloway for the first time ever. Was going to pretend she wanted a Saturday job.

After that, they would chat – her former boss loved children. She had some photos of Esmond with her: a way to buy extra time. She'd steer the subject round to David, oh so casually. Watch the older woman closely, see if she *knew* what part Tracey played in his life.

Familiar door. Familiar shop bell. Familiar scents of cheeses, spices, vinigrette. And the familiar figure of Tracey leaning into the display fridge, scooping something from a salad compartment into one of the individual cartons sold by weight.

'A quarter, you said? That's slightly over. I could… Fine as it is? Oh, OK.' Mrs Melloway liked them to be generous with their measurements. Most customers accepted and paid for the extra weight. When she'd worked here, she'd always tried to meet the customers specifications exactly. Tracey, it seemed, had no such honesty.

Jeanette moved forward as Tracey finished serving the man, and the older woman smiled anew with recognition. 'Hello, stranger. Long time no see.' Was her greeting slightly too bright? Though they'd worked together, she and Jeanette had never been close. She'd been living at home with Mum, then, probably seemed juvenile. Tracey would speak of her children, her husband… Jeanette had never known what to say… to anyone. Mrs Melloway would also find her more outgoing now. She'd never have dared to do something like this when she was in her teens.

'So, Tracey, what have you been up to?' She kept her tone light, forced herself to maintain eye contact.

'Not much,' Tracey said, 'you know…'

'Jeanette!' Mrs Melloway, now, also seemed intent on over-doing things. She hurried from the staff room like a long lost cousin and ushered her into the back. The woman had mainly stayed in her office when Jeanette had worked there, though she had given her a generous bonus when she left to have her son.

'I'm sorry to disturb you like this, Mrs Melloway.' She had to stay in favour.

'You're not. It's nice to have someone to chat to. I usually just have a sandwich at my desk.'

Jeanette felt her stomach contract at the mention of food and lunchtime. She'd been too nervous to have anything before she left.

Now the odours of the shop were combining to make her feel hollow and needy. She would buy something from Tracey's salad section and use it as an excuse to talk to her before she left the store.

'Sit down, sit down.'

Why did some people feel the need to say everything twice? She took a seat on the bench that ran along one wall, and her former boss pulled up a plastic chair. Jeanette put her bag on the floor, unbuttoned her coat, wondered how to start the conversation.

'So, what can we do for you, Jeanette?'

'I...' She couldn't plunge straight into personal detail. 'It's about a job.'

'You want to work here?' The woman looked more surprised than she'd expected. She'd been a good worker: Mrs Melloway had said so at the time.

'When you have a vacancy... it's just for Saturdays. With prices what they are, we're finding it difficult to make ends meet.' David hated statements like that, she thought, and forced back a sudden snort of laughter. He despised cliches – spent half his life correcting the speech of her cliche-mad mum.

Mrs Melloway tugged at a curl from her perm. Jeanette saw a glint of grey. 'I can understand... I take it David hasn't found something else?'

So she knew he was looking for another job. Feeling a blush start at her neckline, Jeanette stared miserably at the floor.

'No, he's not sure what he wants to do at the moment.'

'I couldn't give him a reference. You understand?'

'Why?' She looked up, amazed: he'd always been a reliable worker. Hardly every late, virtually never off sick.

'After what happened – employers ask about honesty.'

'But he *is* honest. You've never had cause to complain.'

The woman's eyes widened, mouth opening: 'You don't know.'

'Know what?'

'That's why I sacked him. He was stealing from me – well, from the shop stock.'

'You *sacked* him?' She gripped the underside of the bench.

'I thought... oh God. I assumed. Jeanette – I'm sorry.' Mrs Melloway leaned over and put a hand on her arm. 'It was just over a week ago. I'd suspected him for some time. It never occurred to me he wouldn't say.'

'What did he take?' Somehow she had to get through this.

'Foodstuffs, mainly. Once some organic wine.' A pause, 'I... wanted to believe I'd got my stocktaking wrong. But I saw him take things, Jeanette. On the last day, there were stolen biscuits in his jacket, so...'

Biscuits, organic wine: things for her and Esmond. Had he felt bad because he couldn't contribute as much as she did to the household accounts? He'd always been a proud man, seeking respect and applause and confirmation. Had he stolen to provide for them in his own confused way?

'And toiletries,' Mrs Melloway said into the silence. She seemed to be speaking to herself now, was looking unfocusingly ahead. Jeanette winced: why would he steal toiletries? Then again, she did have a birthday next month...

She took her purse from her bag. 'I'd like to pay for your losses.'

'Jeanette, no. He was a good worker over the years.' She laid her hand on the girl's arm again, 'And what he took had relatively little value. Take that mascara – it only cost a couple of pounds.'

Mascara. Her throat felt tight, her heartbeat went into overdrive. She'd tried mascara on one of their early dates: he wouldn't forget. Crusty black blobs beading otherwise fine, sandy lashes. David hadn't commented at the time, as they met outside the restaurant. He hadn't had to – one look had said it all. By the end of the evening several lashes had fallen out, had lain above her cheeks like dead insects. Her eyes had felt heavy.

'You're allergic to that stuff' he'd said. And gone into one of his discourses about being yourself, not taking on affectations. About how nice it would be if women didn't have to pretend. 'So much hypocrisy,' he'd said, 'superficial niceness.' His voice had gone brittle.

She'd written his words in her diary when she got home.

He was probably home now – God knows where he'd gone yesterday, and on Tuesday and Wednesday. She'd thought she'd known how his days were spent, only had to worry about the nights. Now everything was changed, everything tarnished. He'd stolen mascara, and it certainly wasn't for her.

'Can I get you anything? A drink? Coffee? Tea?'

Mrs Melloway's voice seemed to come from miles away, to intrude.

'No, really. I'm fine, thank you.' Her voice sounded strained. She inhaled, aware her mouth was too stiff to work right. 'David chose not to tell me. Please don't let him know that I know.'

'Of course not. It's very unlikely I'll be seeing him.'

But Tracey might, Jeanette thought miserably, mind searching for explanations, facts. He had to have been stealing these toiletries for someone – some female – and there was still that mysterious key.

'If… if you wouldn't mind not mentioning it to anyone.'

'You have my word, Jeanette. Believe me – I feel awful about all this.'

That makes two of us. Walking shakily back to the launderette, she wondered where David would go next Tuesday, from eight in the morning till around six at night. Somewhere cheap, or free, given that he was no longer earning. Somewhere warm and safe where he wouldn't be found.

He took the car these days – impossible to follow him. Still, according to the magazines, most men got careless and left clues to their affairs. She knew when he was free to meet a woman, now she needed to know where they rendezvoused. She would just have to watch and wait till she found out.

CHAPTER TWENTY NINE

D rop. Twist. Strike. Follow Up. Run for it. Face mask-like
with tension Jeanette went through the moves again. 'I've
never... I don't have very much co-ordination.'

'It gets better,' Sandra said, walking up to her, 'just relax.'

Relax, when you were grabbed from behind, effectively pinioned.
Relax, with others watching, with the threat of murder and rape on
the streets outside.

'I don't want to scare you,' Sandra, who took the class, had said,
before detailing the various kinds of violence that went on in towns
and villages, 'but it's best to be prepared.' Prepare to be thrown onto
a thin, wide mattress, to feel silly. 'One day you'll be glad you took
this class,' Sandra promised the assembled women and girls.

Privately, Jeanette doubted it. She was rarely out at night on her
own, and was hardly at risk in a busy laundry. And they had a good
lock on the door. David had installed it himself.

'Can I have your bag for a moment?'

'What?' She blushed again, feeling singled out, inadequate.

'Your bag. I want to show the class the weapons it contains.'

Women in a circle, watching. Her eyes sought Wanda's and she
managed a self conscious grin. Sandra unzipped the well-worn shoulder bag.

'Here we have a handful of change – ideal for holding in your fist
as you strike an attacker.' She pulled back her fist, and brought it
forward, stopping just short of Jeanette's nose. 'Or a comb – the
handle can be used to poke your assailant in the eyes, or even up his
nostrils. It will usually make him let go of you pretty fast.'

Nervous laughter: everyone was watching the instructress intently. Sandra went through various movements, using her arms, legs, and bodily bulk.

'You can do this. And this. And this.'

Kicking back, falling, elbowing. Power in the female form.

Then she told them to split into pairs, and practice on each other. Thankfully Jeanette hurried over to Wanda, found them a space in the hall.

'You've got a lot to answer for!' Smiling to show she didn't mean it.

Wanda shook her head: 'You look so placid, yet your body's been a lethal weapon all this time.' Holding each other awkwardly: mock kicks and punches. Strange to grab hold of another woman's flesh. Strange, really, to hold onto anyone other than Esmond. David wasn't the huggable type, and her mother didn't even like shaking hands.

But some people out there liked doing... God knows what.

'There's some real weirdos about,' said a blonde woman wearing clusters of rings. She spoke hoarsely, looked at them wildly. Otherwise the talk at the tea-break was mostly subdued. 'That girl who disappeared after being at college. That's what made me decide to come here tonight.' The speaker's eyes said more than her voice did.

'Same here. I'm sometimes out that way – it's worrying. And the papers were saying she may not be the only one.'

A thoughtful silence. Jeanette cradled her coffee carton, not liking to look at Wanda. Her friend probably wanted to forget about all of this. Or at least not discuss it amongst strangers. Earlier she'd mentioned wearily that the police had been to see her again. Been to see everyone, anyone. A policewoman had walked with her on Tanith's last known journey. Wanda said they seemed to be desperate for a lead.

A lead into a world that had been lacking in risk, in excitement. A lead to explain why anyone would take – then kill? – this thirty year old semi invalid. Tanith had lived a quiet life, signing on and doing her weekly two hours of modelling. Other than that, she appeared to have rested and dreamed.

She'd been applying for jobs: they'd found employment cuttings from the Scottish papers and freesheets. But she hadn't been granted any interviews, hadn't been anywhere different, met anyone strange. Her affairs had either been remarkably furtive or else nonexistent. She had had no known enemies, no jilted boyfriend intent on wreaking revenge.

'So is this the first self defence class you've all taken?' Wanda looked round the seated circle, obviously anxious to broaden out the subject.

'I did a karate lesson once,' a slender woman in baggy trousers volunteered.

'I once went to ju jitsu,' another woman said. She smiled to herself, as if remembering. 'But the men were much better than me.'

'Is that what made you decide to come here, because it's woman only?'

'Sort of.' The woman looked around at the others, pursed her lips. 'A few weeks ago, in The Meadows, this man followed me as I walked over to Newington, to the shops.'

Everyone looked up, then down again. The city was well known for the huge, tree-lined park.

'I wasn't hurt or anything.' The woman looked at them in turn, 'He came from behind – shoved hard.' She took a deep breath, 'Luckily, I sort of fell at an angle, landed on the grass.'

A girl in her twenties with dungarees covered in slogan-bearing badges, leaned forward. 'And he didn't... what was the point?'

'He grabbed my shoulder bag as he pushed me.' A snorting laugh, 'I was on my way to the cashline machine. It only contained five pounds.'

Mugged in The Meadows. This could happen to her, to Wanda, to her mother. Jeanette grimaced at ther friend and sent waves of sympathy to the woman who'd been robbed.

'The Meadows can be a risky place. Last summer I was flashed at,' said the blonde woman with the rings. 'I didn't try to fight back either – just reported him when I got home.'

A discussion, then, about the psychology of flashing. Did exhibitionists go on to other sex crimes? What happened if you stood your ground? Theories, bits remembered from documentaries, friends experiences: one of the students had even covered the subject as part of a criminology course.

192

Jeanette looked and listened, unable to contribute. Suddenly she felt naive and unworldly, and young and very small. Chilling to hear of such things; since she'd married David the Edinburgh streets had seemed so safe to her. Of course, she rarely read the papers, watched the news.

'After this, I'll be too scared to come here,' she whispered to Wanda, only half joking. 'My mum used to warn me every day about men like that.'

'Got to keep things in proportion. Should be safe, 'cause there's two of us,' the student murmured back.

Back, afterwards, to the launderette, its clock showing nine-thirty. Creepy to think of those washing machines silently waiting in the dark.

'I feel like a criminal,' Jeanette whispered, unlocking the door, and switching off the burglar alarm. 'It's in here. I meant to give it to you earlier on.' She put on the lights and Wanda followed her into the backshop. 'It's the pocket, see? Just there…' She kept her voice low. 'He's always rushing about in the flat and the health store. I think he caught it against the handle of the door.'

'Jeanette, you could do this yourself. The main thing's finding thread that's the same colour,' Wanda examined the material, then answered in her normal tone.

The whispery atmosphere broken, Jeanette cleared her throat, spoke more loudly. 'I suppose so… but David likes things to be right.'

Wanda looked up, grimacing slightly. 'It might take a few days – I'll have to go into town for suitable thread. And I've got masses to do at college at the moment. If he's in a rush…?'

'He isn't. He just changed over to his winter coat – that's him till springtime. It's too cold for his jackets now.' She crossed her fingers inside her own duffle coat pocket. 'He won't even notice this one's gone.'

She wished she could ask Wanda not to mention this to David. But she couldn't, not without feeling daft. Wished she could mention she didn't know how the tear had happened. Who knows, she might even have her suspicions allayed. But how could you say that your husband had been sacked and now spent his days at some unknown destination? Say you thought he had a mistress who had torn in a frenzy at his clothes?

And lain with him on the ground in a wood or a forest. She'd found some brown flaky stuff in the turn ups of his trousers when she put them in the wash. Why make love outside when you had the key to an apartment? Unless the lady's husband had been at home? He must want her very much to face such discomfort. She must be very beautiful, very bright.

'Ready to hit the road?' Wanda asked, and Jeanette thought for a moment, then nodded.

'I'll just reactivate the alarm.' Alarmed now – afraid for her child's future. If David decided to leave her, he might not go alone. He'd said before now he wanted his son to have the best of everything. And, with his months at university he could earn more than she could if he decided to work full time. Plus, if his mistress worked, they'd be bringing in two incomes. She, Jeanette, probably wouldn't meet anyone else. She'd never exactly made heads turn – didn't want to. But didn't want to lose her little boy. Didn't want to lose him to a man who was smartly dressed, intelligent. A man who was educated, who could impress a judge. David and the legal system... well, they spoke the same language. She and her mum couldn't argue with the likes of them.

As Jeanette walked up the road she promised herself she'd find out exactly what David was up to. She'd end any affair he was having now, before it went too far. Could remind him of the way she helped to finance his song-writing. Could hint that she'd like for the two of them to go to bed.

There must be ways in which she could save things, make them happy. Show that Esmond needed both his mum and his dad. They could go someplace on holiday – even just a short trip. Make the mistress realise he had a life apart.

'Penny for your thoughts,' Wanda said as they reached her bus stop. In the circumstances Jeanette wondered if they weren't worth much, much more.

CHAPTER THIRTY

He woke suddenly, skin stuck to unfamiliar cotton. He stared up: the ceiling looked different. The contours of his bed had changed.

'Jeanette!'

He shouted her name, and she said, 'It's all right, David.' The voice came from across the room. He looked, and saw a divan, with a sort of large cot at the end. Esmond was sleeping in it, the early sun casting its orange-yellow glow upon his face.

Of course – they were in a bed and breakfast place, in Berwick. They'd arrived yesterday morning, would go home sometime today. Odd, how Jeanette had suddenly insisted they take off for pastures new. Came home from her self defence and announced he should pack a bag. She hadn't cared where they went, as long as they went tomorrow morning. So they'd ended up at Berwick, by the sea. In February. No one else was holidaying at the B & B so they'd had their choice of rooms.

At least the place was cheap... well, free as far as he was concerned. Jeanette, who'd sold some jumpers to women at her keep fit class, had promised to pay all their costs. She was being very nice to him, very – *affectionate*. Had actually joked that they could share the one divan and beat the cold. He'd ruffled her hair, knowing he couldn't manage anything else at the moment. She'd seemed appeased, though, had smiled, and then gone shy.

So here they were – their first night away from home in ages. And he'd had a nightmare, and woken, confused, like a child.

'David... you still awake?' Jeanette asked into the silence.

'Just getting my bearings. For a second I didn't know where I was.'

The story of his life, recently, he thought wearily. He hadn't been to his bank yet – had she noticed he was short of cash? The money was in a building society account which he didn't have a cashline card for. Couldn't access any funds till tomorrow, when the place reopened again. Couldn't reach Tanith till then, either, unless he could find some excuse to go out for a while when they got back tonight. He'd planned to go there to the Secret House on Friday, fool around a bit. But he hadn't been able to find the key.

He'd searched all his jackets, his trousers, the car and his wallet. The jacket he thought he'd left it in had gone absent without leave. Jeanette said she'd put it in for dry-cleaning, that she'd put everything in it on his desk. There was his wallet, tissues, a packet of sweets... but no key.

Maybe he'd dropped the key on the embankment after locking the door? His glow of relief quickly faded. What if someone discovered it, opened the door and found...

Damn the bitch. Damn, he should have killed her. Should have buried her – it would all be over by now. Instead, here he was, in another town with a wife who had suddenly gone clingy.

'Time we were up,' he said. Maybe they could have an early drive home.

'So, what'll we do now?' Jeanette sat up, ran a hand through her hair, and smiled. She looked healthy: he felt old and cynical and worn.

'Have breakfast?' he said, striving for lightness.

'After that, silly.'

'I don't mind.'

Wander around, she suggested, and pay a visit to a historic building. Then they could go to a newsagents, find a cafe, read the Sunday papers and their accompanying magazines. Yesterday she'd had them walk the length of the beach, until Esmond got tearful. It must be strange for him – he'd rarely been away from home.

'Time to wake up, wee man.' Jeanette had got that expression from her mother. It was inaccurate, as usual – Esmond was a *child*, a little boy. Horrible the way people had children then expected them to act as mini-adults. Typical of his mother-in-law, though, not to think things through.

'Up we go.' Jeanette was lifting their son out of his extended cot now. 'He seems a little sleepy.'

His reply sounded pedestrian to his own ears: 'It'll be the change of air.'

Baths, showers, teeth cleaning. By the time they were ready to go down for breakfast, an hour had elapsed. His stomach felt concave, he couldn't remember when he'd last eaten. He was going to make up for it now.

'The full breakfast, please,' he told the thickset woman who owned the place. Had cereal to start with, finished up with two slices of toast.

Jeanette had the same and refilled her coffee cup. 'I'm still building myself up after that self defence class,' she smiled. Looked at him evenly, 'And I've got another keep fit session on Tuesday night.'

For the first time in their relationship he felt comparatively boring. What had he done recently that he could talk about?

'Any time you want to demonstrate your moves...' He held his hands up in mock surrender.

'That would be great. Sandra said we should practice on a friend.'

'Local girl, is she?'

Jeanette shrugged: 'Probably.'

He'd have to make sure he never brought someone like that to The House.

Or tried to – he doubted if he'd get very far. These women were trained to kick you where it hurt and went on hurting. He felt his balls tighten involuntarily at the horror of it. Imagine that tender flesh shrinking, changing hue.

No, after this, he wouldn't drag anyone else up the embankment. Would keep the place for himself, a solo sanctuary. Maybe one day, when Esmond was old enough, he'd tell him about the sunshine on sweet scented wood, the busy insects, its gentler moments. The House would probably be knocked down by then, just a memory nothing stayed the same.

Which was both good and bad, depending on how you looked at it. Good that you got free of your parents, escaped into adult life. Bad because change meant further uncertainty and tension. Culminating in acts for which you might one day have to pay an awesome price.

'Right. Ready for off?' Jeanette put down her cup and smiled at him.

'Yeah. fine.' He stood up, took his coat from the back of his chair. 'Ready, Esmond?'

The boy's head was leaning back, feet sticking out from a chair that was much too large for him. Jeanette lifted him down, and he followed them out of the door.

Esmond had never been much of a breakfast eater. Lunchtime came round: they bought pizza, he pushed his away.

'Maybe it's all the excitement?' Jeanette said uncertainly.

David shrugged, looking at his son's flushed face. 'Let's find someplace quiet where he can sit and draw, have an orange juice.' They found such a place, but Esmond was still querulous and kicked at his chair.

'Should we get junior aspirin? What can you buy on a Sunday?'

Jeanette picked the child up. 'David, he's never been quite like this before.' She put her palm to his forehead. 'I think we'd better go home.'

Monday morning blues were so dark these days that they were practically navy.

'He's not well, David. Can you keep an eye on him?'

Eye, eye… He opened his eyes and she was looking down at him impatiently.

'I've been up half the night. I've got to go to work,' she said.

After she left, David called the doctor to arrange a house visit.

Meanwhile, he waited, coaxing his son with food and drinks. Esmond finally sipped some of the fruit juice. Cried more afterwards, screwing up his face into an ugly mask. What to do? What to do? David smoothed the blankets, muttered platitudes. Went and sat on the lower bunkbed and wished he could escape further than the next room.

Escape to a place where things were right; a place without suffering. Oh, the guilty should suffer, but the innocent should go unharmed. Esmond was a little boy who didn't understand what was happening. Who looked to his impotent father to put things right.

Nothing was right any more, nothing. The doctor came eventually with his stethoscope and thermometer, said that Esmond had mumps. Suggested orange juice could make his discomfort worse and that he should avoid sharp-tasting foodstuffs. Better to give him ginger ale or water; even weak tea.

Water it was, then, at least until Jeanette got home. He couldn't go out for ginger ale, had to stay in the house. Knowing Tanith was in his other House, eating nothing. Unless she'd eked out the nuts he'd left her on Thursday night. Her own fault – she'd never been a hearty eater. Had seemed to go on a diet the moment he brought her to his secret place. Typical woman – changeable, unreliable. Let her go without, then, for a little while.

While he took care of someone who was deserving of it. He brought Esmond a banana, reassured when he nibbled at its tip. Offered him a picture book, but he pushed it away and started crying again. His brow felt hot and sticky, his face was beginning to swell. He phoned the launderette, and gave Jeanette the diagnosis. Asked her to bring in various drinks when she came home.

'Oh, my God,' Jeanette said when she saw him. She squatted by the bed. 'Esmond, it's me. It's mum.' Smoothed his hair back, checked his beaker was full, that he could reach it easily. Moved out of the recess, whispered: 'Have you looked at his eyes?'

He looked over. They were a bit red. The child was squinting.

'What did the doctor say?'

'Don't give him orange juice.'

'Is that all?'

There had been something about the light: drawing the curtains… Hard to remember: being told what to do had made him enraged.

'Um… He said we could close the curtains if his eyes got worse. They've just gone that way. They weren't like that earlier on…' He could tell he was babbling: was beginning to feel exhausted. Maybe he was going down with some illness himself?

'Right. You make the tea. Something simple like bacon sandwiches. I'll sit with Esmond for a while. Then I'll give mum a phone – tell her he'll be staying with me tomorrow instead.'

'With you?' He stared at her stupidly: she was half way out of the lounge, 'But you've got work.'

She looked at him steadily: 'Haven't you?'

He willed himself to look equally steadily back. 'Of course. But… I'm just part time. Mrs M can cope without me. You know what Susan's like every time you go off.'

'I suppose.' She was looking at him uncertainly.

'I'll phone old Melloway at home,' he said, 'let her know I won't be in. In fact, I'll do it now, if you see to the tea.'

As soon as she went out of the room, he dialled the speaking clock: 'Mrs Melloway? It's David. I won't be in tomorrow. Esmond's ill.'

'All right?' Jeanette came back again, voice brittle. This was taking its toll of her, their routine shot down in flames. First a weekend away: new sights, strange faces. Now a feverish child and a curtain-closed, claustrophobic lounge.

He nodded, pretended to listen, said, 'I'll keep you posted.' Hung up. 'Fine. She said to take as long as I liked. You know she loves children. More than she ever liked us.'

'I remember.' She set out three empty plates on his desk, fetched Esmond's tray. 'I'll use that cutter my mother gave us to cut his roll into a fireman shape.'

Her face was subdued in the faint light that emanated from the desk lamp: they'd arched it towards the floor, to keep the brightness low. The scent of bacon drifted through.

He sniffed: 'Is it still under the grill?'

'Shit,' Jeanette said, and made a dash for the door. '*You* were supposed to be doing that.' she said, coming back, glaring accusingly. She transferred one roll from the main plate onto each smaller one, 'We'll have the best ones first. These others are a bit crisp.'

He eyed the remaining rolls with their black-edged fillings warily. 'They'll be fine.' He tried to sound calm, but he felt trapped and headachey.

'Want a rasher of bacon, Esmond?' Jeanette said, and the child began to cry. On and on and on; snuffling, hiccuping. Face all swollen and scrunched up. David couldn't bear to look.

He sat at his desk, instead, and cut his roll in half, then into quarters. Turned it into eighths, laid them in a circle round the plate.

'Are you going to eat that or just torment it? You liked bacon well enough yesterday,' Jeanette snapped.

Yesterday. Berwick, another woman's cooking. Christ, she was beginning to sound like his mum. 'I didn't realise eating it was mandatory.'

She glared. 'Just shut up, David, if you've nothing helpful to say.'

Unknown for her to swear and snap: he felt unequal to it. 'I'll wash the grill.' He stalked out, staring ahead, to the momentary escape route of the tiny kitchen. He cleaned the rack and everything else, scrubbing hard.

Now what? He couldn't go out – she'd get mad at him. He hadn't got to the building society, was down to a couple of quid. He made them both a new pot of tea, brought in a spare mug of boiling water with which to dilute Esmond's.

'You can go read in the bedroom or the kitchen,' she said. 'We've got to keep the light low in here.'

He'd really have liked to get drunk and play heavy metal on full volume. Would have liked to have brooded alone with his dull, dragging thoughts. 'OK. Only I haven't been to the library.'

'I brought in some newspapers,' she said, 'and magazines, and comics. Take your pick.' So organised, thinking ahead, planning.

Once he'd been like that.

Once.

'I think we should take turns sitting with him tonight', she said as he made for the doorway. 'He looks so restless. At least he won't be so scared if we're at his side.'

Horrible thought, horrible. But she'd think he was a monster if he said no. Awful to stay close to that pitiful, wheezing specimen. Such energy reduced to a limp bundle in a bed. 'The doctor didn't say…'

'I'm his *mother*.' She was stronger than him now that it came to something like this.

'Maybe I could pop out to the newsagents, buy a paperback?'

'We spent too much at the weekend, David. The papers will have to do.'

Damn. He'd planned to get in the car, race over to the Secret House. He had the pieces of bacon roll in a napkin, had added a banana, an apple, and put them in the inner pocket of his coat. Four days now since she'd eaten, she'd be getting ravenous. He still couldn't find the key, would have to stave the shutters in.

But not tonight: he'd have to go tomorrow. 'Maybe you should tell your mother to come round in the afternoon, let me get out for some groceries and things?'

'No – I don't think she's had mumps. I remember her saying so when I got it. You don't want to risk a woman of her age getting sick.'

He'd had it. He'd had every childhood disease looking for a dwelling place. Well, you did when you were terrified. He refused to look at the bed.

'I'll sit in the kitchen, then,' he said. 'Give me a shout if you want me.' Wishing his superior mind could make things better. Wishing this closeting illness hadn't happened at all.

At least she was going to work tomorrow and he could stay home all day. If she'd taken time off, he'd have had to stay out for the duration of his health store shift. A long day, spent in a cold, concrete room with a boring companion. No CD system there, no television or flushable loo. This way he had a legitimate reason for staying in the safety and warmth. Things could have been a whole lot worse.

No they couldn't. He opened the first paper, and saw her staring back at him. Fuller of face, with that same, spiky hair. Tanith Boag – till now he hadn't known her surname.

'*Missing for ten days,*' said the caption.

'*Can you help us find her?*' read the subheading underneath.

'David.' He jumped. Jeanette stood at the door. 'Did the doctor say if we could wash him down or something? He seems to be burning up.'

'What? No. He didn't say.' He closed the paper hastily, trying to remember. 'I've still got that medical encyclopaedia. I'll check it out.'

Glad, now, to be doing something positive. Glad to undertake a chore which stopped him thinking about *her*. He hadn't trained her or fucked her for ages. The way things were going, there'd be nothing left to fuck.

CHAPTER THIRTY ONE

No fun, no freedom, no cash, no sex. no wanking. He was home all day with Esmond; she let him go out when she came home from the launderette. By then he was too tired to face The Secret House, to deal with her whinging. He walked, mainly, changed his books at the library, drove to the late night supermarket and bought groceries with the money Jeanette gave him to pay for the things on the list.

Food... and *drink*. God knows, he'd always shied away from the stuff. Needed it now, though, to relieve the grey mist of days. Literally grey, with the curtains shut to safeguard Esmond's eyesight. No music, no television, no phoning girls from the safety of his desk. Now he perched at the breakfast bar in the kitchen. Read and made drinks up, day after day after day.

Drinking rather than thinking – it was all too horrible. Her, there, at his special place, doubtless reeking of urine, of shit. And more sickness here, in his flat: Esmond muttering, kicking. Having strange dreams in which he said flames crept over the bed.

'It's all right, wee man, it's all right.' Jeanette kept repeating that. Each day she came home, said he, David, had done something wrong. Given Esmond too little to drink, forgotten to read him a story. Failed to air the room sufficiently, or aired the room till the place got cold.

'Did you give him the soup I left out?'

'He wasn't hungry.'

'You should have tried, though.'

'He's old enough to know what he wants.' Going on and on about meals – it brought it all back to him. Eat this, swallow that, finish it, start it *now*. Easy to think you had escaped into the sophistication of adulthood. Old demons, lurking, waiting for a moments weakness to make their return.

Five days of seeing his little face change shape and texture. Five days of watching him sweating, swelling, crying out. On the sixth day he started playing a little with his coloured pens, though just dropping one made him start wailing. On day seven he asked if he could watch some TV. By day eight he was beginning to look human again, was eating more, smiling.

A ring at the doorbell: 'Who can that be, Esmond?' David asked. Opened it to find Mrs Landrew practicing her most insolent expression. 'I'd better not invite you in,' he said.

'Jeanette tells me he's on the mend. He needs his granny.' She side-stepped him, her shoulder brushing his, making the rage renew. Hurried in with her too-purposeful walk, clucking at Esmond. Tucking his duvet round his neck, calling him her good wee lamb. 'Has he eaten anything today?'

'Yes.'

'What?'

'Breakfast. Lunch.' *Did she want a fucking menu? Die, bitch, die.*

'Granny knows what's best, lambie.'

No she doesn't.

'See what granny's bought. Upsadaisy. Big wide mouth.'

Sugar loaded rubbish – not the unsweetened biscuits he'd brought from the health store. He looked at the heavy-based table lamp, imagined pairing it none too gently with her head.

Easy, easy. He backed away towards the door, towards relative freedom.

'You're not going out, are you?' Eyes in the back of her headscarf: they never failed.

'I'm going into the kitchen to replenish Esmond's beaker of juice, if that's all right?'

'You don't want him drinking too much. He might have an accident.'

'The doctor said to give him plenty of liquids to flush out toxins. I've been managing perfectly.'

'Mmmm. Jeanette said you got some time off work. Very good of your boss, I must say. In my day, of course, the mothers stayed at home.'

Teeth coming together, clenching: 'Well, we've moved on since then.'

'You *think* you have anyway. The young generation always thinks it knows best.' (Young. Had he ever been young? If only.) 'You'll not be getting many of your songs written, I don't suppose?'

'They're... incubating.' He was beginning to think he'd lost the ability, all concepts fled.

Another stare: one day their eyeballs would remain locked in combat. 'Well, I'll let you get that juice,' she said.

Dismissing him from his lounge. He slammed the door, heard Esmond scream, took long strides through the tiny hallway. feeling trapped in a house full of germs.

'Here. You take a break. I'll sit with him for a bit. I know it's tiring.' The woman had come to stand behind him in the kitchen, was sounding nice. He blinked, looked up warily, rubbed his eyes. Had she really had a change of heart?

'Thanks. I'll make us some coffee, find my library book.'

'Not for me, thank you. The caffeine's bad for you.'

He stood up, made himself an extra strong mug of the stuff, set it down close to her, started to leave the kitchen.

'You can read this,' she said. Thrust it in front of him, so that he had little choice but to take it. 'I'd like it back.'

The late afternoon edition of the evening paper, full of local lowlights. A fire in a warehouse, a hold-up in an off-licence in Leith. And, tucked away in a corner:

'*Tanith – Police Follow Up New Clue.*'

His stomach did something acrobatic. He was glad Mrs Landrew had left the room.

The column inch that followed said Tanith had been seen getting into a car parked at the kerbside. The woman, who'd been glancing out of her window, couldn't tell what colour it was. Probably a saloon type, though. If Wanda was to tell the police that he drove an Escort... His pulse suddenly providing a stimulus that rivalled any caffeine, he pushed his coffee cup away.

CHAPTER THIRTY TWO

Blood, a spot of blood. At least that's what it looked like – a dry brownish stain on one of the sleeves of his shirt. Small, like a single splash or droplet. Quite far down, towards the cuff.

Jeanette stared at the stain, glad that the launderette was temporarily quiet. Had he cut himself shaving? Did he even get dressed in the morning before he shaved himself?

Strange that she didn't know these things after more than four years together. But he was such a private person, so *alone*. In the past she'd sometimes hesitated to speak to him for fear of breaking into his thought patterns. He had a way of making you feel you'd invaded his world.

A world of torn shirts and jackets, potential blood stains. A world in which he no longer worked, in which he lied. Still, he'd been good with Esmond during the last ten days of tears and tantrums. She'd been so worried at times, she'd cried and complained even more than her son.

Poor David. She thrust his laundry into the machine. Poor misguided David. Had he planned on keeping this garment hidden from her, in the box where they kept the clothes that needed special care?

Usually she brought the bulk of their laundry here, left him to do things that needed to be washed by hand. Only his hands hadn't gone near the garments, near anything domestic. He hadn't tidied his desk or put the car through the carwash or even taken back his library books. Hadn't done anything at all.

So she'd done the handwashing herself, part necessity, part favour. In some ways she felt she owed him one – he'd been stuck at home for ten days with a fretful little boy. She'd thought he'd put this shirt in by mistake – it didn't need hand washing. Had transferred it to the weekly launderette bundle, and here it was.

Spinning round now, removing what kind of evidence? A woman on her period whom he'd undressed and lain down with somewhere? He must have... Jeanette felt shaky: she'd never tried it. But she'd read of how a man could stimulate a woman by hand. So he'd... touched her, maybe in the car, parked dark and secret. And she'd writhed and pushed against him and he'd got menstrual blood on his sleeve.

This, then, was the evidence. A menstruating woman who had, on at least one occasion, been with David in a forest or a wood. Someplace where they had leaf-mould, or some similar substance. Which suggested there was a husband back home.

She swallowed a build up of saliva. Be calm, calm. Think clearly. The woman was obviously free during the day, but wasn't on the phone. Leastways, he never phoned her. Well, not from home, anyway.

It wasn't much to go on, in this search for an identikit picture of David's mistress. Was the affair ongoing? Was he going on to see her now? This Tuesday was his first chance in ages, now Esmond was back at her mums, convalescing. She prayed Mrs Landrew wouldn't go to the Health Food Store. It was a possibility, if Esmond asked for one of the biscuits Daddy bought him. If she found he no longer worked there, they'd never live it down.

Jeanette sighed, forced a slight smile as the door opened to admit a customer. She wished it was closing time, that she could lose herself in her exercise routine.

Head moving to the left, then gradually circling. She could feel the fears and uncertainties leaking out of her. Just for a moment everyone moved with the same sure motion, the same purpose, and the world felt instinctively right.

Arms next, stretching them out, up, under, finally windmilling them in slow motion, torso still. Then legs, knees, a slow-march warm up, familiar moves.

'Right, everyone. If you space yourselves out a bit we'll move on to the aerobics section.'

The tempo swift, demanding, but still predictable, still under her control. More passion in this dance disc than she'd ever felt in twenty two years on the planet. Jumping, twirling, working out to anothers wants and needs.

Working out. Work it out. Was it working? Dancing faster and faster, leaping up, skipping forwards, to the side. Wanda had slowed right down, as had the other girl to the left of her. 'Just one more track to go in the aerobics section,' the teacher said.

More, she wanted more. Wanted to keep going like this forever. No complexity: just a body doing the best that it could do. 'We'll start bringing it down in a minute,' the teacher continued, trying to encourage the flagging ones. Jeanette jumped, skipped, jogged, marched, twirled. Reluctantly she joined the others in lying on the floor for the eventual cooldown. Stretching gently, eyes closing. Back to a too-cool atmosphere, a husband's cold lies.

Or hot lies, told out of fear of her reaction? Told to save his pride, their marital face? As if she cared about the job, about his status. She flexed each of her fingers, imagined herself stroking his face. Given time and privacy she'd like to. There was desire there, deep down.

OK, so it hadn't been good in the early days, but she'd been half dead from self-consciousness. A man – the first man in her life – seeing her naked buttocks and breasts. Tracing her lines, noticing every tiny mole and imperfection. Thinking that her tummy was too round, that she was too dry down there, too ugly, too tight.

–Open hands, close hands, circle wrists–

They'd never spent a night in the same bed together. Maybe now, if they could talk about the future, rent a bigger flat. The songwriting obviously wasn't working, money-wise: so perhaps he'd take a full time job. And if she got that manageresses position, she'd be earning extra and...

'... And finish coming up gently.'

She looked up, realised she'd missed an exercise instruction. The other women were halfway to their feet, and neatly rising. Sitting up, she pushed herself forward, exchanging grins with another woman who was equally slow.

'I was miles away,' she said, as Wanda joined her by their jackets.

'Me too.'

'Still no leads?' She opened her eyes wider, inferring.

No. I don't think they're going to find her now.' She hoisted up her shoulder bag, 'It's been too long. It's not – I'd be hypocritical to play the grieving best friend or anything; I didn't even like her that much – but to be... taken away like that.'

'It wasn't your fault. You couldn't have done anything.'

Wanda pursed her lips together. 'I just keep seeing her waving in those last few seconds before she walked away.'

Horrible to be so close to someone who might have been murdered. Horrible to think that it might have been Wanda if she'd taken the same route.

'You can have a lift home, if you like, if you come to the flat. David's at home with Esmond. He'll be glad to get out. I think he's sick of heating tins of tomato soup.'

'No, I'll give him a break. Got to make the most of my bus pass.'

'I'll wait with you,' Jeanette, said, 'Now that we're doing self defence...'

'That's right – you should be good, Another Jackie Chan. All that one to one tuition you got the first week.'

Jeanette laughed, 'I was trying to hide behind another woman. I nearly died when Sandra chose me to practice on.' She grimaced inwardly. David would have corrected her for being melodramatic in saying: 'I nearly died'.

Well, once he would have. She felt a shiver of sadness for the way things were changing for him. Once he'd have told her to think about language, be careful, precise. Nowadays he seemed to have lost all interest in words and meanings. As she became more aware of what things meant, he seemed to care less.

'You did well,' Wanda said, and she had to stop for a moment and think about what the other girl meant. Did well at the self defence class, of course.

'*You* can do the next demo,' she said, smiling.

'Me? I've no one to practice on.'

Jeanette opened her mouth, planning to say she could borrow David. Shut it again – he was being borrowed quite enough as it was.

'With Esmond being ill I've not had much time to go through the movements.'

'Bet that girl in the white outfit has been practicing non-stop.' Funny how talking got easier and easier. Those first two classes she thought she'd told Wanda about everything that wasn't strictly private in her life. She'd imagined the rest of their meetings would be spent in a growing chasm of silence. Instead, as the months passed they'd laughed and joked more and more.

Even the silences weren't too bad, providing they didn't stretch out over much. Quiet times were bearable, if you knew the other person was your friend.

'Esmond'll be missing his chips tonight,' Wanda said, standing back a little as another bus stopped to let off a middle aged couple.

'Mum said she'd make him some instead.'

'It's handy that, your mother living in Edinburgh.' Jeanette felt surprised at the student's words. She'd never considered mum living elsewhere. 'If I have children, I'll probably move closer to *my* folks.'

Jeanette frowned: 'I just never moved away.' People like herself simply didn't, stayed in their locality. Wanda was looking at her through the lamplit dark.

'Haven't you ever considered a change of scene?'

'No. Well, maybe recently. More for holidays.'

'And David?'

'As long as the place is cultured, he says he doesn't care.' She gazed down the street, watched a woman closing her curtains. She looked lonely, silhouetted against the light. 'When Esmond goes to school I'd like us to get away more – *see* things. Touring Scotland would be a start.'

'You don't want another child at that stage? That's what my cousin Norma did.'

This was Mrs Landrew's line; it was unusual to hear it on her friend's lips.

'No, one's enough. You have to think about them all the time. You have to... bargain for freedom.' Good line that. She felt brighter, more alert these days.

'That's what I told Tanith,' Wanda said heavily.

'She had a baby? I thought she was a single girl.'

'She didn't have any – said she wanted four.' A pause, 'I think it was Esmond made her broody. He was so cute that day.'

Esmond? Tanith had seen Esmond? Had it been at the college? Had…?

For long seconds she tried to find strength, tried to make her voice sound normal. 'Tanith broody? What did David make of all that?'

'Mmm?' Wanda craned her neck as the sound of a large vehicle grew nearer. 'Damn. It's a lorry. Oh, I don't know if she told him. I took the two of them round the exhibition and left Tanith in the cafe.'

So David had met Tanith, had spoken to her. Yet he hadn't said anything when she'd mentioned the girl to him days before. Which was weird, even for David. Normally he'd be analysing events. Unless… unless Tanith was his mistress. She was unusual in that she did modelling, and David liked unconventional women and men. She had lots of spare time, craved excitement. She'd been ill, so might well have visited the Health Food Store. And a girl who took her clothes off for unknown artists sounded adventurous. The type, perhaps, to indulge in some outdoor sex? There was only one thing wrong with her analysis, Jeanette thought, feeling her heartbeat go into overdrive: Tanith had disappeared.

CHAPTER THIRTY THREE

He had money again, Jeanette thought. Where had he acquired it? On Saturday he'd driven herself and Esmond to The Savacentre to do the shopping. On Sunday he'd paid them in to Edinburgh Zoo. Was this other woman, this unknown *mistress*, bailing him out?

Someone was – or else he was stealing. To take money, though, seemed worse than pinching some biscuits and makeup from work. David was the kind of man whom women would beg and borrow for. Unfathomable, unreachable, a free-spirited, frustrating dream.

But something had happened, for he was suddenly *there* all the time. Playing the family man, the attentive, educating father. Could unemployment be making him feel insecure?

'Do you like the monkeys, Esmond? There's one coming out – see? That's his house in there. I think he's waving at you and mum.' Filling up the day with lions, tigers, and a pacing polar bear. Both of them speaking at Esmond, through Esmond. She'd enjoyed the animals, the crisp, cold air, but kept wondering when he'd try to break away.

Home, and he helped make the evening meal. Did the dishes afterwards, made them an additional pot of tea. She phoned her mother, chatted for a while, waiting for the door to slam. Waiting for him to say he'd pop out for a magazine, a can of juice, a walk or drive.

Instead he settled down in the kitchen with two of the Sunday papers.

'Anything interesting?' she said, going into the kitchen for some crisps. Surprisingly, he read out a book review. 'Sounds worth saving up for,' she said lightly, before going back into the lounge and switching on the TV.

A lightweight comedy – she was going off those, nowadays. She switched channels, moved on from the news, found a programme about incidents which had changed people's lives. A woman in her twenties spoke about being trapped by her legs in a train crash. For six hours she'd lain there, knowing that she'd want to connect more with other people if she didn't die. Afterwards she'd sold her baker's shop to set up a charity which took disabled children abroad.

An older couple spoke of losing their faith after their son had been murdered. He'd been on his way home from a Scripture Union meeting when he'd been attacked. The youths had gotten off on a technicality. The couple had renounced their religion, felt cheated, betrayed.

The scene switched to a middle aged brunette, a new scenario. The face on the screen looked sad, lost, confused. She said that one Monday her husband had left the house as usual, and not come back again. He'd withdrawn his life savings after consulting his doctor about depression several days before.

'He said nothing to me,' said his wife, 'nothing. I knew he wasn't happy at work, wasn't sleeping well.' The camera zoomed down to her hands, clasped together in her then back to her face, the eyes searching the horizon, blank. 'I had no idea things were this bad, this desperate.' A look at the camera: 'Rob, if you're watching... please come home.'

Psychologists, marriage guidance people. child bereavement counsellors. As the studio panel started its discussion, Jeanette felt the tiredness surge through her in sedative-like waves. Time for another biscuit, maybe several. That zoo was huge and tiring, she needed a lift.

'...Men and women act in this way when they're under stress. Most commonly they return to the place they lived as a child.'

En route to the kitchen she stopped, stared at the screen, heartbeat accelerating. Hurried back to the handset and turned the volume up.

'The distraught person basically wants a simpler way of being. Sometimes they'll go to a place where they were free of responsibility.'

A return to his childhood – why hadn't she thought of that before? Unemployed, the world rejecting his songs, the pain of being caught thieving. It would make sense for him to want to contact his dad. Hurt by fresh wounds, he might want to heal old ones. This would be his last chance to put things right before the old man died.

She sat back in her chair, sipping her lukewarm tea, reflecting. It all made sense – the furtive visits away, the failure to make phone calls from the house. The Frates had been a poor family, needy. She remembered David pointing out, and sneering at, the tenement where he used to live.

So, his father wouldn't have a phone; probably didn't have much of anything. Perhaps he was ill, dying, which would explain that spot of blood. Easy to tear your shirt on a nail in a run down area. Easy, for someone proud like David to lie about where he'd been.

She bet that he felt silly, self-conscious. How could he admit he was seeing his father, perhaps nursing him, after all that he'd said?

'Mean bastard, didn't give a fuck.'

Hard to go back on all that. Simpler, both parties willing, to renew the bond quietly, remake it into something good.

'Anything interesting on?' She jumped slightly as he came into the room, clutched her tea cup.

'No, not really.' Not now this programme was over, leastways. She was glad he hadn't been with her whilst she was watching. If he knew that she'd guessed, he might suffer a loss of face.

If she'd guessed. She had to know for sure – get this worry over with. She sat and thought as David slumped down and stared without enthusiasm at the screen. The tenement row that he lived in as a boy was now uninhabited and uninhabitable. Tomorrow she'd phone the council and see if they knew where the former tenants had gone.

Practically across the road – that's where they'd been decanted to. Jeanette stared at the phone, amazed at how simple it had been. But this was just a starting point, she reminded herself, thinking quickly. The tenants would have long since moved to permanent homes.

'I suppose my father-in-law was just put there temporarily? I mean, if the plan was to do up his original house, and send him back?'

'One moment please.' The sound of computer keys tapping. 'No, when the refurbishment grants were stopped, the tenants were all given the option of staying in the new block.' A slightly self-conscious laugh. 'Then there was some dispute about who owned the land, so the original old houses are still there.'

She hung up, and sat down in the backshop as her pulse slowed and stabilised. Heard the shop door ring, and went out to greet an elderly man.

'You're quiet,' he observed.

'What? Oh, yes. Probably get busy later on.'

Hard to concentrate on what he was saying. She wanted to be free of this place. Wanted to shriek to the skies: *I'm scared, I'm scared, I'm scared.* She'd thought it would take ages to find Mr. Frate, that she'd have weeks of phoning, writing. Instead, he was probably a forty minute journey away.

Do nothing, forget it. Stay with your keep fit and self defence. But if David left her and took Esmond, most of her life would be over. She couldn't bear to think of him being raised as another woman's son. No, she had to see this thing through – it was only one brief meeting. Find out if she'd misjudged him, if he was tending a sick man rather than teasing a sexy woman every few days.

She could go straight there when lunchtime came round. *Should* go there, if she was going to seize the day like that film had suggested. David wouldn't be there today, was looking after Esmond in the house. Whereas on Tuesday, Wednesday and Thursday, when he didn't have childminding duties... She'd do it, she decided. After all, Mr Frate was *her* relative too.

'Susan, I'm going to be late back. Can you cover? You can have tomorrow's shift off, or I'll owe you one.'

'Shopping, is it?' Susan seemed to spend most of her time shopping in the foodhalls.

'Yes. We took Esmond out at the weekend, didn't get things done.'

Questions, details. Funny how people were interested in the progress of a child they hardly knew. She'd never felt that kind of curiosity, rarely identified with others. She always forgot to ask after other children at the creche.

'Off you go, then, boss,' Susan joked. Jeanette smiled wryly. Susan seemed determined to make the most of her few brief hours of power.

A different walk, an unfamiliar bus route. She'd already phoned the bus station so knew approximately where to go. Going to see a relative she'd never met before. Sad, when she had so few relatives of her own.

Safe, known territory replaced by new streets, untried shopping centres. Row upon row of maisonettes, like giant building blocks.

'You get off here, lass. Take that street on your left, and go past the community hall. You'll come to the one you want.'

People were staring. She blushed – she'd asked the driver to let her know when she reached her destination.

'That's great. Thanks.' Calm down, breathe deeply, stay cool. Jumping down from the bus, she started walking. Saw the street signs and realised she was mistakenly heading right. Waited till the bus went out of sight, pretending to tie her shoelace. Feeling silly, shaky, wishing she was back at work.

Turn left to find the right street: the place was poorly signposted. One sign had been partly torn off at one lower corners, the next one had red paint sprayed over it in jagged lines. Still, when she reached the tenements she realised it was going to be easy. They had those security doors, with name-labelled sets of buzzers outside.

Hoping she looked like she was doing a survey of some sort, she began to walk up to each set of name panels. Frame, Fran, Fern – at her tenth or eleventh tenement she found a Frate. Pressed the buzzer and waited. Nothing. Squinted up at the windows, hoping to see a curtain twitch.

Maybe he was ill in bed, couldn't reach the answering system? She felt a hot low rush of guilt: was it his key that David had had?

She sat down on the step, intending to wait for a while and see if anyone went into the building. Leaned back against the security door, and it opened, and she fell back into the close.

A close which smelt of cats – or was it children? A close which had once looked spruce – you could tell by the paint near the ceiling, a glossy dark red. Elsewhere, the walls were scrawled on, etched into, painted: knifes and pens and paintsprays and nails and even nail varnish used by those intent on making their mark.

David had never lived here, but he'd have hated it. Hard, now, to imagine him visiting a dive like this. But she'd come so far, couldn't give up without checking. She'd made up a story to tell the old man, in case he hadn't seen his son after all.

Dusty stairs, a broken first floor window she could hardly see through. He was on the second floor. She wondered if he'd married again. Put her ear to the door, heard a TV blaring. The bell didn't work: she knocked, then knocked again. No response. Determined now, she rattled the letterbox. Heard it bang authoritatively, sounding powerful and sure.

Floorboards cracking, footsteps. She stood back, waited.

'Who is it?' asked a voice. It sounded disgruntled, catarrh congested, ended on a wheeze.

'It's me.' That meant nothing. Start to think, girl. 'It's.. about David.' A pause, a key being turned. The door swung in.

A man of medium height, wearing a once white shirt and mustard coloured cardigan. His shoulders were rounded: his brown cord trousers bagged at the ankles, covered his slippers up to the toe.

'What?'

'I'm David's wife. Can I talk to you for a minute?'

'David?' His hair hung over his forehead in locks of iron grey grease.

'David Frate.' She couldn't bear to say, 'Your son' – he looked so alien.

'Don't ask me about him. I haven't seen *him* in years.'

Didn't the man feel something, *anything?* She realised he wasn't going to invite her in, and was glad. The hall carpet, what she could see of it, looked as if it had never been vacuumed. She stepped back a little, realising the man himself smelt unclean.

So David hadn't been here. That left her second plan.

'I know. It's our son. He's run away.' No response. He wouldn't know Esmond's age and David could have fathered a child many years ago. 'He's... he's nine,' she lied. 'He doesn't have many relatives. I thought he might try to find you, want to stay here.' She took a step back, ordeal over, anxious to get away.

'If he comes here, he'll get a good hiding from me.' Had David really been born out of a union with this man? 'Ran away often enough himself, the little bastard did. Up by that wood yard, half the time. Knew his mother and I couldn't manage that bloody slope.'

'Oh. Well. I'm sorry to have bothered you.' She half raised a hand, let it fall down again as he glared at her.

'Don't put up with any nonsense. Don't let him get the better of you.' She didn't know if he meant his grandson or his son.

She turned to go, and the door slammed unnecessarily loudly. Hurried down the stairs, stepping sideways to avoid a thin black cat. No wonder David had run away – she'd have done likewise. Run from a filthy home to the sweet smell of freshly cut wood.

Wood. Wood mould. Realisation hit her as she stepped onto the street again. Of course, *that* was what she'd found in David's trouser hems that day. So, he was going back to his childhood haunts, and spending his free time there. The question was, was anyone going there with him? Now she knew his destination it wouldn't be so difficult to find out.

CHAPTER THIRTY FOUR

'We regret to inform you...'

Disappointment dragged at his belly, quickly replaced by contempt and a growing anger. Had they even read the stuff, far less considered it?

He'd written these lyrics last summer before Pauline... before asking Pauline out. Penned ten lengthy tracks, enough for a full length CD. And what did he get in return? Wasted hopes and squandered postage. A standard rejection slip by any other name. They'd be sorry. One day, they'd be sorry. In the future they'd want him, and he'd turn them away. Easy to pick on a man when he was down, eating into his savings. Easy to pick on a man who just wanted to stay home and be left in peace.

The doorbell rang, reverberating down the hallway. He breathed in, held. Ignore it. Nowadays it never brought good news. It rang again, he sat silent and unmoving.

'Bell, bell, bell,' Esmond cried. Someone – his son? – was rattling the letterbox: he could hear a woman speaking. Mother-in-law jokes weren't vicious enough, he decided, as he recognised the dulcet tones. He'd try an axe some day.

Stiffly he walked towards the letterbox's flapping gloved hand and coat sleeve. Opened the door quickly, hoping to trap her there. Sorry, M'Lord but she was digitally invading my property.

'You took your time.' He mouthed the words in unison with her as he turned back towards the lounge. Returned to the second post he'd been opening, kept his head well down. The largest envelope was from a music magazine asking him to renew his subscription.

What with? She was standing in front of his desk now, gloved palms flat on its rich, polished surface. Eyes trained on the three remaining envelopes, he ripped open the next piece of mail.

Circulars, requests for money, a coupon for a new improved washing powder. Junk mail for junk people: hollow promises, money-grabbing hype. Nothing personal which said we know you've talent. Nothing which said: we're here for you, please phone.

'Bills again, is it?'

Esmond grabbed hold of her leg, and she scooped him up. David's jaw felt locked, cemented.

She looked down at the boy, 'Your poor mummy works hard to pay those.' He clenched his thigh muscles together so hard, he actually rose slightly in his seat, felt calf cramp threatening. Not that she'd notice. The old hag only saw what she wanted to see.

'So,' he said lightly, 'what brings *you* here on a Monday?'

What brings you here every fucking time I'm supposed to have the house to myself?

'Well, it was a nice day, and I've just got my pension. I thought David'll want a chance to get his writing done.'

'I'm flexible.'

Your move again, bitch.

'I knew Esmond would like to go to the cinema, see that Disney film.' She wasn't looking at him now, aware that she was vulnerable.

He considered saying 'Sorry, we've made plans.' Thought better of it, and nodded his affirmative. Maybe some time to himself would cheer him up. Well, not quite *by* himself: he could do a bit of dialling. Envisage a triple X-rated movie all of his own.

'Right, that's settled.' Brisk again, sure of herself, now that her day was going to be purposeful.

'Don't buy him orange juice from the kiosk. It's full of additives, crap.' He liked saying 'crap', he knew the word upset her.

'And pay their prices? I'm not that daft, I bring my own.'

Still artificial crap, just cheaper. He felt too worn to argue the toss. Argue the toss – Christ, that must be Freudian. The second she left he was going to ring some dusky beauty and have a beautiful wank.

Maybe a double session, even a treble. He could hang up between phonecalls, prepare for another shot. Or shoot. Call it what you will

– it signified pleasure. Sensation, pure and simple, no strings attached.

'That's us, then.' She popped her head round the door. Esmond did likewise: David could see from his shoulders that he was wearing his winter coat. 'We'll see you later,' she added, staring hard.

'Doubtless.' He reached into his pocket, held out a ten pound note, saw her face change. 'This should cover it.'

'No, I...'

'Really, we prefer to.' She disappeared, and he walked smartly after her, put the money in her pocket as she reached the outer door.

'I... you know I like to treat him. I don't spend much on myself.'

'We can't take advantage of that.' Keep it light, light: he'd be damned if he'd be beholden to her. She'd never liked or appreciated him. She never would.

'Well, if you're sure.' She took the note from her pocket and her purse from her large, creased tan shopping bag. He knew she would bring back his change, count it into his hand. Say something about children needing their grannies, needing a lap to sit on. He wondered when their under the surface animosity would break through the ever thinning skin.

The door closed on them, voices retreating through the close, hers pitched low and Esmond's high-pitched. He slid back the netting over the window, watched them stroll past. Peace. Nirvana. Well, almost. Any minute now... Wonderful the power a phone gave you. They'd never had one, all the time he was growing up. But who would he have phoned? Probably no one. He hadn't known how bad his circumstances were. When you were little you thought that all people lived like you, cried and suffered. You thought that dads hit, and mums taunted and grans stayed out of the way.

No Childline back then: he'd asked himself often if he'd have rung it if there had been. Unlikely, when he felt so ugly, so stupid, so unerringly *bad*. After a while, he hadn't expected anyone to care about him, care *for* him. You didn't, when the people who'd created you said that you were their biggest ever mistake.

A descendant, who, mood-wise, kept descending. Getting lower and lower. Rock bottom, the pits, depths of Hell. A boy with nervous dermatitis, who cowered behind old factories. A youth with hunched

shoulders, ever darkening dreams. A man who looked all right, but…
He reached for his desk key, unlocked the hidden tray, slid it towards
him. The colourful directory beckoned: he lifted it out.

Page after page of pornographic potential. The Book Of A
Thousand Orgasms. Way to go. How long since he'd held this – held
anything? How long since… too long, too long.

Would he dial up Prank-Playing Wendy who needed lots of
correction? Or hear out Arching Alicia, whose tongue could reach
places no one elses tongue had ever reached? He moved on to another
page, assessing. He wasn't hard yet, though he'd felt a twinge. This
one had to be good, had to be convincing. He'd tear the phone from
the wall rather than sit through another rendition of 'Je T'aime'.

Cocktail Waitresses: We've Nothing On Under Our Uniforms.
The illustration showed a brunette leaning forward, soft beige
buttocks teasing from under a short black skirt. That will do nicely,
miss. He started to unzip himself. Stopped, and picked up the
receiver. Some of the girls liked to talk you through that bit.

Start talking, baby. He dialled the number hastily, sat back in his
chair. The voice came on, much less sultry than normal:

'*So, you think you're about to enjoy yourself? You've got a nerve
to even call me, you snivelling little wretch.*'

What? This couldn't be right. This didn't sound like a cocktail
waitress. Unless… maybe this one would start off being cheeky, and
another waitress would sort her out. Maybe they'd fight on the
tables, bare bums jutting out at all angles. Maybe two male
customers would penetrate them from behind…

Beginning to lengthen slightly, he stayed with it.

'*… I'll bet your prick is pathetic, the size of a worm. In fact, I
doubt if you're able to get it up, never mind use it. Maybe I won't let
you. If you come without my permission, I'll put you over my knee…*'

Feeling chilled, feeling shaky. Someone break in on this. Someone
stop her. She's got too much control.

'*… and pull your underpants down. I'll give you such a thrashing.
You'll never have been punished like this.*'

The cunt, the vicious, fucking cunt. Threatening him, demeaning
him. He had suffered like this before – more times that he cared to
remember – but never, ever again.

'In fact, I'll teach you a lesson every day. Bend you over a stool and lash your...'

Jesus. He slammed down the receiver, fear and loathing drying the insides of his mouth like calamine lotion. Making his eyelids prickle, the bones beneath his cheeks feel tight. God, he needed a drink – a large one. Make that two.

Hurrying over to the cupboard, he fetched a glass and the vodka bottle. Introduced them to each other, added a tiny splash of orange: he didn't like colourless drinks. They reminded him of the times when he'd only had water available. What had mum called it? Adam's wine. He took a large gulp of spirits, and another. Stupid bloody company, getting the recordings wrong. You dialled up for a mind fuck and got some cunt threatening to all but castrate you. Cocksure bitch – he'd like to see her try.

The second vodka chased the first, the third raced after it. Christ knows the harm a company like this could do. Scaring boys and men, making their pricks go small and ineffectual. Balls climbing up into their bodies, scalding fright. Psychological cruelty, prolonged mental damage. She'd like it to be physical, too.

If she got the chance. God knows, though, with him alive she wouldn't get that chance. Another whore had teased and taunted him on the phone... They were all in league together, turning his first day of the week into a mind-hurting manic Monday. The next bitch he met was definitely going to pay.

CHAPTER THIRTY FIVE

Mondays were great, Wanda mused as she finished early. Last seminar at 2pm, and no baby-sitting till mid-week. Pity there were alterations to be done at home, shrieking for attention. This was the kind of clear winter's day for walking up Salisbury Crags. A day for lifting weights at the College's tiny gym, a day for dancing. Instead there were trousers to hem, waistbands to tuck in, patches to sew. That was dedication for you, that was commitment. The price of living – well, of *restricted grant studying* – didn't come cheap.

Nor did her bus pass. Wanda stared at it as she waited for the service home, realised it was almost out of date again. She'd have to sell some of last year's books and fabrics, find ways to make a little extra cash. If Jeanette got this better paid job maybe she'd get some extra hours looking after Esmond. She'd sounded pretty confidant last week.

It was looking good, almost definite. The Area Manager had told Jeanette they'd already found a suitable shop. They had put in an offer for it and were waiting to hear if the bid had been successful. She'd be manageress if the deal went through.

Wanda sighed as the bus took her through Edinburgh's wintry streets. Why was the afternoon traffic so heavy? She felt caged, claustrophobic as the vehicle trundled most of the way home. Relax, relax – that was the problem. She didn't want to, she acknowledged, putting her key in the lock. Made cheese on toast in the kitchen and quickly ate it. Washed a handprint – her own or Esmond's – from the lounge's door.

The sewing, she must get down to the sewing. She grimaced, washed her plate, cleaned the kitchen surface then the cooker top. She should really put out crumbs for the birds. Start the mending, the sewing! Force herself – to do her best.

Opening the first half of the wardrobe she found the bag with its assorted garments and page of customer instructions. Went back into the lounge and got her sewing bag out with its nice new threads. Wanda threaded the machine needle, shivered then started sneezing. Time to fetch her warmest jumper from the other room.

She opened the second part of the wardrobe and ruffled through the hangers of her more dated clothes. And found a man's jacket – *David's* jacket. The jacket she'd promised she'd mend for him several weeks ago. Well, promised Jeanette, to be more specific. How on earth had it remained there all this time?

Of course. She'd brought it home one night after their self defence class. She'd been tired, hungry, had put it in the little used side of the wardrobe to keep it wrinkle free. Obviously it hadn't gone in the alterations book – wasn't supposed to. No need for Jeanette to be landed with the laundry's handling charge.

She'd do it now, fix it properly. Wouldn't add on a percentage for profit; just charge for her time and material costs. David didn't earn much money, and had given her lifts home sometimes. And Jeanette was her classmate, her newest friend.

Assessing, tacking – he'd certainly ripped this pocket spectacularly. Still, she'd seen worse, *and* put it right. Matching, mending, restructuring, renovating. Getting through today's work, but still feeling restless, slightly trapped. Maybe she should go out to the library, get a few books out? She wanted to get outside for a while, walk and run.

Finishing David's pocket, she went into the foot of the wardrobe, found the carrier bag she'd brought it home in. She could walk over with it this evening to the house.

Be all you can be. After three more hemming tasks, she put her running shoes on. Jeanette usually got home for six – she'd aim to be there by quarter past. Maybe they'd invite her to stay for a while, to eat with them. Nice to have something she hadn't had to prepare herself.

A cool night, a bright night. She jogged, ran, fast-walked, marched and trotted through the Edinburgh streets. This was different, life-affirming, energising. She should do impulsive things like this all the time.

✠

No she shouldn't.

He answered the door and his eyes seemed vague, unfocused.

'Is Jeanette in?'

'Jeanette?'

'I brought this round.'

A pause, then his face cleared. He smiled, held the door open. 'I'm sorry. I was thinking about something. You know how it is.'

She knew how it was – the ways of creativity. You gave yourself up to something, were startled by a voice, a bell. Had to come back from your trance to deal with another reality.

'Been there, done that,' she said with a forgiving grin. Following him into the lounge – he put something away in his desk tray and locked it. State secrets? Probably state of the art songs. 'I'm sorry I interrupted you.' She stood awkwardly on the other side of the desk to him, carrier bag by her side.

'No, I've finished getting organised. Sit down. Tea?'

'I'd love a coffee.' Her toes felt bruised, her cheeks felt breeze-buffed. 'I've walked all the way over here, it took ages. Thought it was about time I got fit.'

Jeanette must still be at work, or out with Esmond. She'd have come through to greet her by now if she was in the house.

'Where's Esmond hiding, then?' she shouted after his back. He didn't answer. Didn't hear her, most probably. She was being completely paranoid tonight.

She looked round the room, surprised that his typewriter wasn't in evidence. This was supposed to be one of his song writing days. Maybe he had taken it into the kitchen or bedroom, wherever the light was stronger? He probably had one of those portable ones for travelling around.

He walked back into the room carrying a tray with two coffees. She noticed his looked especially black. Noticed the open vodka bottle on his desk, and felt a stab of guilt, as if she'd been prying. Jeanette had said that David hardly ever drank.

'I was wondering about Esmond. Is he sleeping?'

'No. Jeanette's mother took him out.'

'Oh, that's nice. Anywhere special?'

'Everywhere's special to her if it's away from me.'

'Happy families, eh?' She knew what he meant – Mrs Landrew had a degree in unthinking condemnation. She felt awkward, though, alone with him like this. He seemed remote, even angry. As soon as she'd finished her coffee she would leave.

'Were you writing today?' His desk surface held three single sheets of paper.

'Just dealing with my correspondence, things like that.'

She nodded. Silence. Jeanette had once been like this – almost wordless. Maybe as she'd become more chatty, he'd grown more quiet?

'I was wondering... I don't see your typewriter.'

'I don't have one.'

'Oh. You mean you word process your songs.' She hadn't meant it as a question, but he took it as one, leaned forward.

'No, I hand write them – I never learned to type.'

Even so. She sat back, amazed, sipped burning liquid. How could you work at something for years and not use professional tools? He could have taken typing classes, bought a book on the subject. Even two finger typing would be a start.

'It's the message that's important, not the medium.' Though he spoke slowly, his speech seemed slightly slurred.

'Granted, but...' She saw the look on his face, cut short her objections, said '...I'm sure you know what you're doing.' Cradled her saucer close to her chest.

'Would you like to read my songs?' He was already going into his top drawer, bringing out a folder, 'You can take some away, if you like.' He handed over his portfolio, sat down. She looked at the first sheet, frowned slightly, looked again.

Jumbles of words, ill-fitting phrases, unlikely metaphors.

'Nude reasoning makes indecipherables tremble. We knowers are free.'

16 lines of obscure nonsense: she read them once, twice, went on to the second page. This was… Was this really the best he could do?

'What do you think? That second one's about the meat industry's propaganda.' So intense, so sure, so misguided, so talentless, so sad.

'Oh, I see – the reference to *killing lunch*.' Laughter was gathering, tickling at the base of her throat. She had to get out of here, and quickly. She didn't want to hurt him, but hated to lie.

'And the third…' He came over and sat on the arm of her chair, arm along the backrest, 'That's looking at the dolphins.'

'The dolphins?'

'They help make depressives more alert.'

God, but she felt alert, heard warning bells. This man had no critical faculties, for all his big words.

'I'll have to be going, David. The alterations…' She felt his fingers on her arm, a pinioning rage.

'People are always cheating me out of their time.'

Uh-oh. Come on Jeanette, Mrs Landrew…

Strange how the once-fantasised touch made her snatch away her forearm. The phone began to ring through the tension-filled room. He walked over to the desk, and picked it up. Listened for a second.

'That's fine.'

She started edging towards the door. He grabbed at her.

She screamed: 'Get off me!'

He dropped the receiver back in its cradle. Lurched after her – she could feel his breath on her neck. Then the hands – oh Jesus, the hands. – one over her throat, squeezing, tightening. The other covering her mouth with its alienness, making her gag.

This wasn't real – it just *couldn't* be happening. She knew this man, he was her friend's husband, she baby-sat his child. If she could just say something, find out what he planned to do, what he wanted. Self defence, defence… Her body consumed by its thudding heartbeat, mind a blank.

Pushing her towards the lounge door, out into the hallway. He'd stopped increasing the pressure: it was constant now. Pulled her into the kitchen, pulled open a drawer, jangled through its contents. She started struggling when she saw the knife.

Don't cut me, don't stab me!

His fingers tightened round her throat till she stopped trying to kick backwards.

'We're going to go out through the close in a minute. My car's outside. I'll put my arm around your shoulders, like we're lovers.' He seemed to choke or hiccup on the word. 'Don't say anything, act normal. I'll have the tip of this thing pressing into the side of your neck.' He jerked the hand at her mouth. 'Understand?' She nodded, looking up at him. They shuffled to the door. Still holding her, he unlocked it, swung it back, peered out. 'In a minute I'll take my hand away. If you scream or try to run for it, I'll cut a vein.'

Probably her jugular vein: she could feel the rage in his body. They were going into the close now – surely someone would see? And whoever was on the phone must have heard her shouting. And Mrs Landrew might be back any minute. So might Jeanette.

Come, someone come. See me, help me.

He was forcing her to move now, his grip undiminished on her throat. Shuffling, two-backed steps to the security door: he took his hand from her mouth to open it, kept the other round her neck. Transferred it round her shoulder, his forearm bent inwards, the knife mainly concealed in his hand.

She knew it was there, though – could feel it pricking her. Sharp steel on fair flesh, cruelly needling the skin. Better, perhaps, if he cut her slightly: people would see the blood, react to it. But he might panic, then, stab her to death.

Outside, an old age pensioner, walking much too quickly. Slow down, slow down. Weren't people of his age supposed to stand and stare? Hadn't he seen that David was holding her all wrong, seen the glint of metal? No one around, then, just grey February streets. An Edinburgh evening, safe as houses. He unlocked the car door, shoved her into the seat.

Her chance to escape, make a run for it. He had to hurry round to the driver's side now. She could be out in seconds, racing down the road to blessed freedom. There'd be a chip shop or something she could go to for help.

Any minute now, any... She felt a hand on her collar as he leaned in through the passenger door. Saw the fist zooming closer, moving towards her head. Then pain sped behind her eyes for hot seconds and the world disappeared.

CHAPTER THIRTY SIX

'He doesn't mind, then?'

Jeanette looked blankly at her mum: stared at the receiver. She'd thought she'd heard Wanda's voice in the background, telling David to get off or get away. Could they be..? No, no, it was ridiculous. Wanda was her friend, wouldn't betray her like that.

But why had David hung up on her so abruptly? He hadn't asked why she'd be late or mention that their son was out for the day with his gran.

Trust Susan to get the books in a mess: it might take hours to fix them.

Mrs Landrew leaned forward. 'He doesn't mind? You told him I've brought Esmond here?'

'What?' She set down the service washes ledger, 'Em, no Mum. He was in a rush. There was someone at the door.'

Lies, damned lies. Her mother was mustering up a glare from the depths of her ongoing suspicion.

'He'll realise Esmond's here, Mum – or think you took him on somewhere else after the cinema show.' She tried to smile, 'Don't worry.' *David won't.*

So much for knowing where he was, being able to keep track of him. Ever since Esmond had recovered from mumps, her mother had been paying surprise visits to the house. Visits which let David off the hook, relieved him of his baby-sitting. Let him go out to see – and do – God knows what.

'Was David writing when you went round, Mum?'

'He was opening his letters – the second post.'

Letters. Love letters? It would explain why he never used the phone. Wanda wasn't on the phone, couldn't afford it. Stop it, stop it. Wanda was reliable, a friend. Her first friend, ever. Her last one, if she kept being suspicious like this.

'You didn't get the chance to tell him your news on the phone, then?'

News. What news? Her brain trudged round. So much had happened – seeing David's dad, getting the promotion today. A manageress, in a big new laundry, with two girls working for her. More money, more fringe benefits, better amenities.

Plus managerial status – David would be pleased when she got the chance to tell him. They needed time alone together to talk. She could buy a bottle of wine on the way home like they did in the TV programmes, sit down and have a celebratory drink.

'Mum, I've got a bit of sorting out to do here.'

'Tell that Susan about that.'

'… and I'd like to make some plans with David.' She waited for the offer that never came. 'So if you could keep Esmond tonight?'

'I've done my bit.'

'Well, I suppose I could have a word with Wanda.' She reached for the phone again. Wanda didn't have a telephone, but her mother didn't know that. She started to dail the operator. *Come on, Mum, come on, Mum, come…*

'But I'll take him as a favour to you. He'll be better off with his gran.'

'Thanks.' She put the receiver down. 'Maybe you could come round for dinner tomorrow? We could go to the cafe – my treat.' Easy to be nice to everyone today, now that she'd be free of money troubles. Scary, though, the prospect of being fully in charge of three people: Susan, who just did lunchbreak cover, didn't count.

Maybe she'd do advanced Assertiveness, ask about how to deal with employees. Hard enough coping with fellow *workers* in the past. When she'd worked at the Health Food Store, she'd never known what to say to them. Still, she had more to talk about now that she did evening classes, read a lot.

'We'll be going, then, get our tea cooked.'

'Mummy will see you tomorrow, little man.' Poor Esmond – he'd been all over the place today.

Following her mother and son to the pavement, she waved good-bye then returned to the launderette. Put the 'Closed' sign up, hesitated, then locked herself in. You couldn't be too careful, surrounded by muggers and flashers. She didn't want to have a story to tell the self defence class on Friday night.

Oh Susan, Susan. The girl had put the alterations details in the service wash book. Jeanette wondered if she'd entered in the service washes anywhere at all. They'd had this problem before, and she'd put an extra large label on the cover of the service book to distinguish the two. And still they had time-consuming mix ups like this. Could Susan actually read? She couldn't bring herself to ask: the girl was on some kind of disability pension. She could only work a certain number of hours.

Pulling up a chair, Jeanette sat by the counter and copied the details onto the correct pages. Whitened out the errors using liquid paint. Swept and washed the floor and wiped the surfaces. Left the place and began to walk briskly home.

Nice to get away from buses, from shops, from dark, dank closes. Nice to hug thoughts of her new job to herself. Taking a slightly different route, she went into the off licence, stared at the wine section. Chose something called 'Riesling' which was light coloured and under ten pounds.

She threaded her purse from hand to hand as the man wrapped the bottle. She didn't care how it tasted – more what it symbolised. A new start, a better social life, increasing options. Like the 'after' part of an article about improving yourself.

If she could phrase it right, maybe David would come to work with her – she couldn't admit it would be *for* her. He needed to keep his self confidence, his pride. Swinging the carrier bag with the wine in it, Jeanette began to walk faster. In the days to follow they'd work things out.

She walked in. None of the lights were on. The house felt empty.

'I'm home,' she called loudly, hoping for a reply. Walked into the kitchen, set down the wine, put the kettle on. Walked into the lounge, saw the two coffee cups, the bag. *The bag she'd given Wanda that night they'd gone back to the launderette.* She'd forgotten all about that. Now she looked inside.

David's jacket, mended at the pocket. So Wanda *had* been here, they'd had a coffee, had... had what?

'Get off.' That's what she'd said: they must have been playing. Teenagers regularly shrieked and jumped on each other on the pavement outside. Not that Wanda was a teenager, but she was capable of acting like one. She wasn't the inhibited kind. David would like someone uninhibited, sexy. Someone pretty and free.

Free to take Esmond – Christ, she already took him. They always seemed so right and ultra relaxed together. Esmond had drawn a picture of Wanda and she'd put it on her wall.

Walls, boundaries, uncertainties. When is a friend not a friend? When she takes your man. Becomes your son's stepmother, a far from wicked one. That night after the cinema she'd said Esmond and she were great pals. Said 'I'll take him off your hands if you get tired of him'. She, Jeanette, would be totally alone.

No way were Wanda and David going to do this, get away with it. No way would she let her little son go. Stomach weak with dread she opened the wine and drank straight from the bottle. Recorked it, liquid fire bringing her instant drive. Voice surprising her with its strength, she phoned for a taxi. Took money from the shopping fund box, just in case. Went outside and waited – her mother had taught her to do that. Said some drivers put their meters on the second they got to your door.

True? False? She didn't care any more. Got in, gave him Wanda's address, sat back in her seat. Watched the streets drift by, quiet now, in the lull after the rush hour. Wished that taxi cabs didn't move so very slow. Almost, almost...

'It's that house, there.' He pulled over abruptly. 'Can you wait a few moments?'

She would be leaving soon – with or without her man.

The driver grunted something and she hurried from the cab, rang Wanda's door bell. Rang again, staring hopelessly at the window blinds.

No lights, no sounds of life or sounds of love. Where could they have gone? Someplace cheap and yet quiet, someplace neutral.

Somewhere they could do what they wanted, take as long as they liked. She looked back at the driver: he was staring at her.

She walked back to the cab; 'Can you take me somewhere else?'

This Wanda whore had better keep a tidy house, or she'd suffer. He watched her stir into consciousness with head rolling moans. Tanith had made the place smell of vomit, shit, of putrefaction. Pale and flabby in life, grey-blue and sprawling in death. He'd buried her body outside ten minutes ago – well, thrown it into the waiting dug-out. Good thinking, that, getting her to construct it in livelier days. He'd kicked a layer of earth over her clothed body. He'd shovel in the pile of wood mould before he left.

For now, he had better things to do , like disinfect the place. Like teach this uppity student bitch a lesson as she came round. Just a few more moments – her lids were fluttering. He watched from the other side of the room as her head came slowly up. The eyes began to focus, widened. Fixed into a stare, then looked down to where her arms and legs were bound. Rope, chair... you're not going anywhere, baby. She tried to flinch her body forward, failed. Whimpered like a tiny animal, looked back at him, eyes searching, seeking, saying pretty please.

Paying him attention now, he thought, as he poured the disinfectant around Tanith's second last resting place. The artist's model had left an ugly almost body-sized stain. The cleansing agents made the place smell like the geriatric part of a hospital, but at least he could breathe without feeling sick.

He wondered if *Wanda* felt sick as she took in her new surroundings. Saw her jacket and jeans in the corner, bra and panties covering her curves. Saw the small fire in the grate: it's growing hunger. Saw the broken towel rail just waiting for reconstruction, felt the heat.

Bad, not to show respect to her superior. Bad to want to sew hemlines rather than praise his songs.

'I know it's in need of work,' he said as she turned her head from side to side and took in the minimal furnishings, 'But the last owner left it in rather a mess.' He snorted, she flinched, her mouth opened, closed again. He walked towards her, knelt down, ran his fingers through her hair. Tugged, just a little, and she grunted, eyes dilating. He wondered just how wide they would get.

'I intend to get you a new door, of course,' he said with mock gentlemanliness. Gesticulated towards the trunk, which was jamming it closed from the inside. He'd had a hell of a job busting the lock to get her in here. Tomorrow he'd buy a new one. Tonight he'd have to nail it shut from the outside.

When he left today, which wouldn't be for hours yet. Mrs Landrew had Esmond, Jeanette had said she'd be late. He could pretend he'd felt lonely, gone for a drive, met a musician. They could have gone to one of those pizza places for an inexpensive meal.

'I used to like you. You know that? I used to like you.'

She opened her mouth to speak, and he slapped her face.

'Shut up. Shut *up*. I'll tell you when you can say something.' He had to protect himself, had to fight off her honeyed words.

Her head flopped downwards and she started to make a dry, hacking sound. Was this insubordination? He might have to punish her with more than mere slaps. But no, his father had often hit him for that – hit him for crying. Said 'I'll give you something to cry about,' gave additional blows.

All she would have to avoid was causing any initial anger. Do what he wanted and when, no matter how much it hurt. He'd take it easy this time, when training her. Have controlled teaching periods, recovery sessions, little chats. He'd learned this from the weakness of Kim, Pauline, Tanith and that disco girl. A little pain each time went a long, long way.

Getting the scissors from the cupboard, he walked towards her. She strained back in her chair then shook her head. Breathed heavily as he cut away her bra at the front, exposing her nipples. Now, that was an excellent plan...

Tanith had smoked. She'd lit up in the car, in the cafe. He had taken away her matches so she must still... Dragging the trunk away from the door, he turned sideways, slipped out into the early evening coolness. Hurried to the grave, pulling his jumper up over his nose and mouth. Gagged several times. New heights of body odour. Well, new depths...

Flicking away the soil with impatient hands he found her windcheater, located the button down pocket. The gin had made his fingers leaden. He fumbled with a hanky, a sweet wrapper, a twenty pence coin and a pack. A pack of ten – what a cheapskate. Four left, though, which was more than enough. One would last a long, long time if he blew it out between sessions. Striding back to The Secret House he pushed the trunk against the door again. She was stiffening, staring. He wanted to deflect attention from himself.

Towards *herself*, towards the body that had caused the problems. The body that had birthed him, the cruel hands that had slapped and nipped. The voice that had started criticising, and never stopped until he'd fled from it. The eyes that said 'We're disappointed in you. You're not like us. You're a horrible mistake.'

Her mistake, for having him, treating him badly. Her mistake for being a brainless, selfish bitch. Now the breasts that had failed to nourish him were exposed. Nipples protruding, begging to be kissed.

Ah, but that was what she wanted – blind affection. Wanted his slavish devotion, whilst she gave nothing in return. No, she'd had her chance for years, had used and abused him. Now it was her turn to sob and shriek and writhe.

Let your body breathe. Hers was breathing rapidly. Up, down, up, down, up, breasts rising and falling, only the jutting nipples staying still. Not for long. He put a cigarette in his mouth, struck a match against the matchbox. Soggy sandpaper. He tried again. She had started to relax a little: he saw the slight bulging of her abdomen, the way her shoulders sagged.

Just a man having a cigarette. She obviously didn't realise he wasn't a smoker. Just a man in need of some stimulus, a mini-high. The third match sputtered for a second, went out again. The head of the fourth flew across the room, unlit.

The fifth spurted into light: he inhaled, coughed a little. He checked the ropes round her arms, legs: still tightly bound. Took her chin in one hand, holding her face towards him. Took the lit cigarette from his mouth and moved it towards her left breast.

CHAPTER THIRTY EIGHT

The taxi was moving faster now, overtaking. They'd been on the road for a while, and the driver hadn't said a word. Not long till she found David, found reality. Found his much-loved woodyard, the embankment he had raced up to escape his childhood home.

He had to have gone there with Wanda – he had to. Even if it *was* too cold to make love outdoors. They could have found a shed, a way in to one of the old factories he'd sometimes mentioned. Maybe there was a back entrance through which you could drive a car. He'd taken the Escort – she'd noticed that while waiting for her taxi to arrive. He obviously knew his way round, could park in a concealment of trees.

More streets, roads, avenues, familiar and unfamiliar. She'd lived in Edinburgh all her life, yet still hadn't been round some of the schemes. No cause to, really – no incentive.

'Down here, lass?' The street sign was hanging off the side of a crumbling wall.

'Yes, that's right.' Sounding more sure than she felt. This was madness. Women hired investigators for this sort of thing. But she didn't have that kind of money, that kind of certainty. The shame of paying a PI to tell you you'd been imagining things…

'What number, lass?'

She didn't have a number so gave him David's dad's one. 'Just here is fine.'

He stared at the row of ill-kept houses on one side, the derelict tenements on the other. 'Want me to wait?'

'No.' She dug into her bag, found her purse, paid the amount on the meter. Added a pound for his trouble, glad Mrs Landrew wasn't around. She got out of the cab as slowly as possible, eyes searching through the increasing darkness, looking for the familiar car.

'Bye.' She raised her hand and flapped it slightly as she went past the drivers window, but he continued to sit there, looking out. Go away, go away. She bent down and pretended to tie her shoelace: *go, please, go, please, go.* After a few seconds she heard the engine start up, and he pulled out. A few minutes later he disappeared from sight.

Carefully she scanned the deserted street. Saw the shell of what had once been a hatchback, saw piles of debris all around. The opposite side of the road boasted a chipped, greying cooker. The Escort's bonnet was visible over its brown-stained top.

Slowly she began to walk towards it, whole body trembling. Presumably he'd gone through one of the three adjacent closes, Wanda at his side. He hadn't bothered to conceal the vehicle, to hide his movements. He obviously thought no one knew where he was.

She'd start with the close that was nearest, go out into the garden. Looking for a slope – that's what Frate senior had said. A slope he and his wife couldn't manage, so it must be substantial. Lucky she'd spent those last few months getting fit. Fit to discover the truth, fit to confront it. Strong enough to have her say. Holding her breath to limit the stench, she hurried through the gaping entrance, and out onto a pathway. Saw the backgreen, and, at its top, a large brick building which the tenants had presumably used to store things in. To its left she could see part of the embankment, a rough path stretching away in the distance across a mini moor. Its breadth stretched the entire length of the street. God knows where its depth went back to. Squinting through the dark, she climbed up the steps and into the long grass of the former washing green.

Dark shreds of cloud swept across the moon, dampness pulled at her ankles. Breathing hard, she walked up until the green suddenly gave way to the embankment's greater slope.

Sloping towards whom, towards what? She stared up at the dried out hill, with its snarls of weeds and blown plant life. Back to nature. Back to nudity? David going back to his roots. Shoes sliding, she held onto big stones that jutted from the earth, found shallow footholds.

And thistles, the size of small trees: her bare hand brushed against one. She almost cried out, fought against it, mustn't spoil the surprise. This was her future she was fighting for, the custody of her little Esmond. She must tread carefully, finding the right toeholds, the right questions, the right replies.

Did he really come here to have sex? It was isolated enough, but inhospitable, ghostly. All those black, broken windows making a backdrop behind her: there could be meths drinkers and squatters staring out. Then she stepped behind the roof of what had presumably been the communal storage house and was hidden from even these.

A wide expanse of dark, the ground felt spongier. She squatted down, dug her nails in, palm filling with splintery brown. Yes, this was the substance she'd found in the turn ups of David's trousers. Evidence of adultery – decaying wood.

Something – *someone?* – rushed through the dark some distance ahead of her. Oh, help, help. She stayed crouched, as low as possible, to the ground. Too loud for a cat. Had it been a large dog, some half mad creature? Easy to believe in spirits on a night like this. Creaks, groans; like a door tortuously closing. Then silence, silence. She stood up, began tiptoeing forward again.

She'd move on like this till she reached the wall or fence that heralded the end of the embankment. Then backtrack and go left from the storage house roof. Walk systematically till she found the wood factories Mr. Frate had said David escaped to. That is, if they hadn't been knocked down years before. Hard to imagine a small, morose boy fitting into a busy factory life. Perhaps, though there had been women there who'd given him biscuits and juice.

On, on, on, slowly, carefully. At last she saw what looked like a large square cabin ahead. The side she was approaching from had heavy closed shutters concealing the windows. Impossible to see as much as a sliver of light. Assuming they had any light – they might not need it. A man would always find what he wanted, her mother had said.

Sweat was swamping her underarms despite the falling temperature. Just do, it, do it. She wasn't in the wrong. Two steps closer, three, scarcely breathing. She smelt then *saw* smoke, a thin grey spiral from the chimney standing out in relief against the blue-black sky. So they *were* in there – they had a fire going. How romantic. They'd probably lit candles too.

Oh, David, I would have slept with you, I would have. Didn't know that you even wanted to. You said you liked bunkbeds, went out on your own, spoke of being free. Said a mother should be pure of spirit, a woman apart from the rest...

Never too late, though: the magazines said so. Said intelligent humans were capable of positive change.

Positive change starting now. She moved silently forward. In a few more minutes she'd reach the nearest side. Then she'd walk round, find the door – she could even look through the keyhole. Maybe just shouting for them to come out would be enough.

Yes, she didn't want to see this, see their nudity. She would shout that she knew they were in there, ask David to come out. Let Wanda find her own way home: she wasn't getting a lift in the Escort. Let the little cheat suffer, for a change. She went momentarily rigid as a strange noise rang out across the bleakness. What was that? Another sound: a female's high pitched babbling. Jeanette froze, listened, too far away to make out the words. Could she be coming. orgasming? Women supposedly went wild in its throes. Shrieking, yelping, sobbing: the articles made it sound like something painful. That cry had sounded like a woman who was in pain.

Another scream – desperate, tortured, horrible. Another and another: frenzied, out of control. Jeanette backed away until she came up against the roof of the storage house. The screams were getting wilder all the time.

Don't let it catch me, don't let it catch me, don't let it... Her lips soundless in the darkness through terror rather than design. Find a policeman, a police station – anyone. Was there a local phonebox from which she could dial 999? For a second the pathway down seemed to have gone, vanished. Then her searching hands and feet found it, found new strength. Heart pounding – was it after her? In front of her? – Jeanette slid down the embankment and began to run for help.

CHAPTER THIRTY NINE

'*Stop. Wait. Look this way, Jeanette. How do you feel about what's happened?*'

Faces filling up every available space around her, cameras whirring, flashes going off in her eyes, in Esmond's eyes. The child scrabbling, screaming. Trying to bend down in the crush of bodies in order to pick him up.

Whispered telephone calls before she got her number changed: 'Bitch. Do you know what it's like to slowly starve to death?'

Of course she didn't know – couldn't imagine. But they sent her pictures of people from the death camps until she did. And photos of women who had undergone breast reconstructions.

Notes saying: 'Your man did this.'

Shit shovelled nightly through the letterbox, shit via parcel post, via first class mail. A nation saying what they thought of Mrs David Frate by emptying its bowels. A nation who couldn't get at him so would settle for her.

So – a temporary move in with mum, a return to her beginnings. A family therapist whom she hoped would be temporary too.

'Children pick up on such things,' said the therapist, Shona. She had dry, reddish eyelids and wore print frocks quite unsuited to the sweeping March winds.

'I've kept all the… packages, and the papers away from him.' He could recognise his fathers picture, even if he was unable to read abut what he'd done.

'How does he seem?'

'He.. It's strange for him living at his gran's.'

Strange for both of us.

'He wants to go home.'

Shona buzzed the creche worker to bring Esmond through from the other room. 'Let's draw a picture. Can you do me one of your old house and of where you live now?' Week after week of Esmond drawing pictures. Jeanette dreaded the day he'd draw one of Wanda or of his dad.

'Talk to Esmond about his dad,' Shona said, sounding like one of the counsellors in the magazines. 'Say that daddy still loves him but has had to go away.' Away to a place where they were doubtless spitting in his food and kicking in his testicles. Away to a place where he'd wish he'd never been born. Yet somehow she couldn't write, couldn't contact him. She'd sat down and tried to write to Wanda, too, but had thrown away page after page.

Nipple reconstruction: what could you say to someone whose husband had made you require nipple reconstruction? One of the papers had said, 'Miss James has undergone personality changes': she hadn't been able to bring herself to read the rest. Read all about it. Booklets, leaflets. Shona had given her some cards which contained 'Touch and Trust' games. Said she should practice them with Esmond, buy what she could afford from a long list of educational toys.

Embarrassing to have to be told all this – shouldn't she know it instinctively? The therapist said most things needed to be learned. Said that Esmond had learned fear after the journalists mobbed the pair of them, but that he would learn to trust again as he made friends.

Friends. She couldn't yet make herself another one. You had to tell friends things, had to explain... She hadn't been able to face the launderette, face the community centre. Had signed on for Unemployment Benefit, spurning the ill-disguised offers of money from the press.

'I can't fathom you – you'd think you'd at least want to get something out of all this. Put it aside for the bairn, one of these trusts.' Her mother: a pale, gaunt, hard-eyed Oracle, keeping strangers with their knowing stares at bay.

If only someone would keep her mother at bay. 'You've not eaten your toast yet.'

'I'm sorry, Mum. I'm not hungry.'

'Think money grows on trees?'

'No, it's just that... I'll give you Esmond's child allowance after I've been to the post office today.'

'You're surely not going out? I've been getting you everything, haven't I? Someone will see you...'

'I'll put one of your headscarfs on.'

'But your picture's been everywhere.'

'Mum, that was *weeks* ago.' Knowing the older woman was probably right, but that she had to get away for a while. Take a walk round the shops, get a book which she'd chosen herself.

'You're not taking him with you.' It was a statement rather than a question.

'No, of course not. It's not as if he wants to go out.'

Getting ready, and for the first time since finding the embankment's cabin she felt hopeful. The weather was getting warmer, Summer fashions would be brightening the stores. She'd take that list of educational toys Shona had given her. She'd get him a teddy bear to cuddle as well, something fun.

If she could get away once in a while, maybe living with her mother would become bearable. Maybe in a few more months she'd feel strong enough to look for a job.

'Mum, I won't be too long. I...' She turned to face her, saw the sudden brown-black darkening of the panes.

Crash. More than a crash – words were inadequate. Darkness taking over the top half of the window then taking it in. Cracking of glass, an implosion of numerous splinters. Muscle and blood and eyes and sinew and bone. A girl. At first she thought it was a dead girl they'd thrown through the window, part of a girl's body. One of David's... but surely they'd found them all? Esmond rushed into the lounge crying, screaming, Mrs Landrew was staring at the obscenity and saying 'Oh my God, my God.'

A dead cat tied to a chimney brick. No written message.

'Take him into the other room, Mum. I'll call the police.' Phoning the special number she'd been given, knowing that she was going to ask them to do more than remove this butchered animal. Knowing that her childhood was irrevocably over, that now she had to protect a child of her own.

EPILOGUE.

Glasgow's miles better. Better than Edinburgh, leastways, where everyone knew her features and her mum's approximate address. No one expected to see her here in this busy city. She felt safer, probably looked more normal, more assured.

'Ready, wee man?' He'd been ready for three quarters of an hour. Rocking back and forward in his new school blazer, nothing like the kids in the adverts with their gleaming grins and shoes. 'Will we go get Jilly, then?'

Mrs Carr, next door, had a daughter, Jilly, who was two months older than Esmond. They were starting school today, would be in the same class. Mrs Carr had tried to take both five year olds to see round the place earlier that summer, but Esmond had run and hid until Jeanette agreed to come too.

'We'll have to go now.' He stared at her solemnly. 'You've got your banana in your bag in case you don't like all of your school dinner.'

She'd have to find a job now that he was going to school, bring in a family-sized wage. It was best to get him used to canteen or packed lunches, used to eating away from home from the very first day.

God, but he looked so little and sad, so helpless. 'Let's go and get Jilly, then, ring her bell.' Meeting the five year old on the landing in her almost identical blazer. Mrs Carr telling her daughter she'd collect her at lunchtime, bring her home. *Guilt, guilt. Don't fuss over him, don't cling to him. Remember when you were little, your lurking mum.*

'Off we go, you two.' Intense August sunshine. A short walk, but a pleasant one, the children hurrying slightly ahead.

'Esmond, have you got your jotters?' Walking, talking. Not sure it mattered: he'd be given ample paper in class. Both children nodded: Esmond looked back at her. He held his beloved pack of felt pens in his hand. 'Don't you want to put them in your satchel?' Some older boys might take them away.

He shook his head, skipped on, the red-haired Jilly ahead of him. She was a stronger child, a larger child: more vibrant, much more *sure*. Easy to talk to, though, laughing, chatty. Well liked by the other neighbours in the block.

Jilly reached the open playground gates, and Esmond joined her. Both looked back, stopped, Jilly pulled a leaf from the hedge: 'Look what I've got, Mrs Dean.' *Mrs Dean* – the surname still felt strange to her. Luckily Esmond had been too young to ever write his name as Esmond Frate. She'd chosen the new surname from a TV character; it had no other significance. New name, new start.

She looked down at the pair of them. 'Remember and not eat any berries or anything. We have to wait here till the bell goes, then Miss Wallace will come out.' They nodded. Stared at two other mothers who were crying. 'I'll be here at the gates for you two when you get out this afternoon at three.'

A stare, a wordless nod. For a moment Esmond looked just like David. She backed away, gave him a little push towards the other kids. Watched as the two of them broke into a run, reached the centre of the playground. Saw Jilly reach playfully for Esmond's pens. Watched them fall, scatter, saw the rage in his sudden stillness. Saw him strike the girl somewhere between her shoulder and her arm. Well, children didn't stop to think: some rough and tumble was inevitable. And yet… Heart beating faster, she walked slowly up the playground. Jilly looked up at her, lip forecasting tears. Esmond was on his hands and knees, scooping up his possessions. Squatting, she reached for a chunky green pen.

What to say? She wanted to help him. Wanted the years and years he'd have to spend here to be fun.

'Esmond, wee man. Jilly was only playing.'
Don't make an enemy out of a friend.

For a moment he stayed rigid, a mini iron man. Then some of the tautness left his face.

'Mum'll wait by the gates till you go in, love.' Throat beginning to feel painful, she backed away.

Heard the bell's peal, gut-wrenching memories. Jeering bullies, friendless lessons: the one adult in her life telling her again and again that the world was bad.

She waved as Miss Wallace came out and began to mingle with the children, arranging them into a watchful two-by-two line.

'She's good,' said one of the mothers to her friend, and Jeanette looked over at her. 'She taught my older boy last year.' When she looked back, Miss Wallace was walking up to Esmond, who was squatting beside a patch of what looked liked marigolds. He'd never had a garden, never seen... She watched as the woman bent at the knee, smiled, said something. Esmond looked over at Jeanette.

Trust, trust... She nodded her encouragement. *Make friends, have people to talk to when things go wrong.* He took a step towards her, turned, looked from one to the other.

She smiled, walked slowly up to the teacher. 'This is all new to him. He didn't go to nursery school.' *He should have gone.*

The woman nodded, smiled as she knelt before him.

'You remember Miss Wallace, Esmond? She's your teacher. Maybe when she sees all your pens she'll let you draw.' Draw him out of himself. She willed her son to accept the woman. Willed herself to love him enough to nurture him yet temporarily let him go. Images of a small, scared boy crouched behind a factory door, with no one to turn to. An older man, bent with hatred, more than ever a recluse.

Go, go – make the first move. Be different.

With a last lingering look at her, Esmond smiled and took the teacher's hand.

New titles from The Do-Not Press:

Stewart Home: C*nt
1 899344 45 4 – B-format paperback original, £7.50

David Kelso is a writer who claims to be so lacking in imagination that his fiction isn't fiction at all. He returns from a faked death to complete a trilogy that necessitates him having repeat sex with the first thousand women he ever slept with. But then he starts to lose the plot — literally...

Stewart Home's brilliant new novel is abrasive and darkly witty; essential reading for psychopaths, sociopaths and anyone else interested in the ins-and-outs of the book trade.

'Home is reconfiguring books as explosive elements — pages so stuffed with ideas that they might go off in your hands.' — Ben Slater, The Independent

Andy Soutter: DN Angels
1 899344 46 2 – B-format paperback original, £7.50

Theo Riddle leaves home and hits the road, looking for love and money. Sheltering in a derelict boathouse on a Devon estuary, he first encounters a strange, passionate woman and then an art dealer heading for the Mediterranean in a stolen yacht. A dangerous adventure; an intriguing collection of psychopaths, hustlers and philosophers. But who is in control? Theo or his new-found accomplice — the cosmic gypsy who claims to have his best interests at heart but who appears to have a sinister agenda of her own?

Gary Lovisi: Blood in Brooklyn Bloodlines
1 899344 48 9 – B-format paperback original, £7.50

Tough Brooklyn PI Vic Powers thought he'd seen it all, but then someone threatens to blow away the only thing he holds dear — his wife. Before long he is on a hellbound train to confront the psychopathic childhood companion whose monstrous games still haunt him. And when pushed, Powers knows that he can be a monster himself...

The first Vic Powers novel from New York's new master of the hardboiled thriller, Gary Lovisi.

'A craftsman who learned his business from the masters' — Eugene Izzi

---

Also by Carol Anne Davis

Shrouded by Carol Anne Davis
ISBN 1 899344 17 9 – C-format paperback original, £7

Douglas likes women — quiet women; the kind he deals with at the mortuary where he works. Douglas meets Marjorie, unemployed, gaining weight and losing confidence. She talks and laughs a lot to cover up her shyness, but what Douglas really needs is a lover who'll stay still — deadly still. Driven by lust and fear, Douglas finds a way to make girls remain excitingly silent and inert. But then he is forced to blank out the details of their unplanned deaths. Perhaps only Marjorie can fulfil his growing sexual hunger. If he could just get her into a state of limbo. Douglas studies his textbooks to find a way...

Also available from The Do-Not Press: RECENT TITLES

Ken Bruen: A WHITE ARREST Bloodlines
1 899344 41 1 – B-format paperback original, £6.50

Galway-born Ken Bruen's most accomplished and darkest crime noir novel to date is a police-procedural, but this is no well-ordered 57th Precinct romp. Centred around the corrupt and seedy worlds of Detective Sergeant Brant and Chief Inspector Roberts, A White Arrest concerns itself with the search for The Umpire, a cricket-obsessed serial killer that is wiping out the England team. And to add insult to injury a group of vigilantes appear to to doing the police's job for them by stringing up drug-dealers... and the police like it even less than the victims. This first novel in an original and thought provoking new series from the author of whom Books in Ireland said: "If Martin Amis was writing crime novels, this is what he would hope to write."

Mark Sanderson: AUDACIOUS PERVERSION Bloodlines
1 899344 32 2 – B-format paperback original, £6.50

Martin Rudrum, good-looking, young media-mover, has a massive chip on his shoulder. A chip so large it leads him to commit a series of murders in which the medium very much becomes the message. A fast-moving and intelligent thriller, described by one leading Channel 4 TV producer as "Barbara Pym meets Bret Easton Ellis".

Jerry Sykes (ed): MEAN TIME Bloodlines
1 899344 40 3 – B-format paperback original, £6.50

Sixteen original and thought-provoking stories for the Millennium from some of the finest crime writers from USA and Britain, including **Ian Rankin** (current holder of the Crime Writers' Association Gold Dagger for Best Novel) **Ed Gorman, John Harvey, Lauren Henderson, Colin Bateman, Nicholas Blincoe, Paul Charles, Dennis Lehane, Maxim Jakubowski** and **John Foster**.

Jenny Fabian: A CHEMICAL ROMANCE
1 899344 42 X – B-format paperback original, £6.50

Jenny Fabian's first book, Groupie first appeared in 1969 and was republished last year to international acclaim. A roman à clef from 1971, A Chemical Romance concerns itself with the infamous celebrity status Groupie bestowed on Fabian. Expected to maintain the sex and drugs lifestyle she had proclaimed 'cool', she flits from bed to mattress to bed, travelling from London to Munich, New York, LA and finally to the hippy enclave of Ibiza, in an attempt to find some kind of meaning to her life. As Time Out said at the time: "Fabian's portraits are lightning silhouettes cut by a master with a very sharp pair of scissors."

Maxim Jakubowski: THE STATE OF MONTANA
1 899344 43 8 half-C-format paperback original £5

Despite the title, as the novels opening line proclaims: 'Montana had never been to Montana". An unusual and erotic portrait of a woman from the "King of the erotic thriller" (Crime Time magazine).

Also available from The Do-Not Press: RECENT TITLES

Miles Gibson: KINGDOM SWANN
1 899344 34 9 – B-format paperback, £6.50

Kingdom Swann, Victorian master of the epic nude painting turns to photography and finds himself recording the erotic fantasies of a generation through the eye of the camera. A disgraceful tale of murky morals and unbridled matrons in a world of Suffragettes, flying machines and the shadow of war.

"Gibson has few equals among his contemporaries" —Time Out

"Gibson writes with a nervous versatility that is often very funny and never lacks a life of its own, speaking the language of our times as convincingly as aerosol graffiti" —The Guardian

Miles Gibson: VINEGAR SOUP
1 899344 33 0 – B-format paperback, £6.50

Gilbert Firestone, fat and fifty, works in the kitchen of the Hercules Café and dreams of travel and adventure. When his wife drowns in a pan of soup he abandons the kitchen and takes his family to start a new life in a jungle hotel in Africa. But rain, pygmies and crazy chickens start to turn his dreams into nightmares. And then the enormous Charlotte arrives with her brothel on wheels. An epic romance of true love, travel and food...

"I was tremendously cheered to find a book as original and refreshing as this one. Required reading..." —The Literary Review

Paul Charles: FOUNTAIN OF SORROW Bloodlines
1 899344 38 1 – demy 8vo casebound, £15.00
1 899344 39 X – B-format paperback original, £6.50

Third in the increasingly popular Detective Inspector Christy Kennedy mystery series, set in the fashionable Camden Town and Primrose Hill area of north London. Two men are killed in bizarre circumstances; is there a connection between their deaths and if so, what is it? It's up to DI Kennedy and his team to discover the truth and stop to a dangerous killer. The suspects are many and varied: a traditional jobbing criminal, a successful rock group manager, and the mysterious Miss Black Lipstick, to name but three. As BBC Radio's Talking Music programme avowed: "If you enjoy Morse, you'll enjoy Kennedy."

Ray Lowry: INK
1 899344 21 7 – Metric demy-quarto paperback original, £9

A unique collection of strips, single frame cartoons and word-play from well-known rock 'n' roll cartoonist Lowry, drawn from a career spanning 30 years of contributions to periodicals as diverse as Oz, The Observer, Punch, The Guardian, The Big Issue, The Times, The Face and NME. Each section is introduced by the author, recognised as one of Britain's most original, trenchant and uncompromising satirists, and many contributions are original and unpublished.

Also available from The Do-Not Press

The Hackman Blues by Ken Bruen
ISBN 1899344 22 5 – C-format paperback original, £7

"If Martin Amis was writing crime novels, this is what he would hope to write."
– Books in Ireland

A job of pure simplicity. Find a white girl in Brixton. Piece of cake. What I should have done is doubled my medication and lit a candle to St Jude – maybe a lot of candles."

Add to the mixture a lethal ex-con, an Irish builder obsessed with Gene Hackman, the biggest funeral Brixton has ever seen, and what you get is the Blues like they've never been sung before. Ken Bruen's powerful second novel is a gritty and grainy mix of crime noir and Urban Blues that greets you like a mugger stays with you like a razor-scar.

Smalltime by Jerry Raine
ISBN 1 899344 13 6 – C-format paperback original, £5.99

Smalltime is a taut, psychological crime thriller, set among the seedy world of petty criminals and no-hopers. In this remarkable début, Jerry Raine shows just how easily curiosity can turn into fear amid the horrors, despair and despondency of life lived a little too near the edge.

"The first British contemporary crime novel featuring an underclass which no one wants. Absolutely authentic and quite possibly important."– Philip Oakes, Literary Review.

That Angel Look by Mike Ripley
   "The outrageous, rip-roarious Mr Ripley is an abiding delight…" – Colin Dexter
1 899344 23 3 – C-format paperback original, £8

A chance encounter (in a pub, of course) lands street-wise, cab-driving Angel the ideal job as an all-purpose assistant to a trio of young and very sexy fashion designers.

But things are nowhere near as straightforward as they should be and it soon becomes apparent that no-one is telling the truth – least of all Angel!

It's Not A Runner Bean by Mark Steel
ISBN 1 899344 12 8 – C-format paperback original, £5.99

'I've never liked Mark Steel and I thoroughly resent the high quality of this book.' – Jack Dee

The life of a Slightly Successful Comedian can include a night spent on bare floorboards next to a pyromaniac squatter in Newcastle, followed by a day in Chichester with someone so aristocratic, they speak without ever moving their lips.

From his standpoint behind the microphone, Mark Steel is in the perfect position to view all human existence. Which is why this book – like his act, broadcasts and series' – is opinionated, passionate, and extremely funny. It even gets around to explaining the line (screamed at him by an Eighties yuppy): 'It's not a runner bean…' – which is another story.

'A terrific book. I have never read any other book about comedy written by someone with a sense of humour.' – Jeremy Hardy, Socialist Review.

Also available from The Do-Not Press

Charlie's Choice: The First Charlie Muffin Omnibus by Brian Freemantle – Charlie Muffin; Clap Hands, Here Comes Charlie; The Inscrutable Charlie Muffin

ISBN 1 899344 26 8, C-format paperback, £9

Charlie Muffin is not everybody's idea of the ideal espionage agent. Dishevelled, cantankerous and disrespectful, he refuses to play by the Establishment's rules. Charlie's axiom is to screw anyone from anywhere to avoid it happening to him. But it's not long before he finds himself offered up as an unwilling sacrifice by a disgraced Department, desperate to win points in a ruthless Cold War. Now for the first time, the first three Charlie Muffin books are collected together in one volume. 'Charlie is a marvellous creation' – Daily Mail

Song of the Suburbs by Simon Skinner

ISBN 1 899 344 37 3 – B-format paperback original, £5

Born in a suburban English New Town and with a family constantly on the move (Essex to Kent to New York to the South of France to Surrey), who can wonder that Slim Manti feels rootless with a burning desire to take fun where he can find it? His solution is to keep on moving. And move he does: from girl to girl, town to town and country to country. He criss-crosses Europe looking for inspiration, circumnavigates America searching for a girl and drives to Tintagel for Arthur's Stone... Sometimes brutal, often hilarious, Song of the Suburbs is a Road Novel with a difference.

Head Injuries by Conrad Williams

ISBN 1 899 344 36 5 – B-format paperback original, £5

It's winter and the English seaside town of Morecambe is dead. David knows exactly how it feels. Empty for as long as he can remember, he depends too much on a past filled with the excitements of drink, drugs and cold sex. The friends that sustained him then – Helen and Seamus – are here now and together they aim to pinpoint the source of the violence that has suddenly exploded into their lives. Soon to be a major film.

The Long Snake Tattoo by Frank Downes

ISBN 1 899 344 35 7 – B-format paperback original, £5

Ted Hamilton's new job as night porter at the down-at-heel Eagle Hotel propels him into a world of seedy nocturnal goings-on and bizarre characters. These range from the pompous and near-efficient Mr Butterthwaite to bigoted old soldier Harry, via Claudia the harassed chambermaid and Alf Speed, a removals man with a penchant for uninvited naps in strange beds.

But then Ted begins to notice that something sinister is lurking beneath the surface

BLOODLINES the cutting-edge crime and mystery imprint...

Hellbent on Homicide by Gary Lovisi
ISBN 1 899344 18 7 — C-format paperback original, £7

"This isn't a first novel, this is a book written by a craftsman who learned his business from the masters, and in HELLBENT ON HOMICIDE, that education rings loud and long." —Eugene Izzi

1962, a sweet, innocent time in America... after McCarthy, before Vietnam. A time of peace and trust, when girls hitch-hiked without a care. But for an ice-hearted killer, a time of easy pickings. "A wonderful throwback to the glory days of hardboiled American crime fiction. In my considered literary judgement, if you pass up HELLBENT ON HOMICIDE, you're a stone chump." —Andrew Vachss

Brooklyn-based Gary Lovisi's powerhouse début novel is a major contribution to the hardboiled school, a roller-coaster of sex, violence and suspense, evocative of past masters like Jim Thompson, Carroll John Daly and Ross Macdonald.

Fresh Blood II edited by Mike Ripley & Maxim Jakubowski
ISBN 1 899 344 20 9 — C-format paperback original, £8.

Follow-up to the highly-acclaimed original volume (see below), featuring short stories from John Baker, Christopher Brookmyre, Ken Bruen, Carol Anne Davis, Christine Green, Lauren Henderson, Charles Higson, Maxim Jakubowski, Phil Lovesey, Mike Ripley, Iain Sinclair, John Tilsley, John Williams, and RD Wingfield (Inspector Frost)

Fresh Blood edited by Mike Ripley & Maxim Jakubowski
ISBN 1 899344 03 9 — C-format paperback original, £6.99

Featuring the cream of the British New Wave of crime writers including John Harvey, Mark Timlin, Chaz Brenchley, Russell James, Stella Duffy, Ian Rankin, Nicholas Blincoe, Joe Canzius, Denise Danks, John B Spencer, Graeme Gordon, and a previously unpublished extract from the late Derek Raymond. Includes an introduction from each author explaining their views on crime fiction in the '90s and a comprehensive foreword on the genre from Angel-creator, Mike Ripley.

BLOODLINES the cutting-edge crime and mystery imprint...

Tooth & Nail by John B Spencer
ISBN 1 899344 31 4 — C-format paperback original, £7

The long-awaited new noir thriller from the author of Perhaps She'll Die. A dark, Rackmanesque tale of avarice and malice-aforethought from one of Britain's most exciting and accomplished writers. "Spencer offers yet another demonstration that our crime writers can hold their own with the best of their American counterparts when it comes to snappy dialogue and criminal energy. Recommended." — Time Out

Perhaps She'll Die! by John B Spencer
ISBN 1 899344 14 4 — C-format paperback original, £5.99

Giles could never say 'no' to a woman... any woman. But when he tangled with Celeste, he made a mistake... A bad mistake.

Celeste was married to Harry, and Harry walked a dark side of the street that Giles — with his comfortable lifestyle and fashionable media job — could only imagine in his worst nightmares. And when Harry got involved in nightmares, people had a habit of getting hurt. Set against the boom and gloom of eighties Britain, Perhaps She'll Die! is classic noir with a centre as hard as toughened diamond.

Last Boat To Camden Town by Paul Charles
Hardback: ISBN 1 899344 29 2 — C-format original, £15
Paperback: ISBN 1 899344 30 6 — C-format paperback, £7

The second enthralling Detective Inspector Christy Kennedy mystery. The body of Dr Edmund Godfrey Berry is discovered at the bottom of the Regent's Canal, in the heart of Kennedy's "patch" of Camden Town, north London. But the question is, Did he jump, or was he pushed? Last Boat to Camden Town combines Whodunnit? Howdunnit? and love story with Paul Charles' trademark unique-method-of-murder to produce one of the best detective stories of the year. "If you enjoy Morse, you'll enjoy Kennedy" — Talking Music, BBC Radio 2

I Love The Sound of Breaking Glass by Paul Charles
ISBN 1 899344 16 0 — C-format paperback original, £7

First outing for Irish-born Detective Inspector Christy Kennedy whose beat is Camden Town, north London. Peter O'Browne, managing director of Camden Town Records, is missing. Is his disappearance connected with a mysterious fire that ravages his north London home? And just who was using his credit card in darkest Dorset? Although up to his neck in other cases, Detective Inspector Christy Kennedy and his team investigate, plumbing the hidden depths of London's music industry, turning up murder, chart-rigging scams, blackmail and worse. I Love The Sound of Breaking Glass is a detective story with a difference. Part whodunnit, part howdunnit and part love story, it features a unique method of murder, a plot with more twists and turns than the road from Kingsmarkham to St Mary Mead.

The Do-Not Press
Fiercely Independent Publishing

Keep in touch with what's happening at the cutting edge of independent British publishing.

Join The Do-Not Press Information Service and receive advance information of all our new titles, as well as news of events and launches in your area, and the occasional free gift and special offer.

Simply send your name and address to:
The Do-Not Press (Dept. SAH)
PO Box 4215
London
SE23 2QD
or email us: thedonotpress@zoo.co.uk

There is no obligation to purchase and
no salesman will call.

Visit our regularly-updated web site:
http://www.thedonotpress.co.uk

Mail Order

All our titles are available from good bookshops, or (in case of difficulty) direct from The Do-Not Press at the address above. There is no charge for post and packing.

(NB: A postman may call.)